JOBE

Alvarez Security Series

By

Maryann Jordan

Jobe (Alvarez Security Series)
Copyright © 2015 Maryann Jordan
Print Edition

Cover Design by: Andrea Michelle, Artistry in Design
Editor: Shannon Brandee Eversoll
Format: Paul & Oat, BB eBooks

ISBN: 978-0-9864004-9-0

Acknowledgements

First and foremost, I have to thank my husband, Michael. Always believing in me and wanting me to pursue my dreams, none of my books would not be possible without his support. To my daughters, MaryBeth and Nicole, I taught you to follow your dreams and now it is time for me to take my own advice. You two are my inspiration.

My best friend, Tammie, who for twenty years has been with me through thick and thin. You've filled the role of confidant, supporter, and sister. You always believed that I could accomplish whatever I dreamed.

My dear friend, Myckel Anne, who keeps me on track, keeps me grounded, and most of all – keeps my secrets. Thank you for not only being my proofreader but my friend. Our friendship has grown and changed and you mean more to me than you can imagine. And yes, my cat is huge!

Going from blogger to author has allowed me to have the friendships and advice of several wonderful writers who always answered my questions, helped me over rough spots, and cheered me on. To Kristine Raymond, you gave me the green light when I wondered if I was crazy and you never let me give up. MJ

Nightingale and Andrea Michelle – you two have made a huge impact on my life. Anna Mychals, EJ Shorthall, Victoria Brock, Jen Andrews, Andrea Long, A.d. Ellis, ML Steinbrunn, Sandra Love, thank you from the bottom of my heart. Susan Stoker and Laramie Briscoe – thank you for always answering my questions and giving me the benefit of your experience and friendship.

My beta readers kept me sane, cheered me on, found all my silly errors, and often helped me understand my characters through their eyes. A huge thank you to Denise VanPlew, Sandi Laubhan, Barbara Martoncik, Jennifer Alumbaugh, Anna Mychals, Danielle Petersen, Shannon Brandee, Stracey Charran, Leeann Wright, Lynn Smith, Kelly Williams and Tracey Markin for being my beta girls who love alphas!

Shannon Brandee Eversoll has been my editor for the past seven books and what she brings to my writing has been amazing. She has gone from editor to friend – a transition that I love! She and Myckel Anne Phillips as my proofreader gave their time and talents to making Jobe as well written as it can be. Both encourage me to stretch and work harder to bring my stories alive!

My street team, Jordan Jewels, you are amazing! You volunteer your time to promote my books and I cannot thank you enough! I hope you will stay with me, because I have lots more stories inside, just waiting to be written!

My Personal Assistant, Barbara Martoncik, is the woman that keeps me going when I feel overwhelmed and I am so grateful for not only her assistance but her friendship.

The cover was created by my dear friend, Andrea Michelle with Artistry in Design, and her talent is evident in every detail. Thank you for working with me, planning with me, laughing with me, and understanding me.

As the owner of the blog, Lost in Romance Books, I know the selflessness of bloggers. We promote indie authors on our own time because we believe wholeheartedly in the indie author community. I want to thank the many bloggers that I have served with, and who are assisting in promoting my series.

Most importantly, thank you, readers. You allow me into your life for a few hours as you disappear into my characters and you support me as I follow my indie author dreams.

If you read my books and enjoy them, please leave a review. It does not have to be long or detailed...just that you enjoyed the book. Reviews are essential to indie authors!

Dedication

For twenty-two years, I worked as an adolescent counselor in high schools, and while the young people were wonderful, one of the problems we faced that crept into our schools was the gang activity. I dedicate this to the many young women who fight against the pull of that environment. Know that there is life outside of the gangs and people who will help you make those choices. For the girls that I dealt with, know that you are in my heart.

CHAPTER 1

J OBE DELARO WALKED back to his bunk after the briefing. As part of an elite Special Forces squad, he was ready for their next mission. From the meeting they just had…it would be soon. Each of his twelve squad members would spend the evening preparing in whatever way worked best for them. Their Captain, Tony Alvarez, would be in his room sending an email to his wife. The twins, Gabe and Vinny Malloy, would be hitting the weights while listening to some pounding heavy metal music. The others each had their own habits and rituals before a mission as well.

Pulling out the letters from his locker, Jobe sat down on the edge of the narrow bed, his long legs stretched out in front of him. Letters from her. The woman he loved. The woman he promised to marry. The one.

He read her last letter, where she talked about finishing her senior year in college. They met two years earlier while he was stationed at the base near the city of Richland where she was attending the university. And the moment he saw her…all bets were off.

Several of them headed to a local watering-hole one

weekend, grabbing a table overlooking the dance floor and loudly ordering their beers. He moved his eyes around the room and caught a flash of a reddish-gold amongst the dancers crowded on the floor. The unusual color of hair had him searching for her again.

Leaning forward in his seat, he spied her. Long hair, the hue of a lion's mane, flowing down her back. It was hard to tell from the crowd how tall she was, but the way her ass moved had his dick immediately standing at attention. Her arms snaked above her head as she slowly turned around, still dancing to the music. And holy hell, her front was just as good as her back.

He jumped up, ignoring the calls of his brothers-in-arms, knowing he needed to make his move or one of them would be on her in an instant. Moving through the crowd, his towering frame made it easy to part the way until he was standing directly behind her.

As she turned around again, she came face to face with him. Or rather face to chest. Her head jerked back as she looked up, her light brown eyes with flecks of gold piercing him. She must have liked what she saw because she continued to dance and within a few minutes they were moving together as though they had been a couple for a long time.

They spent the next half hour on the dance floor before leaving the bar, heading back to her place. And were inseparable after that. Through the rest of his training. Through his deployments. Through everything. And now, in the middle of his missions in

Afghanistan, her letters gave him a lifeline. Back to home. Back to a future with her. He smiled, reading her final lines.

Please come home safe when all of this is over and know that I will be here for you. I've already told my parents to be ready for a fast wedding because I'm not waiting one more second to become your wife! Keep my heart safely nestled in yours. You have all of me, soldier-boy. Always and forever.

"You reading the same letter again, bro?" Vinny joked as he walked into the room, falling down onto his bed. The ultimate player. A minute later he was followed by his twin, Gabe. Another ultimate player. *Love these guys and respect 'em, but there's no way either of them could ever understand what this girl means to me.* Both men were huge, bulging muscles barely contained in their tan t-shirts. Blond hair cropped close to their heads, they were spitting images of each other. Except to the members of their squad who could tell them apart instantly.

Smiling, Jobe just nodded and slid the letters back into his trunk. He sent her a quick email to let her know he would write to her again soon. This was their way of letting her know he was going to be out of contact for a few days.

The consummate professional, he turned his mind away from her and back to the upcoming mission. It sounded easy—get into a village and rescue a captured foreign national. But in this country, nothing was easy. So the squad was trained to be the best. Go in prepared and be ready to take on anything that came their way. Control. Stay in control and then you can control what is happening around you. That had been his motto for as long as he could remember and it served him well.

As Jobe closed his eyes in exhaustion, he tried to shake the feeling that somehow this mission was going to be different. Forcing those apprehensions from his mind, he went to sleep with one thought. *We've got this.*

Two days later, he knew that his control was slipping. The mission had disaster written all over it from the beginning. The intelligence had been wrong and the foreign national had been relocated. Altering their plan, the twelve men moved toward the new location, traveling stealthily in the dark. The rough terrain was no challenge for them as they made their way over the rocky passes and darkened paths.

The new site loomed ahead, a small village lighted by a few campfires nestled amongst the craggy mountainside. Now, with no intelligence about the new location, they planned by instinct. Captain Alvarez was meticulous in his leadership and they quickly developed a new strategy. As Weapons Sergeant, Jobe and the Engineer Sergeant moved in first, circling around the camp as they located the most likely holding place. Vinny, the best marksman of the group, crept in behind them providing cover. Gabe, the Medical Sergeant, stayed behind, watching the activity below and radioing his intelligence to the squad. Tony and Chief Warrant Officer Jacques "Jack" Bryant moved in behind Jobe, as the others spread out to provide the most optimum coverage for success.

The village appeared to be mostly men with a few women moving among the campfires, preparing food. Just as the signal came from the Engineer Sergeant that he had located the hut with their mission, Jobe heard screaming from inside the building he was nearest. A quick glance through the window had his stomach knotted as his face contorted in a grimace. An Afghan soldier was in the corner on the dirt floor, rutting against a heavily pregnant young woman who was crying as she tried to push him off.

A bead of sweat dripped down Jobe's face as he fought the urge to kill the man on sight. The sound in his radio earpiece was the only thing holding him back.

"Steady on," came Tony's voice, knowing the soldier's discipline was needed to take care of the mission first.

Jobe fought hard to tamp down the rage but found he was losing the battle. One of his younger sisters had been sexually assaulted two years ago when he was on his first tour after Special Forces training. His mind flashed back to the memory of his fury and his loss of control came rushing back. Feeling a touch on his shoulder he jerked around, seeing Vinny standing behind him.

Signaling to move forward, Jobe did what he was

trained. The mission needed to be accomplished at all costs. One wrong decision could mean the loss of the mission…and the loss of his squad. Forcing down the rage, he moved to his destination.

Within minutes, the foreign national was rescued from his holding place and the men began moving back away from the village, pulling out in formation. As the first in, Jobe was the last out, passing by the now quiet hut. Going against his training, he peered inside. The man was now snoring next to the woman, a pool of blood between her legs. Visions of his sister crowded his mind. No longer able to control his thoughts, Jobe crept closer to the window. The woman looked up, eyes wide in horror, then moved quicker than Jobe could have imagined. She leaned over, grabbing the sleeping man's gun and placing it to her head.

Before Jobe could blink, she pulled the trigger. The image burned into his memory. Forever.

THREE WEEKS LATER, Jobe walked into Captain Alvarez's make-shift office. Tony looked up as one of his best soldiers moved into the room and stood at attention. Tony considered him carefully. The body was the same. The steely-eyed determination was the same. But the man was different. Hard. Closed. Jobe resisted having to take time off for a psychological evaluation, but he had been too good a soldier to not follow a command.

Tony thought back to the days after they returned from the ill-fated mission. Jobe's anger had turned inward and he had begun a path of self-destruction. He had gone on a rampage, trashing his bunk after getting stinking drunk. The squad members quickly circled around, offering him support but knowing when he needed help. He was too much a vital part of their team for them to give up on and whatever it took, they were going to see that he had what he needed. The three weeks that he was given leave of duty and been forced to meet with the base psychologist had been the right thing to do. But as Tony stared at one of his best, he wondered if it had been enough.

Jobe stood in front of his Captain, determined to hold on to his control. He assured him he was fit and mentally ready to continue as part of the squad and had the backing of the psych eval to prove it. *Nothing matters but the mission. Get in, get 'er done, get everyone out. That's it. Anything else could get my squad killed.* Refusing to allow anything else to crowd into his mind, he strove to regain control. After the meeting he made his way back to his bunk, but changed his course of direction at the last minute. Heading to the communications building, he sat down at the computer and began typing.

First, was a note to his mom letting her know he was allright. Second, was a Dear John letter to his fiancé. Short, simple, to the point. *We're over. Too much to deal with without having to worry about you back home. I don't need the distraction, nor the concern. You'll be better off without me.*

Walking into his bunk, he knelt at the locker and pulled out her letters. The whole stack. Slowly, methodically, without any emotion he began tearing them up. Vinny walked in halfway through the destruction, took one look, and tried to grab them from his hands.

"What the hell, man? Don't do this," he shouted, bringing Gabe rushing in to see what was going on.

The look in Jobe's eyes stopped them. Cold. Hard.

"Talk to us, bro," Gabe demanded. "What're you doing here?"

Jobe shook his head for a moment not saying a word. It became apparent Vinny and Gabe were not going anywhere when they both sat down on the bed opposite of his. The tension flowed off of all three.

Hold on. Just say what you need to say and wait until they leave. Shaking his head, he thought of what the base shrink said. *Control. You feel a loss of control. Well, this is me getting rid of what I can't control.*

"I just gotta do this," he replied. Their silence spoke volumes so he continued. Staring intently into the eyes of two men he trusted more than life, he admitted, "I almost crawled through that window. I wanted to kill that son-of-a-bitch. But if I had?" Holding their attention, he said, "I'da blown the mission. I'da blown our cover and some of us could have died."

"You're human, Jobe," Vinny said carefully. "We

all are. We're stuck in a fuckin' war doing things most people back home have got no fuckin' clue about."

"Yeah, and that's the job we're trained for," he argued back. "We're fucking Special Forces. We don't make fucked up mistakes because we look into the eyes of some woman being raped and see our own sister."

"Vinny said it right. We're still human, Jobe. But you turning away had nothing to do with that man raping her or her killing herself. That's on them, man, not you," Gabe retorted.

"I'm the oldest," he said. The silence once again settled around the trio. "I was on my first fucking tour when I found out my sister was assaulted at a college party. I felt so fuckin' impotent."

Gabe and Vinny continued to sit quietly, letting Jobe have time to gather his thoughts.

"But mama said she was doing okay, getting counseling, and the last time I saw her, she looked good. So I squared it away." He looked down at his hands, pieces of paper still clutched in them. "Seeing that bastard just brought it all back and then seeing that woman blow her brains out…Jesus," he exclaimed, rubbing his hand over his face.

Sucking in a deep breath, he let it out slowly, as he continued to shake his head. "I can't do this," he said, indicating the torn letters in his hand. "I can't be what she needs. What she deserves. I can't be over here taking care of business, wondering what the hell is going on back home. So I cut her loose. Fuckin' shrink told me I had control issues. PTSD. Control issues? What the hell does he know? Of course I have control issues," he bit out. "We're trained to take control of every situation, so you know what? I am. Cutting her loose so she can have a life without worrying about some nut-job returning from the war."

"Bro," Vinny said gently. "You don't have to do this. Or at least not now. Give yourself some time. Maybe you'll feel differently."

Jobe's hand continued to shred the letters one by one. The handwritten missives she had carefully written claiming they were so much more personal than emails. Looking back up at the twins' hard faces, he said, "I've got my job to do. My squad to protect. My family to deal with, even from a distance. That's all, guys. That's all I can handle."

With the last letter shredded, he stood, tossing the remnants into the trash can. Just then Jack Bryant came around the corner. "Tony's calling a tactical meeting. Looks like a new mission, boys."

The three men followed him into the briefing room. Tony glanced at the twins entering first and then his eyes found Jobe's. Clear. Steady. Calm. Hard. The three nodded at him and he began the meeting.

CHAPTER 2

FIVE YEARS LATER

THE POUNDING OF his feet on the path beat a steady rhythm as Jobe listened to his Ipod for his early morning run. The late spring was giving over to summer and it felt like a hot one again. It was only five a.m., but the air was humid with the promise of an afternoon thunderstorm. Sweat soaked his t-shirt and he whipped it over his head while not breaking stride, nor tangling the wire to his earpiece.

Early morning runs were productive for him, starting the day with a chance to exercise his body and exorcise the demons from his mind. Years earlier, after trying unsuccessfully to deal with some of the stress of the war himself, he finally sought counseling.

Understanding how the loss of control could affect someone like him, who believed in the ultimate power of control, was a difficult and long journey. He worked to fill his time with good friends and family, and his thoughts with the positive of what they were doing.

Rounding the corner from the park, he jogged into his apartment building, nodding to the concierge as he headed toward the elevator. Instead of going up to his place, he went down a floor to the gym and pool area. After a quick shower to wash off the sweat, he dove into the pool, swimming a few laps. He loved the feel of the water after a run.

With an easy heave upward, he pulled his body out of the pool and took the back elevator up to his apartment.

Walking into work, Jobe arrived early, as was his habit, and moved through the halls of Alvarez Security. His former Captain, Tony Alvarez, began his company when he left the Special Forces and had filled it with some of his former squad members. The twins, Gabe and Vinny, worked there and the four of them made the core group.

Lily Dixon, one of their computer experts and married to their friend, Detective Matt Dixon, was on maternity leave for several more weeks. BJ, another computer expert, was pulling double duty trying to take care of the software needs while Lily was out. As he walked into the command center of the business, he saw that BJ was already there.

"What the hell are you doing here so early?" he asked, noting BJ's tired expression.

"My twins were up so I took care of them and got them back to sleep so Suzy could stay in bed a little longer. Then she got up, but I couldn't go back to sleep so I just came in."

Jobe shook his head in wonder at how his friend

handled having twins. But then life was definitely changing around Alvarez Security. Tony had lost his wife and baby girl in an accident while they were still overseas and now had met Sherrie whom he had just married. Vinny and Gabe, the quintessential hound dogs, had also settled down. They had gone from leaving bar nights with at least one woman on their arms to now being in committed relationships as well. Gabe married Jennifer, a beautiful social worker who had guardianship of her young brother, and he had taken on the role of surrogate father as well as a husband. And Vinny? Hell, Vinny could close down the rowdiest bar with the best of them, but now spent his evenings with his beautiful fiancé, Annalissa, a concert harpist who played for the local symphony.

Yeah, things are certainly different around here. Pushing the morose thoughts out of his mind, he chastised himself. *Those thoughts aren't morose. They're good changes. Good for my friends.* As he walked toward Tony's office, knowing that his boss was probably at work by now, he pushed back the reflections of how life could have been different.

Rounding the corner, he saw Tony just walking into his office. Jobe could not help but grin—there was a time when Tony would beat them all in. But now? With a pregnant Sherrie at home, he noticed his boss was a bit later getting to work.

"Captain," he greeted, sometimes referring back to Tony's military title.

Tony chuckled, knowing that of all of them, Jobe had the hardest time breaking the habit. "Morning," he replied, noting the time on the clock. "You don't think for one day you could sleep in?"

Jobe laughed and said, "Old habits, sir. I just rise early, work out and then head on in."

Tony eyed him carefully, seeing the straightforward, clear-eyed expression that he wanted to see. All of his squad had experienced the horrors of war, himself included. And each of them reacted differently. Some, like Vinny and Gabe, turned their anger outward, drinking and fucking their way through bars and women for several years. Jobe turned it inward, refusing to think that he could have what he wanted and be a good soldier at the same time. And nothing any of them said made a difference. It simply took time and some good counseling before they could finally see glimpses of the laid-back Jobe again. But by then, the girl he had loved was gone.

The hall began to hum, the two men able to hear others coming in. Doug, who had manned the security cameras overnight, was leaving as Terrance came to relieve him. Other employees came in, checked the orders board and then headed out, usually to install or check the high-end security systems that had been placed in many of the city's richest neighborhoods.

It was apparent when Gabe and Vinny made their way in as the noise in the main room became louder with the twins' banter. Tony saw the grin on Jobe's face and clapped him on the back as they followed the noise to the main conference area.

Tony stood at the head of the table and said, "Shane and Matt will be here in about fifteen minutes. They said the Police Chief wanted to offer us a contract for some cameras and installations. Don't know anything other than that, so we can just start our agenda until they get here."

The men around the table talked until the receptionist ushered Detectives Shane Douglass and Matt Dixon into the room. Old friends, they greeted each other enthusiastically and Matt began showing pictures of Lily and their new baby. He glanced over at BJ and said, "Hell, you don't look much better than I do."

"Yeah, well take your one baby and multiply it by two and that's what I've got," he yawned. "Don't mind saying that I'll be glad when Lily gets back but I sure as hell don't resent her taking all the time she needs."

Jobe sat listening to his friends discuss wives, babies, toddlers, sleepless nights and dirty diapers. It did not escape his notice that he could have had that. And threw it all away. That was the one thing that no matter how many times he talked to his counselor or pounded out the frustration in a long, hard run he could not reconcile—he could not turn back the clock.

Pleasantries aside, Tony asked Shane to start their part of the meeting.

"Ya'll know I spent a couple of years undercover in a drug gang, so the Chief has put us on a gang task force along with our vice duties. The gang activity is on the rise in Richland," he paused, then continued. "Hell, it's on the rise everywhere. Especially among teens, and that's where the Chief is asking for some help."

Matt took over explaining, "There are some places that we know are hangouts and no matter how diligent the street cops are, they just can't be everywhere. The city would like to partner with you to provide installed security cameras in a few areas that would help the police monitor the worst of the activity."

The group discussed the number of cameras and locations, then the details about monitoring the cameras. Shane assured them that no one needed to watch the live feeds; the Chief would just use them to help in investigations as they discovered more about the gangs in the area.

Tony nodded toward Jobe and said, "You know he's my best security technician, so you tell him what you need and it'll be done."

The group continued their discussion for the next hour, agreeing on what would be the proper equipment for the project.

AFTER WORK JOBE drove around to the quaint neighborhood filled with old, but neat, homes. He parked on the street and sat for a moment looking around. Kids still ran in the streets playing ball, bicycles tossed in yards as they roamed between friends' homes. Moms were yelling out of the front doors, telling the kids to go wash up for dinner. Dads were pulling into driveways in their trucks or company vans. Most of the families in the neighborhood were still laborers or worked for hourly wages. Hard-working families that took pride in their homes and made sure the old neighborhood was still a good place to raise kids.

Thinking back to the conversation at work with Shane and Matt, he looked around and did not see any signs of gang graffiti in the area. Letting out a sigh of relief, he jumped as a voice called out to him.

"Son, you gonna sit there in that truck all night or come in and have some supper?"

Chuckling, he jogged through the front gate, along the neat walk with spring flowers on either side and up to the front porch.

"Place looks good, pop," he commented.

Joseph Delaro stood with his son and gazed over the small yard with pride. "Your mother's got her flowers in and I saw her out here yesterday telling the boys across the street to be careful when they play ball."

"Some things don't change, do they?"

Clapping his hand on his son's shoulder, he said, "Never liked too much change, son. Least not with the good stuff. Let's go find your mother before she comes out here after both of us."

Jobe followed his father into the home he grew up in and realized that little had changed over the years.

The furniture had been updated over time. A new flatscreen TV mounted on the wall replaced the old one they had when he was a child. As he walked down the hall, he saw many of the same pictures in frames hanging on the wall, but more had been added. His sister, Hannah and Daniel, her husband and two children's photos graced the space now. His other two sisters, Miriam and Rebecca's college graduation pictures were also there.

He headed into the kitchen and looked around at the large space. That was one thing his mom had insisted on changing. She hated having a tiny kitchen and separate dining room. So she convinced Joseph to knock down the wall and open the space giving the family a comfortable, eat-in kitchen where she could cook and keep up with all the kids doing their home-work at the same time.

He walked in and eyed his mom standing at the stove. He had seen her there so many times over the years he wondered how she had not worn a hole in the floor. Her graying hair was neatly trimmed and she wore a familiar apron over her clothes. Rebecca was setting the table when she saw him first. Greeting him enthusiastically, she walked over to give him a hug. She was now a teacher and shared an apartment with Miriam and another girl. He knew his mom would have preferred the girls to live at home, but was slowly accepting the fact that all of her children were grown.

Rachel Delaro turned from stirring the pot on the

stove and grinned. "Well, it's about time my son comes home to have a meal. You haven't been here for almost two weeks. Not that I'm counting, of course."

He crossed the space and hugged his mom, kissing the top of her head. Soon they sat down to dinner once Miriam got in from work. She was a nurse at one of the city's hospitals and had day shifts this week. Hannah's family would come over for Sunday lunch, but for now the rest of them enjoyed the meal.

The conversation always flowed with his family, the only silences occurring when everyone was diving into the food at the same time. Rachel watched her son carefully—an old habit she acquired when he came home from his last tour. For all outward appearances, her son seemed calm and at ease as he and his father discussed Jobe's job. But she was a mother…and knew that appearances could be deceiving.

Miriam and Rebecca left after dinner. Joseph headed into the living room, settling into his recliner and turning on the TV. Jobe hung back in the kitchen helping his mom wash the dishes. She had never owned a dishwasher, claiming that she did not want a machine to take away the time she spent at the end of a day pondering and praying over her family.

"You still determined to wash each dish?" Jobe asked.

His mother smiled, saying, "You know the answer to that. For every plate I wash, I spend a moment in prayer for the family member or friend that ate off of it.

My mama used to do that and it's just a part of who I am."

He smiled in return, taking the dishes from her hand and drying them before stacking them on the counter.

"I prayed a lot for you Jobe, when you were gone. I knew when things weren't right and it tore my heart out not knowing how to help you."

He shook his head slowly, "It helped, Ma. Even when I didn't know what the hell I was doing, it helped." He caught her sharp look and immediately corrected, "I mean, what the heck I was doing."

She chuckled and said, "You're a good boy, Jobe. Always was. Still are. And if you have to say 'hell' once in a while, I won't fuss."

They grew quiet again as the dishes were put away. Pouring a cup of coffee, she nodded toward the table and the two sat back down. The comfortable silence settled around them, each lost in their own thoughts for a few moments.

Rachel sipped her coffee and peered over at her handsome son. He could feel her eyes on him and finally laughed as he looked up. "Okay, Ma. What is it you want to ask?"

"Hmmph," she said, setting her cup down. She fiddled with the handle for a few minutes before looking back up. "I know that Gabe and Vinny are now settled down and Tony's got that sweet wife of his pregnant." The unasked question hung in the air for a moment. "I was just wondering if…well if there was…you know…anyone you were interested in."

She saw the flash go through his eyes before being replaced with the calm again, and she winced knowing she had caused that second of pain. "You don't have to answer," she quickly stated.

He reached across the table and rested his hand on hers. "It's okay, Ma. You're right, all my friends are settling down and I know you're chomping at the bit for more grandchildren."

She shook her head as she squeezed his hand. "Oh no, son. That's not it. I mean of course I'd love more grandchildren, but Jobe, honey, I just want to see you happy…like before."

Silence once again settled as they sipped their coffee. "Can I ask if you ever tried to find her—"

"No," he bit out sharply, then immediately softened his voice. "Sorry, Ma. No, I didn't. After what I did to her…well, she did often write, begging me to not walk away from what we had. But I never wrote back. Then finally I got one last letter that said that she was giving me what I wanted and that was her out of my life."

She watched her son relate his story, seeing the searing pain in his eyes. "You don't have to talk about it, Jobe. I shouldn't have asked."

He inhaled deeply before slowly letting it out, then continued, "By the time I was getting out of the service and into counseling, I realized I had thrown away the best part of me. Not only thrown it away, but shredded it, stomped on it, and then threw it away."

"I used to love it when you would bring her over for Sunday dinner. Her parents were so sweet too," Rachel reminisced. "I never told you this, but I tried to reach out to them, but they had moved when she graduated and I never knew where they went."

"I thought about trying to find her," he admitted. "Not to contact her, but just to see. With the resources Tony has it would be easy."

Cocking her head as she gazed at him, she asked, "So what's stopping you?"

He ruefully looked directly into her eyes and replied, "I want her to be happy. You know? Met some great guy, fell in love and be living her dreams now in a nice house with a white picket fence. And maybe had a baby or two." He sighed again before continuing, "But since it can't be with me, then I honestly don't know if I can handle seeing pictures of her living the dream with someone else."

She nodded, not saying anything. After a few minutes, Joseph called from the living room asking if anyone was going to watch the game with him. Rachel shook her head in exasperation as she rose from the chair, taking their empty cups to the sink. Looking over her shoulder, she said, "You go on in and sit with your father, Jobe. Me and God have some more dishes to take care of."

THAT NIGHT, LYING in bed, sleep was not coming to Jobe. He climbed out of the bed and softly padded over to his closet. Kneeling in the corner where he kept his Army footlocker, he opened it. Among some of his memorabilia, he pulled out a small packet of letters. The letters that she had sent after he broke off their relationship. After he had destroyed the others. He knew them by heart. The first ones, full of begging promises and tearful pleadings from someone with a broken heart. He shifted them around in his hands until his fingers moved to the one in the back. The last one. The one where her anger had finally won the day and she poured it out on him. Deservedly so.

Replacing the letters back in the chest, he closed it methodically. Crawling back into bed he lay there until the morning light peeked through the blinds.

CHAPTER 3

M ACKENNA DUNN EXPERTLY parallel parked her little car in front of the brick building, set back from the road. She glanced to the seat beside her and saw the curious, but nervous face of her passenger.

"Come on," she said brightly. "Let's get you settled."

Mackenna stepped out of her car and leaned into the back seat to grab the small suitcase and two grocery bags. She led the way up the steps and used her key to open the door. The young woman followed obediently. They passed the front room, occupied with three women at computers and another woman appearing to be teaching them. Across the hall, they walked by a smaller room filled with books on shelves and two comfy chairs, just ready for lounging with a good story.

Mackenna pointed out each room as they passed and then they found themselves in the kitchen toward the back, overlooking the alley behind. There were two other women there, both turning and smiled as Mackenna appeared.

"Carla, Jenita, I'd like to introduce you to our newest guest. This is Gabriella, but she goes by Gabby."

The two women greeted Gabby enthusiastically before Mackenna interrupted to say that she was going to show Gabby her room. They made their way up the stairs in the back and down a short hall with several doors open on either side.

Moving through one of the doors, Mackenna showed Gabby into a small, private bedroom with a closet, twin sized bed, dresser, and chair. Pulling open the blinds to let in the sun, she turned to face the girl.

"I know it's small, but it's all yours for as long as you stay in the program. The other three bedrooms are larger and hold bunk beds. Now, you've already read the rules and have signed the agreement, but I need to know that you understand the importance of following the rules."

"I do, I promise," Gabby said, fear still in her eyes. "I don't want to go back. I want to stay here and be safe." Placing her hand on her protruding stomach, she continued, "And I want my baby to be safe as well."

Opening the grocery bags, Mackenna pulled out toiletries, linens, and other personal items. Lifting the small suitcase onto the bed, she said, "Okay, here are your clothes. We provide these initial personal necessities and if you need something else, you can ask me or Rose. I know you haven't met her, but she helps me here. She's teaching now, but you'll meet her later. The bathroom is just down the hall...you do have to share with the other women here but it should not be a problem."

Placing her hands on her hips, Mackenna stared firmly into Gabby's eyes. "Most important is this. You came to us. You wanted out and you want to learn employable skills. Our program is three months long. We can provide you with basic skill learning, job placement, and can help with your doctor appointments. You have the responsibility to keep your area clean, assist with the kitchen duties, and most importantly…" she made sure she had eye contact before she continued, "you absolutely cannot, under any circumstances, contact any of the gang members your ex belongs to. That was why we took your cell phone and disabled it when you entered our program. You'll get it back when you graduate."

Gabby's eyes grew round as she shook her head back and forth. "Oh no, Ms. Dunn. Never. I promise I never want to see him or have anything to do with him again."

Mackenna held Gabby's gaze for a moment then, satisfied with what she saw, she nodded and turned away. "Dinner's at six. Make yourself at home until then. Your classes start tomorrow and you can meet the other girls at dinner." Stopping at the door and looking back over her shoulder, her face softened with a smile. "And Gabby? I'm glad you're here."

Gabby sat down on her bed, overwhelmed for the moment. She knew she had been given a second chance at life…a life outside of the gangs. Looking at the retreating back of Ms. Dunn, she smiled at the woman in charge of the New Beginnings program. *Maybe, just maybe this will be my salvation.*

Mackenna made her way down the stairs, stopping in the small office that she called hers when she was in the building. She bounced between New Beginnings and the Department of Social Services building downtown. Sitting in the old chair, she powered up her laptop and quickly began scrolling through her emails. It seemed as though her work never ended. Answering the ones that she could, she glanced at her watch.

Dialing home, her mom answered, with a somewhat garbled greeting.

"Hey, I just wanted to make sure you were all right."

"Uh huh," came the reply.

"I'm going to meet a friend after lunch and then I'll be home. Is the nurse still able to stay a little later?"

"Yasss."

"Okay, mom. I love you and I'll be home as soon as I can. Text me if you need."

"Los ya ta," her mom said, working on trying to pronounce the words clearly. It did not matter how she said them. Mackenna knew her mother loved her. The stroke may have robbed her mother of much of her speech and movement on one side of her body, but that was all. The survival instinct was strong and passed on from mother to daughter.

Just then her phone vibrating interrupted her thoughts. Looking to see the caller, she answered happily.

"Hey, Jennifer! Are we still on for an early dinner?"

"Absolutely. I've been looking forward to this. I can't wait to hear how your center is going."

Making arrangements to meet, Mackenna hung up and powered down her laptop. Standing, she headed to the front room.

"How's it going?" she asked the computer teacher.

Rose smiled at her and nodded at the three women hard at work. "They're doing great. We've covered most of the basics and by next week should start with the most complicated reports and spreadsheets that they would need to know how to manage. In fact, I told Jerika that I think she's almost ready to have a job interview soon."

Mackenna's gaze found the smiling girl and walked over to give her a hug. "Fabulous! We'll make sure to train you on interviewing as well as helping you with your resume first. And before you start actually meeting with prospective employers, we'll get some business clothes for you."

Jerika returned the hug with tears in her eyes. "Oh my God, thank you. This'll make all the difference in the world."

"A good job will help you transition out of New Beginnings and into your own place," Mackenna reminded her. The smile on the young woman's face was priceless.

Looking up at Rose, she said, "Okay, I'm heading

out. Got a friend I'm meeting for early dinner. I probably won't be in tomorrow. I've got a staff meeting at DSS."

Waving goodbye, she stepped out into the bright sunlight and glanced up and down the street. A low-riding car with darkened windows drove slowly down the road. She stood there defensively as she watched it stop for just a few seconds in front of the building and then move on. Seething, she called Little John, her night watchman.

"Hey girl," he answered jovially.

"Hey back. Listen, I'm out front and that same car is driving by and I'm positive it's probably one of the gangs just wanting me to feel threatened."

"Now girl, don't you go gettin' all riled up. You can't fight those fuckers alone."

"I don't plan on fighting them, Little John, but honest to God, if they come back then I'm going after them."

"Oh Lordy, protect those fuckers when you get mad. Only you know they don't fight fair and they carry guns. So you gotta promise me, you'll leave them alone."

She heard the worried tone in his voice and assured him she was leaving. "Just make sure you lock up really good tonight when you go on duty and I'll talk to you in the morning."

Looking up and down the road again seeing nothing but quiet, she walked to her car and drove to the little restaurant to meet with her friend.

"MAC, I LOVE WHAT you're accomplishing," Jennifer enthused as the warm, melted mozzarella strung out from her fingers to her mouth. They had met at a little Italian eatery and decided to splurge on the appetizers. Jennifer Malloy was a fellow social worker for the Department of Social Services and handled an elder care center that provided low-cost housing for a group of elderly residents. Mackenna stared at the petite, blonde beauty in front of her, giggling at how much she could eat and stay so tiny.

"I know it can make a difference," Mackenna responded. "The research shows that education and job skills can entice some women to not be sucked into gangs or can get them out and keep them out. But it's slow going. So far, we have seven women ranging in age from eighteen to twenty-one that live there."

"How's the fundraising? I have to keep re-applying for my grant and beg our local politicians every chance I get."

Mackenna wrinkled her nose at the subject. "I know…it sucks. So far the grant money is getting us through and I've got a great teacher and a paid night watchman."

"Night watchman?" Jennifer asked, stopping her fork on its path to her mouth.

Shrugging, Mackenna answered, "I gotta try to keep the girls safe. I'm sure some of the local gangs know where we are, but so far no one has bothered us. But, well…"

"What?"

"The girl I took in today is pregnant. Her ex-boyfriend is in one of the gangs here in Richland. According to her, he doesn't care. She says he's got more bastards among the gang women and isn't about to pay any child support. But…I'm cautious anyway. I mean, let's face it, they don't like what New Beginnings is doing."

"I never thought about that," Jennifer admitted. "I had trouble with my elder center but only because someone wanted the real-estate we are in. But nobody cares if elderly people are living there. I can't believe that when I heard about you starting a program to help rescue girls from gangs and give them a chance at a new life, I didn't think about the dangers."

"The girls have come to us so it's not like we went out and stole them from the gangs. I just wish I had a way to keep them from going in to begin with. But that would involve getting to the girls by the time they are very young."

"Are they actively in the gangs or just, um…you know?" Jennifer asked.

Grimacing, Mackenna said, "Gang whores? Is that what you were trying to say?" Seeing Jennifer nod, she added, "Some gangs let the girls be actual members but they usually have to whore their way into the establishment. And for the most part, they'll never be included like the men. So, yes, many of them are just looking for a sense of family and the gang gives it to them."

"Oh, Jesus help us," Jennifer blurted, pushing her plate back.

"I know. But hopefully, our program will be a small start to allowing some of the girls to reclaim their lives."

"You mentioned a night watchman. What other security do you have?" Jennifer asked.

"Security? Um…well, we have deadbolts on the doors. I don't know what else you mean?"

"Girl, my husband is in the business. Gabe works for Alvarez Security and you better believe, I'm talking to him tonight about this."

"Jen, I've heard of Alvarez Security. There's no way my grant money will cover anything and you know our boss at DSS would have a coronary if I bring it up."

"No, seriously, Mac, they can do it. They covered my center because they do some write-off business and I'll bet they would do it for you. I'll talk to Gabe tonight."

Finishing the food on her plate, Mackenna smiled at her friend's enthusiasm and happiness when talking about her husband. Her smile slipped slightly when she thought of her own disastrous love life. It was practically nonexistent and when she did date? *I have such a penchant for going out with the wrong guy.* Lately, her battery-operated boyfriend was giving her more business than the last boyfriend she had.

"You okay?" Jennifer asked, interrupting Mackenna's depressing musings.

Startled, she laughed. "Yeah, just thinking about what all needs to get done this week."

"I hear you. It's non-stop, isn't it?"

"On top of the center, I have my mom's rehab to worry about. She's still covered under my dad's insurance, even after he died, but it isn't great."

"Oh, I'm sorry," Jennifer said, placing her hand on her friend's. "With all the talk about your work, I forgot what you're dealing with at home."

"Mom's doing great, she really is. Her speech is improving, although me and the nurse are probably the only ones who can understand her now. She doesn't have much movement on the left side, but since she was right-handed, she can still do things fairly easily on that side."

As they settled the check, Jennifer stated, "Well, I'm going to take one worry off of your plate. I'm talking to Gabe tonight!"

Parting company, Mackenna headed home, feeling strangely lighter than she had in a few weeks. *Maybe, just maybe, things are looking up.*

TRUE TO HER WORD, that night as the dishes were

being put away and her brother, Ross, was busy with his homework, Jennifer talked to Gabe about the New Beginnings security issues.

"They've got seven girls that have been reclaimed from gangs and what they're doing is amazing. But honey, they only have a night watchman and some deadbolts on the doors. What scares me is that these girls could be in danger from the gangs that they left. The director, Mac, is a friend and I want to help any way I can."

Gabe listened as his wife described the situation and nodded his agreement. "Sounds like something that Tony would be interested in."

"Good, because I want to make sure they're as safe as you made the Elder Center."

Coming up behind her, trapping her against the counter with his arms on either side, he leaned down and whispered against her lips, "Well, the Elder Center got my very private, special attention." Licking her lips, he plunged his tongue in, tasting the wine and choco-late cake they had for dessert.

"Well, maybe you can't give them the *exact* same attention," she purred as she melted into his arms.

Chuckling as he pulled away, he assured her that he would speak to Tony the next day. Then he added, "And you can show me your gratitude in bed tonight."

"Why, Mr. Malloy," she said, batting her eyes and giggling. "I'd be glad to."

MACKENNA SAT DOWN on the sofa after dinner with her mom as they watched TV. She had her laptop on her legs so that she could work while watching TV at the same time.

Penny Dunn looked over at her daughter. "Ya wok too har," she claimed.

Smiling up as she glanced over, Mackenna said, "I don't work too hard, mom. I'm just surfing the web right now." Seeing her mom's curious expression, she explained that her friend was going to try to get a company to set up some security for the shelter.

Satisfied, Penny went back to watching TV and Mackenna pulled up Alvarez Security on her computer. Reading what all they did, she knew that there was no way the grant would cover any of what they offered. Sighing, she hoped that Jennifer was right and that they would agree to do some pro bono work.

Jennifer had shown her a picture of her husband and Mackenna had to admit that he was gorgeous. The Alvarez Security website had no pictures except for the owner, Tony Alvarez. *God, he's handsome too. But, Jennifer mentioned that he was married to another one of her friends. Damn, all the good ones are gone.* Ruefully, she looked around at the small, one-level house that she and her mom had rented after Penny had the stroke. Her days were centered around New Beginnings and her evenings were with her mom. *Not exactly conducive for Mr. Gorgeous and Available to come walking through my door!*

She saw her mom staring her way again and tried to school her expression. But she was caught with the wistful expression on her face.

"Ya shou go ou mo. Ha fun," her mom said, turning off the TV and facing her daughter.

"Mom, I do have fun. I went out tonight, didn't I?"

Making a face, her mother shook her head. "Whe wa the las time ya wen on date?"

"I have dated. Just not recently," she admitted. "Mom, I'll go out again sometime, just not right now."

"Beca of me?"

"No! Because getting New Beginnings up and running has taken all my energy. Who has time to date with all of that?" They were quiet for a moment before she giggled. "And anyway, after Raymond, all other men pale in comparison."

Her mother joined her laughter, remembering the last man Mackenna tried to date. A boring man with a boring job, who came to dinner and talked incessantly about his work.

"Remember how he kept speaking louder around you?" Mackenna added. "I told him you had had a stroke, but you weren't deaf!"

The two women laughed until they had to wipe their tears, the memory of that disastrous date in their minds. As their mirth slowly dissipated, Penny looked at her daughter again.

"Wha abou—"

Shaking her head quickly, Mackenna interrupted, "No mom."

Her mother sat quietly and Mackenna immediately felt contrite. "I'm sorry. It's just…that ship sailed a long time ago and to be honest, it still stings a little."

The silence echoed around the room, each woman with their own memories filling their minds. Sighing, Mackenna gave an unladylike snort, saying, "Not only did the ship sail, but it caught on fire as it was sailing away. And then it blew up. And then while it was burning, it got caught in a whirlpool and was tossed around. And then lightning hit it as it was going down. And the waves knocked it over. And then it finally sunk to the bottom of the ocean." She sat for a second and then added, "And then when all the tiny pieces hit the bottom, they were obliterated and the dust got totally mixed in with the sand, never to be found again."

Penny lifted her right eyebrow at her daughter's description. "I thin I ga the pictu," she said, her heart aching for her daughter as she watched her lost in memory. Mackenna's expression was not one of anger, but had the look of resignation.

Mackenna shook her head, chasing out the morose thoughts and said, "Let's go to bed, mom. It's late and I know you've got to be tired."

She assisted her mom in getting ready for bed and was excited to see how much stronger Penny's left side was becoming. Her mother beamed as she showed

Mackenna how she could get her nightgown on herself.

Smiling, Mackenna helped her mother to bed and then headed to her own bedroom after checking the house one more time. With her thoughts filled with the past, sleep did not come. *Oh, mom. Why did you have to bring him up?*

After tossing and turning for almost an hour, she got out of bed and crossed over to her dresser. Squatting down, she pulled open the bottom drawer and felt toward the back underneath her out-of-season sweaters. Her fingers reached the packet of letters and she plopped down on the floor with the papers in her lap.

She smoothed her hands over the envelopes reverently, fingering the addresses in his handwriting. The familiar ache began in her chest. The ache of love. Long-ago love. Lost love. A single tear slid down her cheek and fell on the top envelope. It was not the first tear that had ever landed there.

She shuffled them around until the bottom one was on top. The one that ripped her world apart, never to be whole again. A surge of anger rushed through her as she thought of the words inside. Memorized from having read them over and over and over. A thousand times over.

And just as quickly as the anger came, it was replaced with a dull pain residing in her heart. Wiping her tears away, she put the letters back into the drawer and closed it. She sat on the floor for a long time, her hands as empty as her heart.

As much as she wanted to hate him, she could not. But when she had realized the door to that relationship had finally closed, she never looked for him again. The idea of seeing his smile on Facebook, probably with a new girl, or even wife would kill her.

Oh, to hell with him, she thought as she pushed herself up off of the floor and padded over to the bed. Crawling underneath the covers, she began thinking of what needed to be done the next day. *Staff meeting at ten a.m. at DSS. Talk to the boss about more grant money. Go over to a few high schools to talk to the counselors about seeing if they can identify girls that might be at risk for joining gangs. Get back to New Beginnings to check on Gabby.*

As she recited her day a restless sleep finally claimed her.

CHAPTER 4

T HE NEXT MORNING at the Alvarez staff meeting, Tony talked about the contract with the Richland Police to add some security cameras in a few of the areas known to be gang havens.

Jobe admitted to thinking about the gangs when he visited his parent's home the night before. "After talking to Shane and Matt yesterday, I found myself looking around for signs of gang graffiti. The neighborhood where I was raised is kind of run down now, but it still seems like the families there are working hard to keep it nice."

"Let's hope it stays that way," Vinny added. "I went home last night and did some searching on the internet. I feel like a dumb shit not knowing this, but we've got the Bloods and the Crips right here in Richland, along with MS-13. I mean, what the hell, man? And some of these kids are only about ten years old."

Gabe looked over sharply, "Goddamn, that's Ross' age. I can't even imagine a kid his age belonging to one of these gangs."

Nodding to his twin, Vinny continued, "And what he'd have to do to get in. Many of these gangs have either beat-ins, where they get the shit kicked out of them by a bunch of others for three minutes or they have to commit a crime. Anything from stealing to murder."

Tony said, "I've got BJ and Jobe working on figuring out which street cameras can be used and where we need to add some more. We'll also look at using existing cameras for feed for the police department."

"Guys, Jennifer talked to me last night and Tony, I was going to talk to you about it first, but it ties into what we're discussing so I'd like to bring it up now if that's okay," Gabe said.

Gaining the nod of approval from Tony, Gabe continued, "Jennifer's got a social worker friend that's running a small center for reclaiming women and girls from gangs. It's been open for about eight months and is run on grant money, so you know what that means. A shoestring budget and lots of hard work for the ones that are trying to make a difference."

"What's it do?" Jobe asked.

"It houses a few women who have voluntarily left or escaped the gang life and gives them basic job skills and helps them find work. It's called New Beginnings and according to Jennifer, it's doing just that. So far, she said that almost fifteen women have *graduated* from the program and have found jobs and apartments to live in."

Gabe had captured the attention of the rest of the group. Tony asked, "Does Jennifer think they need our help?"

"Yeah. The center currently has seven women there, and they're hoping to expand to more. The social worker, Mac, who's running the place, is a real dynamo, according to Jennifer." This statement brought chuckles from the men around the table, knowing that to a tiny powerhouse like Jennifer, this was high praise indeed.

"They're in an old house, not a great area of town, but of course where they can afford it. Jennifer said that there's a night watchman, who checks to make sure the doors are locked and," he shook his head, "she said Mac claims there are deadbolts on the doors."

"Hell, that's about as safe as you can get," Vinny stated sarcastically, knowing that the typical deadbolt is nothing to someone who really wants entrance.

"So, Jennifer wanted to know if there was anything we could do to make the place more secure. But if we do cameras, I know she would want them to be like at her Elder Center. Something that could be monitored from here and then have security systems in place that would alert the police department."

Tony nodded thoughtfully. "Are these girls still in danger from the gangs?"

"Probably," Jobe added. "From what we've heard, you don't leave gangs…at least not without a cost."

"There's more," Gabe said. "Jennifer told me that the director said there had been some drive-bys. Non-violent, but was pissed nonetheless. They've called the cops but according to Jennifer, Mac's not afraid to run out of the door with a baseball bat."

"Fuck," said the group collectively.

"Jesus, that'll get his head smashed in real quick," Vinny growled.

"If not shot," added Jobe.

"Looks like we've got a job to do," Tony stated.

"Boss, you need to know that there won't be any money from the center. It's run non-profit by a grant."

"We've done pro-bono work before and this is no different," Tony said. Looking around the table, he asked, "Everyone agree?"

With unanimous nods and "hell yeahs," the group began organizing the new mission.

"BJ, I want you to take Terrance and Doug with you as you scope the placement of the camera systems for the city lights. Jobe, I'm moving you to this assignment until it's up and running. Gabe, you call Jennifer and have her get in contact with Mac. We'll meet 'em this afternoon if possible at the center and do our initial consultation. You, Vinny, Jobe and I will meet there when you have a specific time."

MACKENNA WALKED OUT of the morning staff meeting, her head aching with all of the negatives. *No more grant money for this year. It'll be tight, but if Jennifer can point me in the direction of some fundraising activities, then maybe we can make it and even have enough for*

another part-time teacher.

With these thoughts swirling in her mind, she headed down the hall.

"Mac," came the shout from behind. Recognizing Jennifer's voice, she turned smiling.

"I've talked to Gabe, who's already talked to Tony, who's already decided to help out your center."

Before Mackenna could react to that news, Jennifer rushed on. "And, they want to meet this afternoon to see the center and assess the needs."

"Wow, they move fast," Mackenna said, stunned at the quick events.

With a wink, Jennifer agreed. "Oh yeah, all the Al-varez men move fast."

Rolling her eyes, Mackenna gave Jennifer a shoulder nudge as they walked down the hall together. "You know what I mean. So when do they want to meet?"

"Yes, I do know what you mean and I just wish you'd let someone move fast on you! But as far as this afternoon, Gabe said to give them a time and they'll be there."

Mackenna pondered what all she needed to accomplish and replied, "Is three o'clock okay?" She waited as Jennifer pulled out her cell phone and confirmed with Gabe. Receiving her nod, Mackenna continued walking down the hall, grateful to Jennifer, but not wanting to intrude on what was becoming a lovey, personal phone call. *I'm glad for her, but I wish...* Shaking her head, she stepped into the elevators, knowing she needed to rush to get her list of things to complete so that she could be at the center by three o'clock.

ARRIVING AN HOUR early, Mackenna was pleased that she had been able to fly through her appointments. She only went to one high school, but set up a time to talk to all of the high school counselors and social workers at one of their meetings next month to discuss identifying young girls that might be lured into the gang life.

Armed with three bags of groceries, she made her way into the kitchen. Carla and Jenita took them from her and began putting them away.

"Ladies, I've got an agreement with one of the churches down the street that we can have some of their food that does not get eaten after they have their Wednesday night meals. That would provide supper for you all for at least a couple of days and stretch our food budget."

"Perfect," Carla said, putting away the vegetables that were brought in. "And before you ask, Gabby is doing great. She settled in last night and this morning was eager to start the Microsoft Certification program, so Rose already has her in the education room with the others."

Sighing in relief, Mackenna smiled. "So how's the job hunting going for you, Jenita?"

The young woman grinned her reply. She had been

at the center for over two months and was ready to graduate out into the world, standing on her own. "Well, this morning the doctor's office where I interviewed for the receptionist position called back...and they offered me the job!"

With a whoop of joy, Mackenna hugged her. "That's fabulous! When do you start?"

"I begin next Monday and I've been looking into the roommate sharing program you were telling me about. I figure that I will need at least a month of working and then I can transition to a shared apartment. I've found one that will be available next month and it's a three bedroom apartment that I'll be sharing with three other women. Two are sisters and they share the large master bedroom with its own bath, so I'll have my own bedroom that will share the hall bath with just one other person."

The three women continued to hug as Mackenna realized what a monumental moment she was experiencing. She felt it every single time. When someone who three months ago left a gang in the middle of the night determined to change the course of their lives and was now doing just that...*amazing. Absolutely, fucking amazing!*

Smiling as she stepped back, she remembered the afternoon's appointment. "Ladies, in about an hour we'll have some visitors. There will be someone here from a security agency to assess what we need to make sure our building and its occupants are as safe as they can be."

Carla nodded, admitting, "I'm glad. That car has been by again this morning. I'm worried that it may be here for Gabby."

A flash of anger flew through Mackenna's eyes. "I was afraid that because she's pregnant, it might be a problem. Those goddamn fuckers come back, I swear I'll kick their asses!"

"Um, I hate to bust your badass bubble, but girl? You're not big enough to take them on and you'd be foolish to do so," Jenita said, knowing that Mackenna had a penchant for acting on instinct at times.

"Yeah, well, I just refuse to let them hurt her," was the only reply. "Let's go upstairs and make sure the rooms are ready in case the visitors need access to the whole building." With that, the three women headed out of the kitchen.

THE ALVAREZ SECURITY MEN drove down the street toward their destination in two of the company SUVs. Eyes peeled, they each expertly surveyed the area. It was in an older section of town with a mixed community of stores and brick buildings. Several old churches dotted some of the corners and while there was a hum of daily activity, it was not difficult to imagine that it would be easy pickings for someone with nefarious intent.

The New Beginning's building was unassuming,

located in the middle of the block and set back slightly from the street. A small placard was on the door, but other than that there were no other distinguishing features. Jennifer was just pulling up in her car at the same time and walked over to greet the men, moving straight into Gabe's embrace.

Jobe's gaze immediately took note of the problem areas. *Little front lighting. No peephole in the door. Unlit walkway from the street to the front stoop. No security bars on bottom floor windows.* As he stepped out of the vehicle, he saw Tony shaking his head. *Yep, he sees it too. A security nightmare for these women.*

"We're a little early," Jennifer said, "so let's go around the back and you can see the whole outside of the building."

The men made their way around the perimeter, noting the narrow space between the center and the buildings on the sides. There, a small courtyard held a picnic table and umbrella, an old grill, and off to the back were the trash cans that were next to the fence leading to the alley. Again, Jobe's eyes quickly assessed.

No lights on the back. A simple padlock on the fence gate leading to the alley.

Jennifer led them through the back door into the kitchen. The area was large, but seemed immediately dwarfed by the four huge men. A woman entered the room from the hall and gave a start. Jennifer jumped in, "I'm sorry. We're here to see Mac. She's meeting us to talk about some security."

"Oh yes, of course. I'm Rose. I teach computer classes to the women in the classroom upfront. I think that—"

Just then, a scream coming from the front of the building startled the group. Jobe, closest to the hallway, sprinted forward as he heard a woman's voice yell, "Call the police, Rose!" He caught a glimpse of a slender woman's back, hair pulled up on her head, as she raced down the stairs and made it to the door ahead of him, grabbing a baseball bat next to the door.

Throwing it open, Mackenna charged out onto the stoop, wielding the bat in the air. "I'm calling the police you fuckers. Get outta here," she screamed at the same low-riding car, this time with the passenger side windows rolled down and several guys hanging out giving her the finger.

"You can't hide forever, bitch!" one yelled.

"Bring it, you bast—umph," she grunted as she was grabbed around the waist from behind and lifted off of the ground, her back slammed against a tall, hard body. Her reddish-gold hair fell out of the makeshift twist and tumbled down her back.

"Are you fucking crazy?" asked the enraged voice of the man who had picked her up easily, his arm binding her tightly. "You provoke those bastards and you're just asking for trouble," he growled.

Realizing that the front stoop had become crowded with whom she could only assume was Tony Alvarez and more of his men than she knew was coming, she saw Jennifer, wide-eyed looking at her.

"Mac? Are you okay?" Jennifer asked, glancing at Jobe holding on to Mackenna, a strange expression on his face.

"Let go of me, you big oaf," Mackenna said, struggling against the unforgiving vise grip of the man holding her.

She found herself immediately released but instead of freedom, she was whirled around to face her would-be rescuer. And stared into the face of the man who had haunted her memories. His face, older and harder than she remembered. His build...heavier, even more muscular. And his expression? Shock. Pure shock.

Her chest heaving as she tried to catch her breath, she pushed against him almost tumbling backward down the front stoop stairs. His hands automatically reached out and grabbed her upper arms, saving her from falling. Not wanting him to touch her, she pushed again.

"Settle," he growled. "You're gonna fall if you keep this up."

Righting herself, she straightened up trying to regain her dignity. *Don't let him see you stare. Don't give him that.* Steeling herself, she turned toward the man matching the internet picture of Tony Alvarez and held out her hand.

"You must be Mr. Alvarez. I'm Mackenna Dunn, director of New Beginnings."

Tony, Gabe, and Vinny stared at her as though she

had sprouted three heads. The woman who one minute ago was wielding a baseball bat threatening street thugs was now attempting a composed and serene expression. And for some reason had rocked Jobe's world by the stunned expression on his face. Then it hit all three of them at the same instance. Mackenna Dunn. The name they had heard over and over when stationed in Afghanistan. At least before…

Tony, quickly recovering, took her hand and shook it gently. "You're right, Ms. Dunn. I'm Tony Alvarez, but please call me Tony."

Mackenna nodded, replying, "Mackenna. Although some just call me Mac." She gave Jennifer an evil eye, but Jennifer only laughed.

Tony introduced the twins, Gabe and Vinny, and then nodded behind her and said, "And this is Jobe. Jobe Delaro."

She knew she had to glance behind her but for all the world, she could not bring herself to do it. *Maybe he'll just disappear. Be gone. Maybe he was just an illusion.*

"Hello Mackenna," came the very real voice behind her. His simple words moved over her like lava. Smooth, flowing. *And will burn me if I let them!*

Taking a fortifying breath, she turned back around avoiding his gaze. *Show him I don't care.* She lifted her eyes to his penetrating stare and her mind stumbled as much as the words trying to come out of her mouth.

"H…Hi…um…hello, Jobe."

He stared back into the face of the most beautiful woman he had ever seen. Her red-blonde hair still appeared to be a lion's mane. She'd put on a couple of pounds since college but from where he was standing they looked great on her. Light, brown eyes that tried to focus anywhere but at him. *Of course, they would want to look anywhere but at him.* His mind locked up, wondering what he could possibly say to her.

"Ms. Dunn?" came a woman's voice from inside the building. "Are they gone?"

The group in the front turned and saw a young pregnant woman standing in the hallway, fear present on her face.

Mackenna pushed past the others, running into the house, dropping the baseball bat at the same time. Encircling the girl in her arms, she reassured, "Gabby, it's fine. They're gone."

Jenita and Carla came down the stairs, pale but smiling. "You are one badass mama," Jenita said.

Jobe growled as he followed her inside. "Don't encourage her. That was a stupid, senseless move and you know it," he said, punching each word out.

Mackenna turned and stared coldly at him. "I do what I have to do to make sure those punks stay on the street and outta my building."

"And you think some tiny girl with a baseball bat is going to do that?" he roared. "Fuck, Mackenna, those guys could pull out a gun and shoot you right on the front stoop or jump out and knife you."

"I'm doing what I can and part of that is letting them know they don't scare me!" she yelled back.

"They don't give a fuck what you think, but if you disrespect them, they will come after you!"

Mackenna was shaking with anger and Jennifer grabbed Gabe's arm, hoping he would stop the screaming match, but Tony beat him to it, taking charge of the situation.

"Ms. Dunn, we're here to help and so let's sit down and discuss what your needs are." Turning to Gabe and Vinny, he said, "You two continue the building inspection and report back here when you have a cursory idea of what we can provide. Jobe, you'll join me with Ms. Dunn."

"It's Mackenna, and why can't Gabe stay?" she answered boldly, her chest still heaving with exertion.

"My company, my rules, Mackenna," Tony stated plainly.

The look in his eyes brooked no argument as she drew herself up, the professional façade back on her face. "Of course. If you'll follow me to the kitchen, there's a table large enough for us to sit at. Rose, take Gabby back into the classroom. Carla and Jenita, please continue with what you were doing."

Moving down the hall, she led them to the table where she sat gracefully as though she had not a care in the world. Inside she was seething. And aching.

Heart pounding, Jobe felt out of his element. *And I never feel out of my element!* He noticed that Tony and

Mackenna sat across from each other, so he slid into the seat next to her. Better to survey her without having to see the censure in her eyes.

"Okay, first things first," Tony said. "Never, under any circumstances, run out of here with a bat. That was completely foolish and dangerous."

Mackenna started to protest, but he interrupted.

"They could have hopped out the car, been up on your stoop in probably five seconds, had that bat out of your hand and beat you to death with it."

She blinked slowly as her stomach churned.

"You're working with these girls so you must have done some research about gangs and I don't care if they're members of a national gang or some punk-ass local group—respect is their mantra. You disrespect them, they will take you down. Do. You. Understand?"

She nodded, realizing how foolish she had been. "I'm not usually reckless," she replied softly. "I just got so mad." She blinked fast, trying to keep from allowing a tear to slip.

Tony's voice softened. "You're doing a good thing here, Mackenna. Let's keep you safe so that you can keep doing it."

Tony began the conversation about her security needs, but Jobe could not keep his mind on the words that were spoken. *Ms. Dunn. That's her maiden name.* He quickly glanced at her ring finger and found his breath leaving him as he noted she was not wearing an engagement ring. His palms began to sweat as he thought back to the last letter she wrote after he had ignored all her pleas to not break up with her...where she admitted he had shredded her but that she would work every day to erase the memory of him from her very soul. *And I let her. What a fucking prick.*

Tony had asked Mackenna about the center and what her major concerns were. His eyes cut over to Jobe but realized his most steely soldier was staring openly at his former girlfriend.

Mackenna could feel Jobe's eyes on her but refused to look at him. Wishing Jennifer had come with them into the kitchen, she knew her friend was outside grilling her husband on the scene she had witnessed.

"If it weren't for the latest drive-bys, I would feel very safe about the center. The neighborhood isn't bad and we haven't had any problems. But our new girl is pregnant by someone in a gang and I'm wondering if that's causing their interest. I...I don't really know what to tell you. I have no idea what we should have as far as security goes and I have to be up front—there's no money in the grant for anything."

Tony began explaining the basics of security, the lighting at the entrances, cameras installed, and even bars on the first-floor windows.

Mackenna's head began to pound as Tony continued to list the things that he would recommend while the man who had ripped her world apart five years earlier was sitting next to her at a kitchen table as though he had every right to be there. *Don't look. Don't give him the satisfaction of even talking to him. No, wait. That makes it seem like I care. I don't care. Well, I don't want him to think I care.*

"Mackenna," came his warm voice from beside her.

She could not help herself. She turned and forced herself to stare at him in the eyes. She had thought that having him cast her away while he was overseas had been the hardest thing to bear, but at this moment she was not sure. Facing him was pure agony.

The silence in the room was deafening. Jobe could hear his own heart pounding and was sure that he could hear hers too. *If only—*

Just then the others entered the kitchen from their outdoor assessment and sat down at the table as well. Jennifer appeared stunned, so Jobe was sure that Gabe had filled her in on some of their story.

The others, determined to keep the conference professional, began immediately planning. Mackenna felt as though she had fallen down the rabbit hole—one minute she was threatening some thugs and the next she was emotionally assaulted by the past. And all the while, these other people in her center were taking charge, making plans as if she were not there.

Jobe looked at her, realizing that even after five years he could tell what she was thinking. Only the girl from his past was facing off with his co-workers with a toughness that he had never seen before. *What's happened to you?*

The meeting came to an awkward end and Tony assured her that they would begin work the next day with the equipment that they had and the installations would continue after some special orders came in. Walking them back to the front of the building, she noticed that Jobe was right behind her. Not close enough to invade her space...but close enough to let her know that he was still there. And still affected her.

She shook Tony, Gabe, and Vinny's hands and gave Jennifer a heartfelt hug. Her friend whispered in her ear, "We'll talk. It'll be okay, I promise." Nodding, she let them walk down the stoop. Steeling herself to be professional, she turned with her hand out.

"It was nice seeing you, Jobe. Thank you." *God, I hope that sounded icy enough.* Forcing herself to look into his eyes, she saw the smile on his face.

Taking her hand in his much larger one, he did not let it go. "It was very nice seeing you again, Mackenna."

Just as she was pulling her hand back, Tony called out from the street. "Gabe's going with Jennifer in her car, so Vinny and I'll ride in this one. You can have the other one yourself."

Jobe grinned as he nodded, silently conveying his thanks to his buddies. *They know what this means. They know she was put back in my life for a reason. Don't have a clue what that is, but I'm sure as shit gonna find out.*

Mackenna's expression was one of shock that his co-workers would just leave them like that. She watched as they drove down the street and then felt pressure on her hand. Jerking it back, she realized that he had been holding it while she gawked at the others leaving.

"Yes, well…um…I have to get back to work."

"Then I'll see you tomorrow when we come," he replied.

"No! I mean, that I won't be here. I'm sure that you can do all that you need without me. You can just see…um, Rose. The teacher. She can help you. I'll be…somewhere." *Jesus, I'm babbling.*

Smiling, he could tell that she was nervous. *Nervous good or nervous bad?* He was not sure, but he intended to find out. "Tony's gonna need you here. You're the one who'll have to sign for everything, so you'll need to be here. At least for part of the installation."

Drawing herself to her full height, she still had to lean her head way back to look him directly in the eyes, saying, "Fine. I'll be here. Now if you'll excuse me." Turning she walked on unsteady legs back into the center, closing the door behind her. As she heard him walking down the sidewalk, she peeked out of the window. Black, tight t-shirt stretched across his back. Tall, muscular. Thick hair that just beckoned fingers to be run through it.

Closing her eyes, she drew in a ragged breath. *Why did you have to come back into my life? Why couldn't you have just stayed a memory?* She leaned her forehead on the pane of glass, as her heart ached for the millionth time as she wiped away another tear. Lifting her head, she saw him sitting in the driver's seat. Staring. Directly. At. Her.

CHAPTER 5

J OBE OPENED HIS apartment door at the knocking, knowing before he did who would be outside. Vinny, Gabe, and Tony all stood in the hall. He threw open the door, wordlessly inviting them in. *How many times over the years have we done this?* Shutting the door behind him, he watched as they settled onto his oversized sofas. He also noticed Tony eyeing the whiskey bottle on the coffee table.

Walking over, he sat down in one of the chairs facing the sofa and nodded toward the bottle. "In answer to the question on your mind, no, I haven't been drinking. But yes, I've been thinking about it."

"Fair enough," Tony replied, leaning back in his seat.

The silence blanketed the room, each man holding on to their own thoughts. Finally, Vinny was the one to break the ice.

"So what's the deal? You gonna be okay with this assignment? 'Cause if you're not, I've told Tony that I'll take it."

Shaking his head, he said, "No, I've got it. There's no need to worry about me."

"You had to be stunned, man. I didn't know who she was until I saw your face. Then her name hit me about the same time it hit everyone else."

Gabe admitted, "I'm sorry. When Jennifer kept talking about someone named *Mac,* I just thought we were meeting some guy. I mean, I can't swear that the name Mackenna would have registered with me, but at least we would have been a little more prepared."

Tony, having sat quietly watching Jobe, finally said, "You want to tell us what you're thinking?"

Jobe snorted as he answered. "I've been thinking of her since I left the center. I have no idea what place I can carve out in her world, but I'd like to try. If she'll let me, that is."

"But?" Vinny prompted.

"But there's a lot for her to have to forgive for us to even be acquaintances, much less friends," Jobe replied. "And I don't have a clue how to go about trying to get her to forgive me."

"Hell man, every one of us has come to you for advice about our women and now you're the one who should have the answers," Vinny exclaimed.

"So what do you think I should do?" Jobe asked, looking at his closest friends.

"I think she deserves the truth," Gabe answered, as the others agreed.

"The truth? I should tell her that after what I saw, I lost it? That I've been successfully dealing with PTSD, but at the time I was so overwhelmed that the idea of being with anyone was horrifying to me?"

"Yeah, that's exactly what you should tell her. The honest to God truth," Tony stated firmly.

Jobe sighed as he leaned back in his seat. The silence once again filled the room. "It sounds so fucking pathetic now. Over there, the idea of maintaining a relationship was overwhelming. Monumental. Unattainable. Now, looking back? Jesus, I took the pussy way out!"

Tony leaned forward, holding Jobe's gaze. "You did what you had to back then to survive. We all did in our own ways. There was no right or wrong. We just did what we had to do to keep going in any way we could. That's what you need to tell her. That's the conversation you need to have."

Jobe nodded slowly, sucking in a huge breath. "I know. Even if she never forgives me, she deserves to know that. I owe her that."

"Now, I gotta know if this is going to be a problem on the job. I think you're the best man for taking care of her security, along with Gabe. But just because this is a pro bono case, Mackenna is still my client and I gotta know that a professional job can be done."

Jobe wanted to be insulted that Tony even had to ask, but his Captain would demand nothing but the utmost best from everyone. Looking him in the eye, he nodded. "I've got this, sir. You'll get nothing but the best from me."

Tony grinned as he stood and said, "Just what I

expected." As he walked to the door, Gabe and Vinny both nodded to Jobe before leaving.

Gabe admitted, "Listen, I told Jennifer what I knew but told her that the story is yours to tell Mackenna if and when you choose. She understands that because that's what I finally did with some of my experiences."

Vinny agreed, "Same here. It took a while for me to unload some of that shit off on Annalissa, but she gets it now. Just remember—you need us, we're here."

With that, the three friends left leaving Jobe alone with his thoughts…and memories.

MACKENNA GOT TO the center early the next morning, having not slept the night before. Her hair was pulled back in a ponytail that stuck out of the opening in the back of her ball cap. *Good—I'll show him that he's not worth my getting fixed up for.* She stilled for a moment, her eyes closed as her knuckles ached from gripping the counter fiercely. *Be strong. Never let him see that he devastated me.* Just then, she heard the sounds of several men outside. Taking a deep breath, she pushed off of the counter and went out to greet them.

Hours later, Mackenna was wondering about her sanity for agreeing to the security work. Jobe had managed to do his job and be where she was at every turn. When she was in the kitchen, he needed to fill their water canteen. When she was in her office, he needed to measure the window in that room. When she went upstairs to check in the bedrooms, he was hanging outside their windows, attaching monitors. When she decided to work in the back for a while, he managed to need to be at the back gate.

When he asked a question, she curtly answered, giving no more of a response than was necessary. She noticed that Gabe stayed outside and allowed Jobe to interact with her. *Why? Why is he trying to have a conversation with me?* The more she thought about it, the more her head hurt.

Finally, she grabbed her purse and headed for the front door, waving at Rose, who was giving her a sympathetic look. Mouthing *I'm leaving* to her, she stepped out onto the stoop. Right into a large body working on a camera over the front door.

She did not even need to lift her eyes to see who it was. She was staring directly at his chest and knew instinctively that it was Jobe. *Fuck my life*, she thought.

Plastering a smile on her face as his hands came down to grab her shoulders to steady her, she tried to ignore the spark she felt. "I'm leaving now, so you'll have to pester Rose if you need anything."

"Pester? Is that what you think I've been doing?" his warm voice slid over her.

"No, I'm sure you give all your clients this much attention," she answered sarcastically and then immediately wondered if he did.

"I've got to confess that I've never given this much

attention to any other job," he said, his eyes twinkling.

She found herself wanting to slap the smile off his face, but could not think of a retort worthy of the situation so she turned and started down the steps.

"Where do you have to run off to?" he called out after her.

She turned slowly and stared at him coldly. A long minute passed before she spoke, "I have responsibilities besides just this center. Things that have to be taken care of."

He sauntered down the steps to where she was standing. She wanted to move, but her legs were rooted to the sidewalk. Just the look of him still made her heart beat erratically.

"Are you sure you can't stay for a while?" he asked softly.

"No," she replied sharply. "I have to get my mom to a doctor's appointment."

"Your dad can't take her?" he asked.

Jerking out of her Jobe-induced trance, she reared back as though she had been slapped. "No, Jobe, he can't. He's dead." Turning she stalked toward her car, leaving him standing where she left him.

LATER THAT AFTERNOON, Jobe walked through Alvarez Security toward BJ's workstation. "BJ? Got some digging I'd like you to do."

"Sure man, what's up?"

"I know when Gabe was trying to get some info on Jennifer, Lily wouldn't do it saying that a woman wouldn't like someone finding out stuff without talking to them first. But I'm desperate."

BJ chuckled. "Yeah, I heard you all are working with a woman you'd once been engaged to." He looked at Jobe for a second, seeing pain flash through his eyes. In a softer voice, he asked, "What do you need? I've got no problem giving you whatever you think'll help."

"Grateful, man," he replied. "I got along real well with her parents although I only met them a few times. They lived a couple of counties over in Charlestown and she was super close to them. I wrote to her when I got my shit together, but she was graduated from college and none of my letters to her former address ever got delivered. I'd even tried her parents' address, but they were returned." He looked at BJ ruefully, saying, "Of course her parents probably hated my guts, so they might not have even given the letters to her. She told me yesterday that her dad was dead and I want to know what else I missed before I step into another hornet's nest."

Gabe and Vinny walked in about the time that BJ typed in the names. Within a few seconds, an obituary popped up. "Man, I'm sorry, but her dad died about four years ago."

"Does it say how?"

"Says after a year-long battle with cancer."

"Ah, fuck. That means he was probably diagnosed right about the time that I broke up with her. God-damnit!" he cursed.

Tony walked in just at that moment, taking the scene in. "What's going on?"

Jobe turned, rage on his face and bit out, "Her dad was diagnosed with cancer about the time I broke up with her and then died a year later. I had no idea because I was so fucked up with my ideals of honor and duty!"

Looking at the men standing around BJ's computer, Tony then focused on Jobe. "My office. Now."

Used to following commands, Jobe walked behind Tony into his office taking the chair indicated. Gabe and Vinny entered as well. Tony eyed them as he walked behind his desk. Looking over at Jobe, he lifted his eyebrow in silent questioning.

Jobe nodded his acquiescence. "We're all brothers, Captain. It's fine if they stay."

Tony motioned for the twins to come in and they quickly took seats. Looking at Jobe, he said, "Talk to us."

Jobe ran his hand over his face. "Guys, we just talked about this last night. I know what I've got to do, but finding out about her dad just ripped me."

"Yes, we did just talk about his last night," Tony agreed, "But part of your ongoing PTSD counseling is talking to us when you feel overwhelmed."

Jobe thought about his symptoms for a moment.

Every case is different, but he had not found many in his situation during the counseling groups he had attended over the years. He rarely suffered a nightmare, although occasionally he would have the sharp memory pierce his consciousness. While others were no longer able to hold down employment, he threw himself into the missions while still in the Army and now working for Tony he gave one-hundred percent every day. He was controlled enough to keep himself away from overindulging in alcohol, risky behavior, or even promiscuousness. He kept himself physically fit and mentally sharp, almost to an excess. And these three men knew that better than anyone.

Taking a deep breath, Jobe began talking to the brothers-in-arms that were there. That understood. That cared.

"Somehow I told myself that she'd be better off without me, because I couldn't give the team what it needed, try to be there emotionally for my sisters and parents who were going through their own problems, and plan a future with her. At that time, I saw no future."

"And now?" Tony prodded.

"I work hard, but I'm no longer seeing it as the on-ly way to get through the day. I exercise, but no longer until I drop. I talk to my sisters but realize that I can't keep them in a bubble and safe every second of the day. Hell, Hannah was assaulted but has dealt with it the best she can. She's happily married and has two kids.

So yeah, I feel like I'm much better."

They sat in silence for a moment, until he continued. "But how do I explain to the woman I loved, that I just simply fell apart for a while. I went nuts, ripped up her letters, and threw myself into my job at the expense of our relationship? It made sense when I did it. Hell, it made sense when we talked last night. But now, knowing that when she was trying to reach out to me, her dad was dying and I just ignored her. Maybe the best thing is to take myself off the job, Tony, and leave her in peace."

Vinny eyed his friend and said, "I never believed in one woman for one man. That shit seemed like something from a Disney movie and we sure as hell know our lives weren't Disney movies. But when I saw Tony and Sherrie together, I knew that was something special. Different. And when Gabe got with Jennifer? Fuck, any of us could see what that was. And me? Annalissa is everything I never thought I would want and never thought I could have. But she's it. Do you get what I'm saying?"

Jobe held his gaze but shook his head slowly. "Not really, man, except that you all found it."

"I saw her face when she looked at you. And when she tried not to look at you. Yeah, she's angry and confused, but Jobe, don't think for a second that she doesn't still feel something for you."

Gabe nodded. "Vinny's right. Even when you were with her today, I could see it too. She's hurting, no doubt. But this girl's worth fighting for. Worth giving it your all to take care of and make her happy."

"Oh, there's no doubt that she's worth it," Jobe admitted.

Tony had been sitting quietly, letting his friends talk through the situation but now observed one of his most valuable team members and said, "Jobe, you've never backed away from a mission. Not even when you were vulnerable. You planned, you knew what you were heading into, and you had the most *Never Say Die* attitude of any of us and that's saying a lot. I'm not saying make Mackenna your next mission. But you owe it to yourself and to her to see this through till the end. Until you can be friends or more or you decide that it is totally unsalvageable."

Jobe smiled for the first time knowing they were right. She was worth giving it everything he had.

COMING IN EARLY the next morning, Mackenna greeted Little John, who was just getting ready to leave.

"You're here before your regular time," he said. Eying her carefully, he added, "Heard there was some excitement around here the other day."

"Yeah," she admitted, pouring a cup of coffee for both of them. "I'm afraid I let my anger get the best of me and I acted rather foolishly. And in front of the security team that came by." She saw him give her a stern glare, so she quickly added, "Don't worry. I learned my lesson. No more baseball bat escapades."

He chuckled, shaking his head. "I know it's wrong to say this, but honest to God, I wish I coulda seen that."

She smiled for the first time since yesterday as they sat at the table. A comfortable silence settled on the two as they sipped their coffee. She looked up after a few minutes, seeing him staring at her.

"You got something else to tell me, girl?"

Pursing her lips, she said, "I suppose that one of the women told you about seeing my ex here yesterday."

"Someone may have mentioned something about that," he casually admitted.

"Yeah, right. They probably couldn't talk about it fast enough!" she complained.

He gave no response and she weighed her words carefully. "We met in college. He was in the Army. Special Forces. Was serving in Afghanistan. I was here planning our wedding and he was over there deciding how to break up with me. He finally just decided that the modern method of a break-up email was best. So I emailed and wrote letters numerous times, begging him to stay with me. To no avail. Over and done with for him, I suppose. Haven't seen or heard from him in five years and boom, he shows up yesterday working for a security company here in Richland. I think that just about sums it up for you."

She took another sip of coffee hoping he would not

see her shaking hands. He noticed.

"You know I was in the military?" he asked. Her gaze jumped up to his in surprise. "I was just infantry. Regular Army. Nothin' special like the Special Forces." He paused for a second, before continuing, "But seen some bad shit where I was."

She leaned across the table, placing her hand on his large one. "Little John, I can't image that there's any job in the military during wartime that wasn't special. I had no idea you had served."

He nodded. "Yeah, I guess when the bombs go off they don't care if you got a high rank or a low one, they'll kill you just the same." He took another sip of coffee, watching the young woman in front of him, still obviously affected by the young man's appearance yesterday in spite of her attempts to say otherwise. "You know, war changes a person. Some come back and are able to put it in a place in their minds where it don't torment 'em every day. Others?" he shook his head, "Others don't come back so good. Maybe it's their bodies that got fu—I mean messed up, and for some it was their minds."

"Why are you telling me this?" she whispered.

"Well, where I sit, a man don't give up a woman like you for nothin'. He musta had a reason but just 'cause he never told you what it was don't mean it wasn't there."

"But how could I have known if he never told me?"

"Don't know, sugar." He sighed deeply as he rose

from his seat and walked over to the sink to rinse out his cup. Turning, he grabbed his car keys off of the counter and was almost to the door when he looked back at her sitting at the table. Sad. And alone.

"Only you can decide if he's worth a shot at eventually telling you. And only you can decide if it's worth moving past. But Mac? The woman sittin' in front of me is still hurtin' a whole lot. If this man's opinion is worth anything, you deserve to either see what's there or put it to rest for good."

With that, he nodded as he walked out of the back kitchen door, and ran right into Jobe and Gabe standing just outside. He could tell by the expressions on their faces that they had heard the conversation. Or at least part of it. He stood for a moment, holding Jobe's gaze…and liked what he saw.

"Gentleman," he said in greeting. As they acknowledged him as well, he turned and looked back at the building saying, "Yep, you gotta a lot of work to do here. But it's worth it." Dropping his gaze back to Jobe's, he continued, "But then I'll just bet you already know that."

BY LUNCHTIME, MACKENNA once again found herself surrounded by Jobe, everywhere she turned. She had to admit that a few times she caught herself looking when she did not think he would notice and wish he had gotten uglier with time. *No such luck. If anything, he's more gorgeous.*

Finally, she made her way to the kitchen to make a sandwich when he wandered in once again. Her gaze moved to his before looking back down at the counter. She did not want to talk to him, but found herself automatically asking, "Do you and Gabe want something to eat?"

"You don't have to fix lunch. And Gabe left to go work on another job."

Her gaze jumped back to his in surprise. "He's gone?"

Jobe nodded as he filled his canteen with water again. "We've got several jobs going on today and one of the other men called in sick, so he left to work on that project."

"Oh." That single word sounded stupid, but it was all she could think of to say. Her mind racing, she finally just pushed the sandwich over toward him and began making another one for her. "You might as well eat something."

Jobe watched her in silence for a few minutes, as he chewed the food gratefully. *At least she didn't throw it at me.* He had managed to move about the house to keep maximum contact with her, trying to balance not crowding and yet making sure she knew he was around. He watched as she moved to the table and sat down, nodding at the chair across from her.

Taking the silent invitation, he sat and continued

to eat. Deciding to start with a safe topic, he said, "I'm really impressed with what you're doing here."

He noticed that she gave a small, almost imperceptible nod. *Good.*

"Thank you. I hope we're doing something right. At least it seems as though we are." She felt awkward but just could not seem to bring her gaze up to his.

"I'd say you're definitely doing something right. You always had such passion to help others and it really shows." As soon as the words were out of this mouth, he realized that he should not have made a reference to knowing her in the past. It was too soon, by the stiff expression on her face. *Well hell, time to go for broke.*

"Mackenna, I'd really like to talk to you sometime. There's a lot I'd like to tell you and hope that you'll at least give me a chance."

She sat stiffly, staring down at her plate. The words of Little John ran through her head, but all she could think of at the moment was the pain. The searing pain that she never wanted to feel again.

"I...don't think that's a good idea, Jobe. It was...um, a long time ago that we were...um, friends and well, that's where it should stay." She stood up from her seat and took both plates to the sink. "You have a job to do here and I'll say that I'm grateful. But as for anything else? Well...um, I don't think that's a good idea."

She faced the window over the sink, hoping he would just walk out of the kitchen and continue his work so that she could leave with her dignity intact.

Jobe had other ideas. He moved to stand behind her, his arms reaching around the counter on either side of her effectively caging her in. His body did not touch hers, but even after years he could feel her heat. The shampoo scent of her long hair was different than what he remembered but stirred him just as much.

He leaned forward so that his lips were close to her ear and whispered, "Mackenna, I get that what I did was unforgivable. But swear to God, I couldn't seem to help what I was doing. I've spent the past years regretting that decision and by the time I tried to write to you again, you were gone. Then I told myself to leave you alone and let you have your life. But now that our paths have crossed again, I'm gonna take that chance to at least have you look me in the eye without hating me."

He could feel her body stiffen, making sure to not lean back into him.

"I don't hate you anymore," she choked out. "But I sure as hell don't like you."

"Fair enough," he admitted. "But I consider that a start."

"No, it's not a start for me. It's still part of the ending."

He touched his lips to the top of her head and pulled away walking toward the door. Looking back, he said, "I'm sorrier than you'll ever know, Mackenna. But

I'm not giving up on at least having the chance to talk to you." With that, he turned and walked out of the door.

CHAPTER 6

TITO MONTALVO SAT on the ratty couch in his apartment which also served as his office. Local leader of the Sixers, he usually had plenty of people around to do his bidding and today was no different. Jazzie and Waldo, his right-hand men, were lounging in front of the TV arguing over what to watch. His mind ran through the things that needed to be done by the end of the weekend, but visions of Gabrielle kept running through his thoughts. *Bitch. I offered her a chance to be my main pussy and she fuckin' leaves.*

He looked over to another gang member, a real up-and-coming go-getter. "Tank? Get over here."

The large, Hispanic man lumbered over, eyes on the leader. "You need somethin', boss?"

"You in the car the other day where Gabby's hanging out?"

"Yeah. She's in some house where some other girls live. Looks like some kind of school, with some white bitch running the place. Bitch came out with a bat the other day, but some big fuckers followed her so we left."

"Keep an eye on Gabby. Don't make no threats,

but you report back to me what you see. And if that skinny ass white bitch thinks she's gonna disrespect the Sixers, she's got a real surprise comin' her way."

"Sure thing, boss. You want me to start now?" Tank asked.

"No, fucker. I want you to sit on your ass for a while first," Tito growled sarcastically.

Duly chastised, Tank headed out of the apartment. Tito moved to the kitchen table and snapped his fingers. Jazzie and Waldo turned off the TV and joined him. Getting down to business, they began their meeting.

Tito had every intention of making the Sixers one of the biggest street gangs in Richland but knew the competition was stiff. Crips and Bloods were at war with each other, leaving some of the picking ripe for his group. The money coming in from drug sales was good, but Tito wanted a bigger slice of the pie. Even if that meant cutting into the piece from the national gangs. And that was dangerous. He wanted more...and had a plan on how to get it.

"I want our girls back on the streets running drugs. They need to put out to do it, fine. But the money's in the drugs, not their pussies."

Jazzie reported, "Gotta tell you, boss, that a few girls saw Gabby get out and they're wondering what you're gonna do about it."

"I'm not gonna do shit right now. That bitch wants to work at McDonalds flipping burgers for fuckin' minimum wage? Let her. You show these girls that they can make bank running my dope. And they want to score johns at the same time? Fine with me. Their pussy can bring in some more money."

"We're being watched, boss," Waldo added. "I seen the cops hanging around our old meeting places."

Tito glanced over, bored with the conversation. "I don't give a fuck what the cops think they got or don't got. They ain't got me and if we keep working it like we have been, they ain't gonna get me."

He sat for a minute, his plans formulating in his mind. "Tank's gonna get some info for me and when he does, I want you two to roll."

Jazzie and Waldo both nodded, understanding what he meant.

"You want us to take anyone with us? Anyone need in?" Jazzie asked.

Tito thought for a moment and then grinned. "Yeah. Take that crazy ass, motherfucker Poco with you. He's eager to get in. He lasted a beat in, so let's give him a job to do with you two."

The two associates grinned. "You got it, boss."

Tito leaned back in his seat, pleased that everything was going according to his plans. Everything except Gabby. *But that bitch will soon see what happens to people that try to help her get away from him.*

MACKENNA PULLED INTO her driveway, noticing a strange black pick-up truck parked on the street in front of the house. It was not unusual since most of the neighbors parked a car on the street, but she wondered who it belonged to.

She juggled the grocery sacks on her arm as she turned the key in the doorknob and walked into the house.

"Mom? I'm hom—"

She stopped mid-sentence, staring dumbly at the scene in front of her. Penny sat in one of the chairs in the living room…with Jobe sitting on the sofa sipping a glass of iced tea. With mint. Mackenna blinked. Twice. Still not believing her eyes. *What the hel—*

"Mackea, loo who ca ta see me?" her mother said proudly, smiling at having a visitor.

Mackenna, still too stunned to say anything, just stared. Her mother's smile began to droop, so Mackenna quickly forced a smile on her face as she held her mother's gaze, refusing to look at Jobe.

"I see, mom. Um…let me get the groceries put away while you…um…visit." She hustled into the kitchen before her mother could see her frustration. *Why is he here? What is he up too? And why in the hell did she have to let him in?*

Hands shaking with anger as she tossed the frozen items into the freezer, she then shoved the vegetables into the refrigerator. So filled with her own thoughts, she never heard anyone approach.

"Mackenna?" came Jobe's voice from behind her.

"What?" she shouted as she raised up, hitting her head on the still open freezer door. "Auggghh!" she screamed as she fell to the floor holding her head, sure that blood would start running everywhere.

Jobe rushed forward, kneeling, and quickly assessing the knot on her head. "Oh doll, I'm sorry. Here let me see."

She wanted to push his hands away from her and tell him not to call her 'doll', but the splitting pain in her head had her hoping she was not going to throw up on his shirt.

He slid down taking her in his arms, with one hand wrapped around her middle and the other grabbing the frozen peas that were on the floor and holding them to her head. He said nothing but rocked her for a moment, allowing the pain to slowly subside. He felt her body begin to relax into him, but did not know if it was because she was comfortable with him holding her or because the pain had her addled. *Probably the latter*, he assumed. In a few minutes he knew he was right when her body went stiff as she struggled to get out of his hold and try to stand.

Refusing to let her fall, he held onto her as she stood before reluctantly letting go. He saw the trail of a few tears before she quickly brushed them away.

Before either could speak, Penny walked into the kitchen, seeing the freezer door standing open, Mackenna with a pained expression on her face, and

Jobe holding on to the pack of peas.

"Ya shudn leave tha freeza doo open," her mother chastised, much to Mackenna's chagrin.

"I was just closing it, mom," she said, trying to keep the exasperation out of her voice. She glared at Jobe, but his handsome face never lost its smile.

"Ya stay fa dinna?" Penny asked as she shut the freezer door.

Jobe watched Mackenna's eyes widen at her mom's suggestion and he wanted nothing more than to do just that. But it was too soon. *One step at a time.*

"Thank you, Mrs. Dunn, but I have to be getting back." He walked over giving Penny a hug, allowing her the time to lift her right arm to hug him back.

"I'll walk you out," Mackenna said, a forced smile on her face. "Mom," she yelled, "I'll be right back and then fix dinner."

He stepped to the side to allow Mackenna to exit the room first and tried to keep his eyes off of her ass as she walked ahead of him to the front door. *Oh yeah, she's pissed.*

Mackenna managed to wait until they were off of the stoop and walking toward his truck when she whirled around, poking him in the chest with her finger.

"What the hell do you think you're doing, coming here like this? Invading my privacy, not to mention invading my mom's privacy?"

He glanced down at her small finger and lifted his

hand to gently remove it from his chest and hold it in his hand. "Your parents meant something to me and I felt like shit when you told me your dad died," he said.

She stepped back but did not pull her hand out of his grasp. "You'd have known about it if you'd never left, so I don't care how that made you feel," she accused.

"You're right, I would have. And for that, I'm so sorry, doll. But I wanted to see your mom and let her know that I was sorry about her loss. Your parents had a marriage like mine did...strong and happy. And I couldn't take away the fact that I didn't know, but I could pay my respects."

Still glaring, she sifted through his words searching...and finding truth. "You still shouldn't have just dropped in. Mom's...better, but..."

"I know, but she seemed fine with the visit. I know what you're thinking. That I also didn't know about her stroke," he said, still gently rubbing her hand with his fingers.

"Were you able to...um...understand her speech?"

"Yeah, actually very well. I realized right away that she had had a stroke and she seemed self-conscious at first, but we began to talk."

Mackenna's eyes darted away, clouding with sadness.

"I kinda got the feeling that she was lonely," he added. Her gaze jerked back to his, the sadness replaced with anger again. *Damn, it's like walking on a verbal landmine!*

"I'm doing the best I can, Jobe. We moved to Rich-land so she'd be closer to the rehab center and I managed to rent this house that has everything on one floor. She really didn't want to live in an apartment with no view of trees or flowers. I know the neighbor-hood is kind of crappy, but it was the only thing I could afford. She had a day nurse that was with her full time and has made so much progress that the day nurse only has to be here three mornings a week."

"Doll, I wasn't criticizing. It just seemed like she was happy for the company," he assured, but noticed that she was still upset.

"I know she needs to get out more, but I can't do that and work full time. And if I'm not working full time, then she might not get the health care that she needs. Don't you see," she pleaded angrily, "I'm doing the best I can?"

"I can tell you are. She's happy an—"

Suddenly Mackenna jerked her hand out of his, seeming to realize for the first time that he was still holding it. "Don't call me doll. And don't patronize me. And…and…just go away," she said, trying to hold back the tears that were prickling behind her eyes.

Jobe looked down at his feet for a moment, before sighing. "I really fucked things up, didn't I?"

"Yes, you did." Both stood, nervously looking at each other. Mackenna stared at the large man in front of her, opening himself to doubt and recrimination. The ex-girlfriend in her wanted to rail at him some more for breaking her heart. The counselor in her wanted to know what had changed the man so much that he would turn his emotions off to the point that breaking up with her was all he could do. And the woman in her wanted to take him in her arms. Still. After everything, she wanted to hold him once again.

Forcing her arms to stay at her sides, she lifted her chin and said, "I do thank you for visiting my mom and for expressing condolences about my dad. I need to go in and make sure she's all right and fix dinner."

He saw the proud stance, recognizing it as one he had adopted many times. The corner of his mouth turned up in a small smile. "You're welcome. I hope to visit again sometime."

She neither accepted nor denied, for which he was glad. *At least she's not throwing me off of the property.*

With her body still stiff as a board, he walked by, touching her hand once more as he passed her on his way to his truck. The feel of her soft skin stayed with him as he drove away.

Mackenna stood on the walk for a moment after he had left, her hand still warm from his touch.

AFTER DINNER, MACKENNA was washing the dishes when her mom moved behind her, wrapping her right arm around in a hug.

Smiling, she said, "I love you, mom."

"Lu ya too, baby ga."

"Oh, I haven't been a baby girl in a long time," Mackenna protested.

"Ya alwa be to me," her mother said, with one last squeeze.

Sitting at the table, Penny peered at her daughter. "Tak ta me?"

Sighing deeply, Mackenna faced the window looking out into the small backyard at the setting sun. "Something happened over there, mom. He never told me and wouldn't tell me. He just sent me a Dear John email and no matter how many letters or emails I sent back begging him to not break up with me, he stayed firm."

She turned, leaning her hip against the counter and stared at her mom's sympathetic expression. "I was going to wait for him...fight for him. But that next month dad got cancer and it just seemed like the next year was a blur. I was finishing college, sitting with dad when he had chemo and trying to help you help dad. And then a year later, daddy was gone. By then, I didn't care what Jobe Delaro had gone through. I was worth more. We were worth more than just him tossing us away."

She gave a little shrug and finished wiping down the counters. Her mother was quiet and she wondered what was going through her head.

"Ya da wa in Vie-nam," she said, struggling with the words. "He came bac not good."

Staring at her mom, Mackenna realized that she had never heard this story. "Do you know what happened to him, mom?"

Shaking her head, Penny replied, "Na. He sad. Na sleep. Som-ti mad." Lost in her thoughts for a moment, she then said, "It hur ta see him like tha."

"What did you do? How did you survive?" Mackenna whispered.

Her mother gave a lopsided smile. "I jus lov him. Tha wa all I knew ta do."

As her mother stood, Mackenna embraced her, holding tight. "I love you, mom."

Later that night after her mother had gone to bed, Mackenna pulled her laptop onto the bed with her and began looking up sites on PTSD and soldiers. So much of the information she had seen before, both on the news and in articles, but none of it seemed to fit Jobe. So many talked about disengaging from work or friends. *That's certainly not him.* Depression. Lack of energy. *Nope, not him either.*

Then she dug a little deeper and found that the symptoms could vary considerably from patient to patient. Detaching from loved ones. Difficulty imagining a future. Fear of losing control. Becoming workaholics. *Now that describes him.*

Reading a little more, she was vaguely aware of the

sounds of a car backfiring on the street, piercing the quiet of the night. Then the shattering of glass. *Shit, it's gunfire!*

Dropping to the floor, she threw open her door and crawled toward her mother's bedroom. "Mom, Mom, don't move," she screamed. Her mother's room was at the front of the house and she could see the window was shattered. Crawling through the glass on the floor, she glanced at the bed finding it empty.

"Mom?" she screamed again.

"I hea," came her mom's voice from behind. "I wa in ba-room."

"Stay down," Mackenna yelled as she crawled back to the hall, hugging her mom. Once out of the sight of windows, she grabbed her cell phone dialing 911. Quickly explaining the process, she pulled her mom back down the hall.

Instinct kicked in; assuming this was a gang drive-by she wanted to warn the center. Little John did not answer the phone, so she scrolled through her contacts to see who she could call. *Jennifer. She can tell Gabe, who can have someone check the cameras.*

She dialed Jennifer and told her what had happened, but before she could get out what she needed, Gabe came on the line.

She told him that the police were on their way to her house, but she was scared for the center. He assured her that Alvarez Security would take care of the center but wanted her to stay put until the police arrived. "Are you away from the windows?" he barked.

"Yes, we're in the hall. I hear the sirens now."

CHAPTER 7

JOBE PULLED HIMSELF out of the pool as he finished his late night swim, working his body to exhaustion in an attempt to ease his mind. Just as he reached for his towel, his cell phone buzzed. It seemed an odd time for Gabe to be calling.

"Yeah?" he answered.

"Get over to Mackenna's. There's been a drive-by shooting. She and her mom are okay. Tony's sending Terrance and Vinny to check on the center and the rest of us are meeting at her house. He's coordinating with Matt and Shane."

"Goddamnit," he growled. Grabbing his gym bag, he jerked off his trunks and pulled on his boxers and jeans after quickly toweling off. Throwing on his t-shirt, he then slid his feet into his boots. Snagging his keys and wallet off of the bench, he headed out to his vehicle.

WITHIN A FEW MINUTES of getting off of the phone with Gabe, the police had entered the house immediately finding Mackenna and her mom. Penny was unharmed but shaken, while Mackenna's knees and hands were bleeding from the broken glass she had crawled through.

An ambulance arrived about the same time that the house began to fill with others. Mackenna was taken to the kitchen so that the EMTs could work on her cuts. One of the policemen walked in to inform her that the detectives from the Drug Task Force would be in to see her as soon as she was patched up. Nodding, she had just looked down at her legs when two men came into the kitchen accompanying her mother. Assisting her mother into a chair, they introduced themselves.

"Ms. Dunn, I'm Detective Matt Dixon and this is my partner Detective Shane Douglass. We're with the Richland Police Department's Gang Task Force. Your mother has already answered some ques—"

"Please don't tire her out. I can answer your questions for you, Detective," Mackenna quickly interrupted. She noticed his warm eyes and could tell that he understood this was difficult on her mom.

Mackenna explained her work with the New Beginnings Center and admitted that she had called the police several times when she felt that there was a possible threat. Before they could continue their interview, she heard a commotion at the front door.

"It's okay, Officer. Alvarez Security is allowed in," she heard someone say.

"Where the hell is she?" came a familiar voice, now

raised in anger. Before she could respond, Detective Douglass yelled, "Back here."

Within a moment, her small kitchen was made smaller. Jobe came sprinting into the room, followed by Tony, Gabe, and Jennifer. While she looked on incredulously, the two detectives greeted the Alvarez men as old friends.

Jobe's eyes landed on hers immediately and he did a quick body scan. The EMTs were still working on her cut hands and legs, but they appeared to be mostly bandaged. His gaze took in her baby-blue sleeping shorts and matching camisole underneath the blanket she clutched. Her face was pale and eyes were wide with shock.

He slid his gaze over to Penny, noting a similar expression on her face. Walking over to her, he squatted down so that he could be at face level.

"Mrs. Dunn? We're going to take care of everything now," he said softly, noticing that her face relaxed slightly. He introduced the others and then, giving her shoulder a squeeze, he stood and nodded at Jennifer, who moved to sit next to Penny.

Jobe stalked over to the table where Mackenna was perched. His gaze dropped to her legs and hands as the EMT finished her bandaging.

"I picked out the glass and got them clean. I'd advise seeing your doctor to get an antibiotic just in case of infection. You up on your tetanus inoculation?" the EMT asked.

Mackenna's eyes never left Jobe's as she nodded her answer. As the EMT moved away, Jobe stepped into his place, moving closer than he would have allowed anyone else to stand.

"Ms. Dunn?" Detective Dixon interrupted. "I've just talked to Tony and Gabe here and have an idea of what's going on at the center."

She gasped, looking over at him. "Is there a problem? Did something happen there?" she asked, trying to hop down from the table. Finding her way blocked by Jobe, she glared at him. "Let me up," she ordered.

"Not likely, doll," came his response. "No way are you going charging over there after what just happened."

"No, no. It's fine," Matt said. "I just mean that you've had some suspicious cars drive-by over there, although without any violence."

"That is if you discount Ms. Dunn's penchant for chasing gang members with a baseball bat," Tony added.

That statement brought another round of questions from Matt and Shane, and much to Mackenna's embarrassment, a great deal of chastising.

"I get it! I know it was stupid, but I was just so angry that I reacted. Which is really crazy because I never let myself get that angry." She glanced over at her mother and the realization of what could have happened swept over her. Pushing against Jobe again he stepped back so that she could move, gathering her mom in her arms. In a moment, she felt her mom's right hand soothing her back. As the adrenaline wore off, her cuts began to hurt, and she tried valiantly to not cry in front of the group of men.

"Who di thi?" her mom asked, looking up at the men in her kitchen.

Mackenna noticed the glances between the others before Shane answered. "Ma'am, there was a painted sign on your front walk. Sixers."

Penny appeared confused as she heard Mackenna's sharp intake of breath.

"Gabby's gang," Mackenna said. Turning to look at her mom, she said, "I'm sorry. My work has brought this to our door."

"Ms. Dunn, we're going to need the information you have on all of the girls that you serve at your center. We need to know which gangs they're from and anything else you can provide. But we can get that tomorrow," Matt explained.

Shane spoke up, "You can't stay here tonight. The police will be processing the crime scene for a while and it's not safe."

"We've got them," Tony said. "They're under Alvarez Security protection as well as yours."

Shane and Matt nodded appreciatively. Looking back down at Penny, Shane said, "Then ma'am, you couldn't be in better hands."

Tony and Jobe shared a look, silently communicating who was taking charge. Tony nodded and turned to Gabe. "Call Vinny. We'll meet at the agency first thing in the morning. Jobe can bring Mackenna in later."

Jennifer gave Penny a hug before walking over to her Gabe. She looked up, whispering, "Can they come home with us?"

Gabe gave his wife a gentle squeeze as he whispered back, "Jobe's got it. Why don't you take Penny to put some things in a suitcase? Check to see if she has any meds she needs."

Jennifer smiled at Mackenna as she hugged her and then walked down the short hall with Penny.

Numb from the evening's events, Mackenna just stared wordlessly as she watched her friend leave the kitchen with her mom.

"Mackenna?" Jobe stepped in her line of vision bringing her attention to him. "Can you walk? Did you cut the bottom of your feet?" He watched her slowly shake her head and he pulled her up from her seat. "Come on, show me your room. We need to pack some things for you since you can't stay here tonight."

She moved silently to the bedroom just down the hall from the kitchen and walked inside. Her eyes took in the room. *Was it only an hour ago I was here?*

Jobe walked to her closet and pulled down a small suitcase. He knew she could come back for her belongings but wanted to make sure to get what she needed for a day or so. He grabbed a pair of jeans and a few tops from hangers and placed them in the suitcase.

Seeing her still numbly standing in the middle of the small room, he walked over, putting his hands on her shoulders.

"Mackenna, why don't you go to the bathroom and get whatever you and your mom need from there. I'll grab a few more things here to last you a day or two." He watched her nod, shock still evident on her face as she walked across the hall to the bathroom.

Wanting to be out of the house as soon as possible, he turned to her dresser and opened a few drawers. He grabbed a few pairs of socks and in the next drawer found some panties and bras. Trying not to think of her in only those items, he shoved them in the suitcase as well. Kneeling to the bottom drawer, he found a few sweaters and pushed them to the side.

His fingers touched a thick sheaf of papers and he glanced down to see what it was. Letters. A bundle of letters. His heart began to pound as he slid them forward. Letters from an APO box return address. *My letters. My fucking letters. Jesus Christ, she kept my letters.*

Hearing her steps in the hall coming from the bathroom, he shoved the letters to the back of the drawer and pushed a sweater in front of them. Standing quickly, he was just putting the last of her things in the suitcase when she came in, arms full of toiletries.

Making their way out of the house, Gabe and Tony assisted Penny while Jennifer moved back to check on Mackenna. They got them settled in Jobe's pickup and all pulled out about the same time.

TWENTY MINUTES LATER, they parked in an underground garage. Mackenna, who had been focusing on her mother, glanced around in surprise.

"Do Gabe and Jennifer live here?" she asked.

"Gabe used to, but they now have a house."

"So who lives here?"

"I do. Well, Vinny and his fiancé live here also, but we're heading to my place." He hopped out of the truck and walked to the passenger side where he assisted Penny from the vehicle.

"Why are we here at your place?" Mackenna asked sharply, the numbness wearing off, being replaced by anger.

Jobe speared her with his gaze. "I've got a spare room. This building is secure. If you won't think of yourself, think of your mom."

"That's a low blow," she seethed quietly.

Penny walked over to Jobe, putting her hand on his arm. "Than ya." She looked at her daughter, who moved over and took her arm.

"I'm sorry, mom. Let's go," she said, as Jobe grabbed their two suitcases and headed toward the elevator.

TITO LOOKED DOWN at the girl he was banging, then jerked his eyes away again quickly. *Fuck, she was ugly.*

Looking away meant he could keep pounding her pussy. She had survived her own beat-in and now was going through the next phase. Her face was still puffy from the beat-in and her split lip still raw. He lowered his eyes to her enormous breasts, bouncing in time to his thrusts. Huge, dark nipples ending in points as large as thimbles beckoned. Leaning down he pulled one into his mouth, biting down hard enough to have her scream out. Grinning, he kept pumping until with one last thrust, he emptied himself into her.

Pulling out of her, he nodded to the other men in the room. Laughing, he said, "I got the tight shit—who's next for the sloppy?"

The men knew their order. The same order as their rank in the gang. This was the only way to get her membership and if they had to hold her down, she could forfeit all she had done up to this point. So, she kept her mouth shut and Jazzie pounded to the raucous laughter of the others.

As soon as he was finished, Waldo stepped up. Jazzie followed Tito out to the other room and they sat until Waldo joined them, zipping his pants up as he walked over.

Jazzie grinned up at him, asking, "Anything left?"

"Hell, my dick's so big, even you plugging her holes didn't make a difference. Now she knows how a real piece in her ass feels."

Tito nodded for Waldo to sit down, indicating that their ribbing was over. Spearing the two with a hard gaze, he asked, "It done?"

"Yeah, man. We got it good. She'll know she's been made."

"Poco?"

"He was shittin' to get out there. Let him mark her walk and he took some shots too."

"Good. Gonna wait a couple of days and then make contact with Gabby. That bitch'll come around once she's seen what I can do."

The conversation was interrupted by a scream from the next room. The three smiled at each other.

"Think she'll make it?" Jazzie asked.

"Don't give a shit. If she does, she's in." He looked over at Poco standing guard in the corner. Jerking his head to the other room, he said, "Hear you did good last night. Go get yourself some."

Poco grinned. With a nod of respect to Tito, he headed to the other room. Time to reap the rewards of being in.

Tito stared at Tank, still in the corner on guard. "You did good," he acknowledged. "You keep that up and I've a place for you that's more than just standing guard."

Tank smiled, his handsome face nodding at the acceptance. Then he walked outside, keeping his eyes open for any signs of a breach in their meeting place. Intelligent eyes searching, always on the lookout.

JOBE MOVED AROUND the kitchen, trying to quietly fix breakfast. He looked up when he saw Penny standing at the counter, her belted robe around her thin frame.

"Good morning," he greeted. "Did you sleep okay?"

Her lopsided smile answered his question and she looked beyond him to the stove before saying, "Ya bur-in ta bacon."

"Shit!" he exclaimed, taking the bacon out of the frying pan and laying it on paper towels.

"Tha okay. She li it crisp," Penny laughed.

"Yeah, well, I guess this will be a little extra crispy," he said ruefully, pouring them both a cup of coffee.

"Than ya fo eve-thin," Penny said, sitting at the table with her coffee in front of her. She stared at the young man that had stolen and then broken her daughter's heart.

Jobe held her gaze, hoping that he met with her approval. Not for what he had done five years earlier, but for what he hoped to repair now.

"It will take time ya know?" Penny admitted to him.

Jobe sat down at the table across from her and nodded. "I want to talk to her Mrs. Dunn. I want to try to explain to her what it took several years of counseling for me to understand. But I need you to understand also," he said, his eyes imploring hers. "I don't expect us to get back to where we were. I just want to be in her life again because she was the best thing to happen to me outside the Forces. I'll take just having her forgive me."

"She ma su-pris ya. I don thin she eva stop lovin ya."

He peered deeply into her eyes, seeing only truth and comfort there. Smiling, he admitted, "That'd be more than I deserve. But if it's true...I'll take it!"

They settled comfortably eating breakfast, each lost in their own thoughts. He thought back to last night when they arrived. After giving the two women a quick tour, he set their bags into the guest room. His friends had turned their second bedrooms into offices, but Jobe left his as a bedroom since he often had a sister or Army friend dropping by.

Mackenna and he had silently worked side by side as they dressed the bed with new sheets. He saw the strain around her eyes and said, "I know you're not happy about this, but I'm the only one who has a spare bedroom right now. Your mom needs rest, so I'll let you get her settled in."

She had actually looked at him in gratitude which zinged right to his heart.

"Anything you need?" he asked, stepping closer. He noticed her licking her lips as her gaze moved from his eyes down to his chest and then back up. All he wanted to do was take those lips, suck on them until she was warm and wild. Blinking to clear his mind, he held her gaze.

"Hmmm?" she asked, her forehead crinkled in

thought.

"Is there anything I can get you to make you or your mom more comfortable?" he repeated.

An adorable blush crept up her face, as she jerked to attention. "No. Um, no thank you."

With that he had left the room, given Penny a quick hug and walked into his bedroom, closing the door. And proceeded to lay awake all night. Thoughts of what they were, what they could have been, and what he wished they could be swirling around in his mind.

MACKENNA LAY IN BED, her mind on overload. When she first woke up, she could not remember where she was. Then it all came rushing back and her heart pounded in fear. *Gunshots, glass, her mom, the police. And Jobe.* Sighing, she gazed around the neat room and wondered how on earth she had gotten into this situation. *We could have gone to a motel. But that's not secure. We could have gone with Jennifer and slept on their sofa. But that's not fair to their growing family. We could have…oh, hell, this was the only real choice.*

Sitting up in bed, she saw her belongings neatly stacked in the corner with her laptop bag on top. Remembering what she had been looking up last night before the craziness exploded all around, she let her thoughts wander back to Jobe. *Loss of control issues. Workaholic. Pulling away from loved ones.* As much as her mind wanted to continue to hate him, she realized that something traumatic happened to the man she loved.

Too much time had passed to ever go back to what they were, but she could not help but wonder if perhaps he would share part of his past with her. *Just so I can put it all to rest, once and for all. Only then, I might be able to move forward.*

Getting out of bed, she threw on the robe that was laying on the floor and walked down the hall. The sight that greeted her was as bizarre as the entire past twenty-four hours and, yet, seemed oddly right.

Jobe and Penny were sitting, chatting over breakfast as though they had been doing so for years. Both looked up as she watched them, their smiles real and unforced.

"Goo mo-nin," Penny greeted as Mackenna walked over to kiss her mom.

Jobe rose from his seat and headed to the stove. He was filling up her plate as she moved next to him. "You don't have to get this," she said, softly. "I can do it."

"I know you can, but I'd like to," he replied, smiling at her.

"You've done so much already," she protested, taking the filled plate from his hands. As their fingers touched, her breath quickened.

"I've done very little for what all I need to make up for," he said.

"Is that what this is?" she asked. "Guilt?"

He snorted as he poured her coffee. "I'm filled with guilt, doll. But no, this is doing what I want to do just because I want to help take care of you and your mom."

Not knowing if he was referring to last night's events or something else, she remained quiet. Taking the coffee in one hand she walked over to the table, sat next to her mom and dug in greedily to her breakfast.

Jobe reminded her that she was going to be going with him to Alvarez Security to meet with Tony and the detectives.

He caught her concerned glance at her mother and quickly said, "I've made arrangements for Penny for today. She'll be well looked after."

Penny seemed to be happy with whatever plans had been made, so Mackenna did not dispute Jobe taking charge. At least for the moment.

CHAPTER 8

J OBE PULLED HIS pickup truck into the driveway of his parent's home. Mackenna glanced sharply at him, but his face gave away nothing. By the time he rounded the front of the vehicle and assisted Penny to the ground his mother was already bounding down the porch steps with his father close behind.

Rachel and Penny hugged and greeted each other like long-lost friends while Joseph stood to the side beaming. As Mackenna slid over to the passenger side, Jobe plucked her easily off of the seat and set her down on the ground, letting his hands stay around her waist a moment longer than necessary.

Before she could process what was happening, Rachel bustled over and pulled her into a hug as well.

"Oh, my dear Mackenna. We missed you so much. And when my Jobe called to tell me what happened last night, I was beside myself! We insist that Penny stay with us until your home is safe to go back to."

Joseph gave her a hug as well, his head nodding in agreement with his wife's proclamation.

"I...um...I...she has to have...um," Mackenna blathered, not able to form a coherent sentence.

"My Miriam is a nurse and she can be here in the evenings for whatever Penny needs," Rachel enthused.

Mackenna looked toward her mother for assistance, but Penny's face just glowed. "Mom? Um, what do you want to do?"

"I wou love ta stay if tha don mind," she said.

At that moment, Mackenna realized how much her mom had missed out since the stroke. When they moved to Richland, her mother lost contact with many of her friends and other than her and the nurses, Penny's world had shrunk. With tears in her eyes, she hugged her mom, whispering, "I'm sorry mom. You haven't had many friends lately have you? Of course we can stay."

"Oh no, bab gir. Only room fa me. Ya stay wi Jobe," her mother whispered back.

Mackenna pulled back and saw the twinkle in her mother's eyes. Glancing to the trio standing a few feet away, she saw the same twinkle in Jobe's parents' eyes as well.

Softly, her mother spoke wisely, "It is time fa ya to de-ci. Are ya goin ta forgive or not."

"It's not that easy, mom," Mackenna whispered back, noticing the others stepping back to give them some privacy.

"Eva-thin worth havin, is worth fightin fa," her mother said.

Mackenna took a deep breath and nodded. "We'll see, mom."

With a last goodbye, Mackenna turned to get back into the truck. Jobe hugged his parents before handing Penny's suitcase to his dad. As he moved he saw Mackenna already sitting in the seat, her head down.

The ride to Alvarez Security was quiet, each lost in their own thoughts. Jobe glanced nervously to the side, wondering what was going through her head. Finally, when he could not take the silence anymore, he opened his mouth to speak. Before he could get a word out, she began to speak.

"Last night, I was on my computer when I heard the shots go off."

He continued to drive, waiting to see what she was going to say next.

"I was looking up some things on PTSD."

His heartbeat increased as he gripped the steering wheel tighter. *Here comes the part where she says she can't handle dealing with a fucked up me.*

Mackenna, aware that he was not going to say anything, continued, "I was thinking that maybe we could talk sometime if you still wanted to."

Jobe let his breath out slowly, trying to control his pounding heart. He had no idea what she meant by that statement, but he was willing to take it as far as she was willing to listen. "I'd like that. Whenever you want," were the simple words that came out, afraid to say anything more.

She sighed as they drove into the underground garage of Alvarez Security, looking on in curiosity as he pulled his truck in line with other large vehicles. "Maybe tonight, when all of this is over."

"Okay," he said. "I'm ready when you are."

She turned and peered at him, seeing the familiar face that had haunted her for so long. *Whatever happened to you, I've gotta know. I've gotta know everything so that I can decide what the hell I'm going to do.*

MACKENNA SAT IN the large conference area of Alvarez Security, eyes wide as she peeked around in curiosity. The huge room held computers, partitioned off areas, white screens on the walls, as well as other equipment against the walls. Doors leading to offices and other rooms holding God knows what else were in sight as well.

"Mackenna?" Jobe prodded.

She jerked, blushing as she realized that she had been asked a question. Pushing her hair behind her ear, she apologized to the others around the table. "I'm sorry. I'm so distracted. Please, what did you ask?"

Shane smiled as he repeated, "Can you tell us when you first became involved in gang work?"

"I'm not involved in gang work," she explained. "That was never my intent, although it's a by-product." Seeing the confused expressions of the others, she continued. "My thesis was actually in women's studies at first. Looking at the home lives of why some girls drop out of high school. What I found was that for many of them, they were involved in gangs. If they weren't getting the love and support from home, they often turned to the family atmosphere of a gang."

"Family atmosphere?" Gabe asked incredulously.

"Yes, family," she replied. "Not the sort of family that we associate with the word. But group. A community. A sense of belonging. Even ownership can feel good to someone who hasn't had that."

"But..." Vinny started but found himself unable to speak his thought in mixed company.

"I know what you're thinking," she said, a sad expression crossing her face. "Most girls are still beat-in as an initiation. And where the males have to rob or even kill to get in all the way to prove their obedience, the females have to have sex with multiple gang members. And again, it's not our way of thinking about family, but for most of the girls...it's what they know."

Matt questioned her more. "So tell us about the center."

"With my research, I found that the only way to get women to break out of that lifestyle is to be more independent. So localities who offer GED assistance, career training, etc. in a safe environment have a better chance of getting some of these girls out of gangs and working independently. So my grant does that. The city leases the center and the grant pays for the teacher, the night watchman, the food, and then I get donations for everything else."

"And the girls there? How do the gangs feel about them being there?"

"Honestly, it hasn't been a problem. Several of the girls had not joined a gang completely, so I guess it was no big deal when they left." She hesitated, then looked at the men around the table. "You also have to understand their world. Women aren't valued as human beings. They're drug runners or prostitutes. The gang members may not have realized the other girls were gone until it was too late and no one ever came looking for them."

"Until now," Shane stated.

She sat quietly, thinking about the situation and how it had gotten so far out of hand. Leaning back, she let out a heavy sigh, rubbing her temples as a headache was forming.

"You want some water?" Jobe asked. "You need a break?"

She offered him a small smile but shook her head. "No, I'm just frustrated."

"So, now?" Shane prodded.

"The last girl we took in about a week ago, is pregnant. I was excited to get her because she'd contacted her former school counselor to let her know that she'd like to get away. This was exactly what I'd wanted. And she's great. Smart, motivated, doesn't want her child to be born into the gang life. But suddenly she would get afraid and I'd see a car with dark windows drive by slowly. I wasn't scared; I just thought maybe someone was trying to see what we were about, but there was nothing threatening at first."

Mackenna hated to admit the next part, but knew that the police and Tony's group needed all the information. She was looking down when she felt Jobe lay his hand across her shoulders. Instead of feeling awkward, it felt comforting. Right. Normal. She found herself wanting to lean into his strength, but held herself back.

"What's going on in that mind of yours, doll?" he asked softly.

This time, even he calling her doll did not make her angry. *What's happening to me?*

Jobe had not meant to let the endearment slip out in front of everyone and steeled himself for her rebuke. It never came. Instead, she just sighed as she glanced up into his face for a moment before turning back to the group.

"This is where I have to show my stupidity," she admitted.

Tony smiled, saying, "Don't worry about it. Everyone in this room has had moments when they didn't act in the smartest way."

She peered at him carefully, measuring his words. "I very much doubt that, Tony. I have a feeling that when you all were in the Army, your missions were well planned out and executed. And you two," looking at Matt and Shane, "if you screw up then people die, so I doubt you make many dumb mistakes. My dumb mistake could have gotten my mom killed!" Her eyes filled with tears and no matter how hard she battled them back, they slid down her face anyway.

Jobe immediately wrapped his arms around her, shooting a look at the others. They all stood to take a break as he held her carefully, letting her cry as she clung to his shirt. "Go ahead and cry, doll. Get it out," he murmured into her hair, stroking her back. As much as he hated her hurting, the feel of her in his arms meant everything to him. He would take whatever this woman would give him, but what he really wanted was her in his arms every day.

After a few minutes, the men returned. She pulled herself together and glanced around in embarrassment at the spectacle she had made of herself.

"No one's looking. You're fine," Jobe whispered, giving her a tissue.

After a minute, she nodded that she was ready to continue. The men would not let her apologize, instead quickly letting her know how much they admired what she was doing.

Grateful, she continued, "Even though I've studied the women and what they need, I have only researched gangs peripherally. I know how they use women, and I know the basics of how they function. I certainly know they aren't to be trifled with, but there are so many and so varied that I haven't studied them in depth."

Taking another deep breath and letting it out slowly, she said, "And that was where I screwed up. When the car drove by the other day, I acted foolishly. I grabbed the baseball bat and charged out onto the stoop in a threatening manner. If it hadn't been for Jobe and the others showing up right then, things could have gotten ugly. And now, not only have I put the center at risk, but I've put my mom at risk. All because I didn't spend enough time learning about the different gangs that the girls come from."

"Do you know about the Sixers?" Matt asked.

She shook her head and admitted, "Not really."

"There's a local gang run by Tito Montalvo. He's an especially nasty piece of work but, he's making a name for himself and the gang, and word on the street is that he's looking to join with one of the major international gangs. From what our informants have told us, the girl you took in? Gabrielle? She's pregnant by him."

Mackenna's mouth made an "O" but no words came out. She turned to look at Jobe, but his face was hard and she could see the tick in his jaw.

Finally finding her voice, she said, "But Gabby just said that the baby's father was in a gang and he'd fathered so many bastards, one more wouldn't make a difference. Since he would never be paying child support, she wanted to get out and start a new life for herself."

"I'm not knocking what she said and maybe in her mind it's the truth, but she may also be running scared and just didn't want to say anything," Shane surmised.

"So you can let go of some of the guilt, Mackenna. You disrespecting them was part of it, but to be honest, I would assume that Tito's stepping up his show by trying to get this girl back by threatening you."

Running her tongue over her dry lips, she said, "I can't put my mom at risk, but I can't shut down the center. Can't let him win! Can't let him get his hands on her again."

"We can't get to Tito at this point, but your neighbor was out walking his dog and had stepped behind a tree to let his dog take care of its business when the car pulled up. He saw the member who jumped out and spray-painted your sidewalk with the Sixers' name. The kid then got back in the car when the shots were being fired. There's a streetlight right there and your neighbor got a decent look at the kid, so we're working on an ID now."

"But there's nothing that can be done about this Tito guy?" she asked, frustration pouring out in her words.

Shane shook his head. "Right now, we've got nothing positive on him."

"I...I don't know what to do," she said, turning her gaze back to Jobe. "I have to work with those girls, but mom..."

"We just needed all this information to make sure that we know what we're up against. And best how to protect you," Matt said, closing his notebook.

Before anyone else could speak, Tony added, "She

falls under Alvarez protection as well."

Jobe smiled at his boss and accepted the smiles of the others. *She's mine to protect and mine to care for.*

Mackenna sat, shocked, not saying anything, not knowing what that meant. She looked up at the others, noting the men around the table. Gabe, Vinny, and Tony had served with Jobe overseas. *They knew him back when...when we were still a couple.* Whatever had happened had not lessened their obvious care and respect for him.

Jobe watched her face as she moved her eyes around the room. Tony and the others were discussing the security needs for her and the center. He could see her mind working furiously, trying to analyze the problem and what needed to be done.

"Mackenna?" he interrupted her thoughts. She turned silently toward him. "You're going to be safe. You and your mom...I promise." Seeing the expression of doubt that flew across her face, he continued quickly, "I know that you don't have a reason to believe my word right now. But you will. I can't change the past, but I can change the future." With that he leaned forward, planting a soft kiss on her forehead.

CHAPTER 9

ARRIVING BACK AT JOBE'S apartment building, she followed him inside. Nervous, she walked over to the living room and stared out of the huge picture windows. Dark clouds were forming in the background and she wondered if they were going to have a thunderstorm. She could hear him move to the kitchen and open the refrigerator. Other noises came from the area and curiosity got the best of her.

She headed toward the sounds, sliding up on a bar stool. Jobe was standing at the stove, deftly turning the crisp bread in the frying pan. He glanced over his shoulder at her and grinned. *That panty-dropping grin that used to make her melt.* His dark hair swept back, tanned skin, muscular arms straining at the short sleeves of his t-shirt. Afraid to allow her eyes to drop lower she realized that she did not need to. The vision of his body was burned into her memory forever.

"Grilled cheese?" he asked.

She could not help but grin back. "Yeah, that'd be great." Moving to the refrigerator, she grabbed two water bottles and set them on the table. In a few minutes, he slid the toasted sandwiches onto two plates and tossed a bag of chips onto the table between them.

Jobe noticed her eating with relish. He had always liked that about Mackenna – no pretense, no whining about her weight, just a real woman. His dick twitched, but he willed it back down. *Who knows if I'll ever have her like that again, but I sure as hell can keep her safe.* But if he was honest…he wanted her…and not just for sex.

"When do you think I can go home?" she asked, interrupting his musings.

"I'll find out from the police when they have finished processing the scene and then Tony'll get your security installed. It's safer for you here right now."

She nodded absentmindedly, then looked up quickly. "And the center? I took today off but need to get to my office at DSS and then to the center tomorrow."

He would love to forbid her from continuing the work at the center just because he was afraid for her, but knew that she would never do that. "We have security people there tonight to make sure the women are safe and then we'll finish tomorrow getting the security system in place."

He watched her carefully while she ate. Her mind seemed elsewhere, but at least she was no longer protesting staying at his home.

"Do you think your mother would be insulted if I called to check on mom?" she asked.

Smiling, he said, "Not at all. Mom knows you're worried."

While he cleared away the few items on the table

she made the call, which seemed to ease her mind. By the time she and her mom had chatted Mackenna was smiling again, the worry lines on her face erased.

She piled up on one of the overstuffed chairs while Jobe made himself comfortable on the sofa as they watched baseball for a while, cheering for the same team. Numerous times he glanced over thinking how familiar the scene was. When they had been together years before, it was always the simple times that he loved. And remembered. And regretted losing. Turning his attention back to the TV he noticed her occasionally looking over at him, and he wondered if she remembered the same thing.

Mackenna tried not to stare at the man sitting on the sofa, his long legs stretched out in front of him as he watched the screen. *I worked so hard to put him out of my mind. Erase the memories. Forget the happiness.* But they came slamming back. The fun times, the moments of shared enjoyment, the sex. *Nope, not going there. He could destroy me once again if I let him.*

By the time the game was over, the hour was late. She headed to the bathroom to get ready for bed, her body strung as tight as a bow. Quickly finishing, she stepped into the hall toward the guest room, almost running into him coming from the front.

He reached out to steady her shoulders then dropped his hands, the touch of her almost burning his skin. His eyes slowly moved down her body, perusing every inch, memorizing it once again. Her long hair, thick and wavy, fell across her shoulders. The colors of red and blonde shimmered under the lights. Her porcelain skin, pink cheeks and clear, light, brown eyes were as familiar to him as his own reflection. The soft swells of her breasts above the pink camisole hinted at the covered treasure, her nipples showing through the material. A hint of peach skin showed from her middle above the matching sleeping shorts. Her hips curved enticingly, leading down to toned legs that seemed amazingly long considering her short stature.

As his eyes made their way back up to her face, he noted with pleasure that she seemed to be doing the same thing. Her gaze had dropped to his naked chest and he saw the long, slow perusal as it continued down to his boxers. He knew the evidence of his desire was present, but refused to move as her eyes jumped back up to his, a delightful blush coloring her cheeks.

As much as he wanted her, he knew the time was not right. Sucking in a deep breath and letting it out slowly, he stepped forward, leaned over and kissed her forehead. Holding his lips there longer than he should, he whispered against her skin, "Goodnight, doll. I hope you can sleep." Stepping around her, he made his way into his bedroom, partially shutting the door.

Mackenna stood where she was for a moment, trying to still her rapid heartbeat. *What just happened?* The attraction was obviously still there. For both of them. *Was there more? Could there be more? Could I trust him with my heart...or maybe with just my body?* The dark hall gave no answers, so she turned and went into the guest room.

Lying in bed, her mind swirling, she found herself restless. Memories of the lovemaking between the two of them heated her body, and the thoughts had her squirming as she tried to still the need building between her legs. Pressing them together tightly, she finally slipped her hand down into her shorts, moving her finger around her drenched folds. Sliding a finger inside, she moaned as she imagined it was him. Her body humming, she slid her other hand to her breasts, tweaking each nipple until she thought she would explode. Wishing it was him. Wanting it to be him.

Finally, she pinched her clit at the same time as the other hand tugged hard on a nipple, rolling it as she pulled, and that was all it took to throw her over the edge. Her orgasm ripped through her, sending spasms from her core outward. *What just happened?* She had not come that fiercely with any other lover. The reality sunk in. *It was him. Just the thought of him makes my body react.*

Rolling over to her side, only partially sated, she finally fell asleep.

In the room across the hall, Jobe smiled although his cock ached with need. Hearing the sounds of the beautiful woman in the throes of an orgasm, it took all of his willpower to stay in his bed and not charge over to show her how it could be between them again. *But not tonight. She has to come to me. It has to be her choice.*

Now, if only his dick would understand.

Getting out of bed, he made his way into the master bathroom, turning on the shower. A few minutes later with the water pounding his back, he jerked off to the memory of their past lovemaking. *And what he hoped would be their future again.*

TITO WAITED IN the basement of the old store his uncle owned, drinking beer. It had been his secret meeting place and only the top members of his gang knew its whereabouts. The entrance from the grocery store above was blocked and well hidden. A passageway from the building next door allowed freer movement in case the police were watching.

He waited with Jazzie, who knew his boss wanted quiet. The police had been sniffing around all day, making them on edge. A noise from the secret entrance drew Jazzie's gaze as Tank opened the door and allowed Waldo and a few others to come in.

Tito sat stoically, acknowledging their hand-signs as they entered. They quickly found chairs around the table looking to their leader for a call-to-order. He wasted no time getting down to business. As Tank started to close the door, Tito stopped him.

"You got another man out there?" Tito asked.

Tank nodded. "Dez."

"Leave him out and you can come in. Might learn

something, big man," Tito ordered. Tank nodded again, words not being necessary when an order is given. He moved to the corner of the room, showing respect and staying alert.

Tito turned to the ones sitting and growled, "I wanna know what the fuck the police know about the fuckin' bitch."

No one looked anywhere but at him, not wanting to disrespect him in any way. Waldo spoke first. "They been lookin' into us all day knowin' we put the hit on the bitch's house. They ain't got who did it."

"They came by the store, but my uncle told 'em I was here working last night. Since that was exactly where I was and there were witnesses, I got to give them a fuck off." A slow smile curved the corners of Tito's mouth, the gold outlining his front teeth glistening between his lips. "Where's the bitch now?"

At this, Waldo hesitated a second. "Not sure. Got a feeling those security people took her."

"And Gabby?"

"Still at the bitch's place. But they got cops swirling all around."

Tito was silent, thinking the situation over. "It's all good," he finally said. "We made the bitch scared. She'll know not to fuck with us anymore. And Gabby'll know what we can do. Ain't nowhere I can't get to her."

"What's next?" another member asked.

"Nothin' to the bitch at the moment. Let her get

complacent before we move again. We'll let Gabby know I got my eye on her. She'll come around."

With that, the next order of business was discussed. The younger girls that had been beaten and fucked into the gang were ready to start drug running.

Jazzie gave his report. "Got 'em paired up with others that been doin' it. They're learning the pick-up and drop-off sites."

"Got any still in school?"

"Yeah. Some have dropped out."

"Get 'em the fuck back in. Need to keep our shit selling in schools. They're either gonna sell the shit or sell their pussy." Chuckling, Tito added, "Hell, tell 'em they got a choice." His eyes cut over to Tank, still standing in the corner. "You man. You deal with some of the girls. Get them up and running drugs or selling pussy, but you make sure they know the money's in the drugs."

Tank nodded once again, a rare smile curving his lips.

"I'll tell 'em to get back in school. They need their education," Waldo added.

At that, the men all laughed. Relieved to see Tito's good humor returned, they finished their meeting and headed out one by one through the secret entrance until only Tito and Jazzie were left.

Tito downed the last of his beer, wiping his mouth with the back of his hand. His mind went back to Gabby. "I actually pursued her," he said, talking as much to himself as to Jazzie. "She was no gang pussy. I was gonna make her my number one. Hell, I was gonna put her in charge of some of the other bitches."

Jazzie knew this—he had heard it before. Though proud that the Sixers' leader trusted him enough to let him in, he hoped no one else saw Tito this way. *No one else needs to see him so pussy-whipped.* He wished the girl was dead—her and that brat she carried. The boss was not weak in any area except for the hold that girl had over him. *If she were dead, then the boss could get back to himself.* And Jazzie knew he could keep him in enough pussy to drown out the memory of that leaving bitch. *And speaking of bitches...*a new idea began forming in Jazzie's mind. *Tito wants the center's bitch out of the picture so he could have Gabby and I want Gabby out of the way so Tito gets back to club business...maybe I can figure out a way to get both bitches out of the way.*

Tito finally rose from the table and headed upstairs to the grocery, Jazzie following dutifully behind...planning all the while.

CHAPTER 10

WALKING INTO THE CENTER early, Mackenna and Jobe found Terrance and Little John in the kitchen. Terrance's gaze met Jobe's and with a nod he indicated that all was well. Mackenna introduced Jobe to her night watchman and she noticed the two men sizing each other up. After a few seconds, Little John gave a huge smile, indicating he approved of him.

Rolling her eyes, she mumbled under her breath as she headed upstairs. The women were in the process of getting ready for the morning and greeted her enthusiastically, having heard about the drive-by at her house.

"Don't mind telling you, I was scared that night when those great, big men showed up and camped outside," Jenita said.

"I'm sorry," Mackenna replied. "It seemed necessary until the police could determine what was going on."

"Do they know anything?" Carla asked as several of the others came into the hall.

"Well, according to the graffiti on my sidewalk, it was the Sixers."

A gasp met that response, and the group turned

toward Gabrielle. "Oh my God, then it's my fault."

Mackenna walked over, placing her hands on the younger girl's shoulders and said, "Honey, you aren't the only Sixer member that's come here."

"No, I'm sure that they're after me."

"But why?" Jenita asked. "I mean, no offense, but you weren't even a full-fledged member."

Mackenna's gaze took in Gabrielle's evasive expression and the way she twisted her maternity shirt in her fingers.

The silence in the hall was deafening as the other girl's circled around. Mackenna could feel the tension building and she was determined to diffuse it quickly. It would not be the first time that an argument broke out between the women staying, coming from different gang backgrounds. Most of the time, they all got along, bonded by a common goal. But the gang mentality was strong and occasionally came out when emotions ran high.

"Everyone finish getting ready," Mackenna ordered. "Check the list to see what chores you have today and what duties you have." Turning to Carla, she continued, "I know you're going back to the restaurant to work later. I'd like you to take Yesinia. They've agreed to take her on too. Teresa, you've got a job interview with Shopmart this afternoon. Make sure you're ready." Looking at the rest of them, she said, "Those of you still in training with Rose, she'll be here a little early today, so get ready. If you're on the housekeeping rotation, you know what to do."

Smiling at them all, she looked at Gabrielle. "Let's talk in my office please," she said in a tone that brooked no disobedience.

As she and the young woman made their way downstairs, she saw Jobe staring up at her smiling. As she rounded the corner, she was surprised to see Gabe and Vinny behind him, their eyes twinkling as well. Giving them a curious glance, she headed to her office and shut the door as soon as Gabrielle was inside.

Jobe's eyes never left her, admiration in his expression. Hearing her take charge and the realization of what all she handled had him smiling in pride.

Gabe laughed, saying, "She's like a drill sergeant, bro."

"Shit," Vinny growled behind him. "If you don't do everything you can to make that woman yours...again...then you're a complete dumbass. 'Cause that girl's got it all, man."

Jerking around to see his friends staring at her office door, knowing they were just as impressed, made him a little jealous. "I'm trying, man. I'm fuckin' trying."

Gabe clapped both of them on the back, announcing that they needed to get to work. They relieved Terrance of his duty and saw Little John off as well, before completing the job of wiring the security system.

Inside her tiny office, Mackenna stared at the young woman sitting across from her, pondering her words carefully. Gabrielle appeared nervous, trying to look anywhere but at her rescuer.

"You're safe here, you know?" Mackenna started. Gabrielle nodded, finally making eye contact. "But I must remind you of the contract you signed the other day when you agreed to come live here."

At that, Gabrielle's expression changed to one of confusion, knowing she had accepted to a great many things to escape Tito's grip. Licking her lips nervously, she admitted, "I...I'm...not sure what you're talking about."

Nodding, Mackenna said, "I know there was a lot we had to go over. What I am specifically talking about now is your agreement to not be in contact with anyone from the gang—"

"I haven't, I swear!"

Holding her hand up, she continued, "And that you would be honest in everything that you told us about your former life."

At this, Gabrielle paled slightly, but remained silent.

"Upstairs, you seemed sure that the Sixers were after you. Now, if you were not a full-fledged member, I highly doubt that they would risk arrest for attempted murder." Seeing Gabrielle's wide-eyed expression, she was glad that she had her attention. "Now, you told me that your boyfriend was in a gang, so I am assuming that you told the truth?"

Gabrielle nodded silently.

"Who was your boyfriend? You indicated that he was a member of a gang, but also said that he wouldn't care if you left. Was he of some importance to the gang and not just a member?"

"Ms. Dunn, I'm being honest. He's a member of a gang...the Sixers. But I can't tell you his name. It would be too dangerous."

Mackenna's incredulous stare pinned the young woman to her chair. "Too dangerous? We're already having danger now. My house was shot at and my mom's life was at risk." She saw tears well in Gabrielle's eyes. "Honey, I don't blame you as long as you're being honest. I have to think about the safety of the whole center as well as my own life and I need as much information as you can give me."

"I should just leave," Gabrielle said dejectedly. "It would be for the best."

"No!" came the vehement response. "Then you let him win. I don't want you to leave. I just want to know what I'm up against here."

"If I tell you, you have to stay quiet. We can't involve the police."

"Honey, the police are already involved."

"Will you at least promise to not go to them unless they ask?"

"I will promise to hold on to the information that you give me until I decide that it needs to be shared," Mackenna said.

Biting the inside of her lip in indecision, Gabrielle

finally relinquished. "Tito. Tito Montalvo is the father of my baby."

Pretending the name meant nothing to her, Mackenna continued to wait for more information.

"He's the leader of the local chapter."

Mackenna sat back with a whoosh as the air left her lungs quickly. *So it's true…the father is the leader? Of the Sixers? Right now the most notorious local gang?* Her mind raced with the implications, thinking of what she had learned from the detectives.

"You can't tell the police," Gabrielle's shaky voice pleaded. "If you do, I'll die."

"What are you talking about?"

"If the police find out what I've told you, then they'll question me. I swear to you that I don't know anything about his dealings with his gang or activities at all. I was never around it and he never talked about it. But if they think I've talked…my life…and the life of my baby won't be worth anything."

Mackenna ran her hand through her hair in exasperation. "Gabby, they already know. I don't know how, but they do. You're going to have to stay here in the center where we have security. I can't take a chance on you even going to the corner store."

"I'll do anything, I promise," the young woman cried.

What a messed up situation, Mackenna thought. *This is taking my work into a whole new direction. One I'm not very happy with!*

Allowing Gabrielle to leave the office, Mackenna stayed where she was, pondering her options. *If Gabrielle really doesn't know anything about this Tito's activities, then she can't help the police. And as long as she stays here and the Sixers see that the police aren't involved, then maybe they'll leave us alone.*

She sat in her office for the next hour, making calls about the upcoming GED examination and getting two of the women signed up for it. She fielded a call from Tony's wife, Sherrie, a paralegal who was assisting her with fundraising.

Carla stopped in to let her know that she was reasonably sure that one of the other women was pregnant also. Mackenna looked at her incredulously. "You've got to be kidding?"

"She's been throwing up every morning. I'm sorry, but I thought you'd want to know."

Sighing deeply, she agreed. "Yeah, I'll talk to her and then make an appointment with the Health Department."

Carla smiled and turned to walk out of the office. At the door, she glanced over her shoulder and said, "You're doing a good job, Ms. Dunn. I know it sometimes doesn't seem that way...but you are."

Mackenna watched the dark haired beauty walk out and close the door behind her. Carla would soon be leaving them, having completed the integration back into society and training program. With a smile curving her lips, she went back to work.

ON THE OUTSIDE of the building, the Alvarez men had been joined by BJ, who was ready to check the connections to the security wiring.

The center had been set up with cameras on the back and front of the building, as well as ones pointing toward the street and back alley. Tony had hired men to put in bars on the first-floor windows and the front door had been replaced, complete with a new latching system.

As the men were finishing their work, the conversation turned to the inhabitants of the center and what Mackenna was accomplishing.

"In theory, it sounds a lot like what Jennifer is doing with her elder care, but I gotta tell you, man, my wife's is a helluva lot safer," Gabe expounded.

Jobe ran his hand through his hair in exasperation. "Yeah, I know, but it's what's she's been working for. I can't demand she give it up." He looked away for a moment, then added, "Hell, I can't make any demands on her. I gave up that right. All I can do is try to protect her in whatever way I can."

Vinny stared at his friend for a long time. "Bro, you gotta get over yourself. The past is done with. You gotta get in there, talk to her, and try to move on."

Jobe turned to the Vinny and asked, "You ever tell Annalissa about your experiences? About the music that died for you?" Seeing Vinny's evasive expression, he then looked at Gabe. "And you. You ever tell Jennifer about that boy? The one that haunted you for-fuckin-ever?"

Both twins drew in sharp breaths, knowing how touchy the subject was.

Vinny answered first. "Yeah. Eventually, but...not at first. In fact, not until much later."

Gabe chimed in, "Same here. I told Jennifer about the kid over there, but not until after we were married. I thought about it, but the time just wasn't right."

Jobe gave a nod as though his point had been made, when Gabe continued, "But our situations were different. We were just meeting women who hadn't been in that past with us. Mackenna was. Hate to dig it in, but it's not the same, bro."

BJ entered the conversation, saying, "I got no idea what went down with you two other than what you've told me. But it sounds a lot like Suzy and me."

Jobe turned to BJ, remembering what it was like for his friend when he was working to get his girlfriend back. "So, how'd you two do it?"

"Our situations were reversed. Suzy left me and I had no fuckin' clue why. After a while I gave up but, I gotta tell you, it marked me. Losing the one you love and thought you'd marry? Not ashamed to admit it gutted me. When our paths crossed again, I wasn't sure I wanted to wade back into those waters again. Hell, once bit by a shark, who wants to take a chance again?"

By this time, the others were listening as well, their

minds moving back to two years before. They had all advised BJ to go after Suzanne and find out what had happened. And it worked...for him.

"But I knew she was worth fighting for, so I waded back in. She told me why she left and we talked. Hell, we talked, argued, cried...but when it was all over with, we knew that we were supposed to be together. It wasn't easy, but I knew she needed to get it off her chest and I needed to forgive. That was the only way we could move forward."

Vinny eyed Jobe, asking, "You talked to her yet? Told her what happened?"

Shaking his head, Jobe admitted, "Not yet. I was going to and then all of this latest shitstorm happened. Now, I don't know. She's got so much on her plate. Do I really want to dump on her?"

The others could not give him a good answer, each thinking that Jobe was always the one they turned to when they needed help. Finally, BJ spoke up, "Yeah, Jobe. You do." He saw the looks the others gave him and he quickly amended, "I don't mean dump on her, but you gotta look at it from her point of view, which had been mine. I had no idea what had happened. She doesn't either. One minute you're engaged, the next...you break it off. And it sounds like you broke it off clean."

Jobe winced, knowing it was the truth.

"She deserves to know it all. Now I'm not saying she's gonna forgive and forget and everything's gonna be fine. She may hate your guts."

This time Vinny winced as much as Jobe. "Fuck man, you know how to give someone hope, don't you?"

BJ ran his hand through his hair and glanced away for a minute. He then turned to Gabe and said, "Do you remember what ya'll told me back then? You said that if you find a woman that you can't live without, you do not let that walk away." He paused, pinning Jobe with his stare. "You gotta let her know what tore you apart and then work like hell to make it right." With that BJ moved back to the van to continue checking the security system feeds.

The other three watched him walk away, then Gabe and Vinny turned back to their friend. Jobe nodded, "I get it. Loud and clear."

Their conversation was interrupted when an SUV pulled to the front of the building. Matt, Shane, and a female police officer got out and started walking toward the group on the stoop. The looks on their faces indicated that the news wasn't good.

"Jesus," Jobe swore, knowing whatever was coming was going to upset Mackenna, as he and the others met the detectives on the front walk. "This just keeps getting more fucked up by the minute."

Mackenna was walking toward the front door to see what Jobe and the others were talking about when she saw Matt and Shane coming toward them. Steeling herself for whatever was next, she stepped out onto the stoop and looked down at them all.

"Detectives," she greeted, noticing the others looking at each other. "Can I help you?"

"Ms. Dunn," they both said at the same time. "This is Officer Petit." The young, female officer nodded her head in acknowledgment as Mackenna greeted her also.

"Do you all want to come inside?" she invited.

"Is Selena in there?" Matt asked, referring to one of the women staying at the center.

Blinking in surprise at the question, she said, "Yes. She's getting ready for the computer class to start. Why?"

"We'd better talk out here first," was the only response given.

She shut the door behind her and walked down the steps into the group, stopping when she reached Jobe.

He looked down at her, realizing she choose to stand next to him. Whether or not it was a conscious choice, he was glad. He slid his arm around her shoulders, giving her a reassuring squeeze.

Matt said, "Selena's been identified as a witness to a gang crime that the River Street Kings committed." Seeing Mackenna about to protest, he quickly continued, "She's not involved—not a suspect. But it appears that she may have information."

"What do you need to do?" she asked, hoping her voice was not quivering as much as she felt inside. She felt another squeeze on her shoulder and could not help but lean in slightly toward Jobe.

"Mackenna," Shane said. "We need to take her

with us—"

"But why?" she cried out. "She's doing so well here. She knows us. She—"

Jobe leaned in and whispered, "Doll, she's not safe here. You can't keep her safe and if it gets out that she's a witness, then no one's safe here with her."

Shane nodded, "That's right. Officer Petit will be escorting her to a secure location."

For a moment, the others stood around, uncomfortably shuffling their feet, knowing that the realization was cutting into her.

She blinked rapidly several times, then lifted her chin and said, "Will you allow me to speak to her first?"

Matt agreed but added that Officer Petit would have to accompany her. She gazed over at the officer and said, "If you'll come with me, I'll introduce you to Selena."

The two women silently went up the steps and through the front door, closing it behind them. The men let out a collective sigh.

"Goddamnit!" Jobe exploded.

His friends looked at him sympathetically, knowing that Jobe was going to be picking up the pieces when it was all over.

Twenty tense minutes later, the door opened again and this time Mackenna and Officer Petit were with a pretty, young woman who had obviously been crying. Jobe's eyes were not on her though…he was staring at the woman in his heart. And her tear-streaked face. He started toward her, but she caught his gaze and gave a slight shake of her head.

Mackenna needed to complete her task without falling apart any more than she had already. She had allowed the policewoman to explain the situation to Selena, but the girl's tears and pleading to stay in the center had gutted Mackenna.

The trio walked passed the men and over to the vehicle that Matt and Shane drove up in. The two detectives got into the front seat as Selena turned to hug Mackenna goodbye.

"Thank you," she choked out, "for saving me."

The tears ran unchecked down her face as she hugged Selena. Finally letting go, she watched as the officer and Selena settled in the back seat before they drove away. She stood on the sidewalk, her body quivering as she pressed her fingers tightly against her lips in an attempt to stem the sob that wanted to escape.

Gabe, Vinny, and BJ left, having to walk by her on their way to their vehicles. Each touched her shoulder quickly, in a show of support while understanding her need for privacy. Only Jobe remained.

She turned, seeing him on the sidewalk near the steps of the building. They both stood, not moving, staring into each other's eyes.

Let me in, doll, his expression implored.

Take my pain, was her inner response.

Suddenly, she launched herself at him, running at

full speed. He caught her easily in his embrace, holding her tightly.

Not caring who saw or what they thought, she let the sobs release as she poured her heart out in his arms. He cradled her head against his chest, next to his heartbeat, hating the reason she was there, but loving the way she turned to him in need.

"I'm not making any difference," she cried. "It's all going to hell."

"That's not true," he shushed. "What you're doing is amazing," he reassured, but her head just shook against his neck. After a minute of crying he heard her speak, but her voice was muffled by his shirt. He leaned his head down while still holding her tightly, asking, "What, baby?"

"Take me home," was the choked response. She lifted her gaze up to his, the red-rimmed eyes pleading, as she whispered again, "Take me home."

CHAPTER 11

THE RIDE BACK to Jobe's apartment was made in silence, as he occasionally spared a glance to the passenger side. Mackenna was leaning against the door, her head on the window, eyes closed. He wanted to comfort her...say something to make it better. But one look at her and he knew she was not ready to hear anything yet. *Maybe I can get her to eat something and take a nap. She looks like she's going to drop.*

The minute the apartment door was closed she whirled around, launching herself at him again. Only this time it was not in tears. As he caught her, she wrapped her legs around his waist and pulled his face to hers for a kiss.

And did not let go.

Jobe, caught off guard, held her up with one hand under her ass and the other around her waist. The unexpected kiss was urgent—hot and wet, and she was not coming up for air. He gladly accommodated, allowing her to rule the moment as he enjoyed the feel of her soft lips moving against his. Her tongue slipped inside and warred with his.

His knees almost buckled with desire as she sucked

his tongue into her mouth and began to grind her soft core against his jean-clad cock. Already at attention, it was painfully swollen against his zipper and he wondered if it would have permanent marks.

He pulled her back gently, saying, "Doll, you gotta slow down. We need to talk about a lot of things."

"Fuck talking," she murmured against his lips, as she continued to move her hips into his pelvis.

Pulling back again, he tried once more to slow her down. *She doesn't want me, she just wants a body right now.*

By creating a slight space between their chests, she reached down grabbing the bottom of her shirt and whipping it up over her head. His eyes dropped down to her full breasts spilling out of her bra before raising his gaze back up to hers.

"Oh, no, doll. We're so not doing this now."

She pulled him, latching onto his lips again and he felt his resolve slipping.

She murmured between kisses, "I just…need…you. Please…"

"Mackenna, I don't want us to use each other for sex. We meant too much to each other at one time."

Jerking her face back away from his, she stared him down, seeing his labored breathing. "Talking's for later. Right now I need a body to let me know I'm still alive. I just want to stop hurting. Please, do that for me."

Seeing his tortured expression, she instinctively knew he was trying to do the honorable thing. *Fuck honorable.* "Jobe," she said softly, gaining his attention. "I didn't go to just anyone. I'm here with you. I. Need. You."

With that, he pressed her firmly again, one hand behind her head as he took over the kiss. With her legs wrapped around his waist tightly, he shifted his other hand to her bra clasp and quickly unsnapped it. She tossed the offending material away as he walked them toward the bedroom.

The heat between them was explosive and he angled his head for better access to her warm mouth. Sucking her tongue, he moved expertly around, feeling every crevice as he memorized her taste again.

By the time they made it into his bedroom she had grabbed his t-shirt and was tugging it upward. Their lips separated only long enough for that piece of clothing to be discarded as well. Before it landed on the floor, he had pressed her naked chest against his.

His hand fisted in her hair, holding her close as he devoured her lips. Hard. Demanding. As though neither of them could get enough. His tongue delved inside of her warm mouth again and again, capturing her moans.

She squirmed in his arms, her nipples tight and aching as she pressed them against his chest. As her core rubbed against his swollen cock, she cursed the material between them. She tried to slide her hand down to his jean zipper but found herself flying through the air before she could get it down.

Having reached the bed, Jobe gave her a little toss onto the mattress before he jerked his jeans down. He saw her eyes widen for a second before a smile lit her face. She quickly unzipped her pants as well and he peeled them off of her before she could finish. *Slow. I should go slow. This should be special,* his mind interrupted, but before he could act on that thought, she slipped her panties down and opened her legs to him.

She saw the momentary hesitation in his eyes and vowed to erase it. Her body was on fire with need. The need to feel something besides fear. Something besides sadness. Something besides hurt. She saw his gaze move from her face down her naked body, stopping between her legs. Sliding one hand down, she fondled herself as she ran a finger through her wet folds. His eyes dilated with lust as she continued to hold him captive with her movements.

Jobe pulled his boxers off, his erection springing free. Palming himself as she continued to play with herself, he knew his cock was ready to explode.

"Just fuck me," she pleaded in a whisper, her need overtaking all other thoughts.

Crawling over her body, resting his weight on his arms, all rational thinking flew from his mind. Placing his aching cock at her entrance he peered down at her face as he plunged inside in one swift movement. Her warm, tight sex welcomed him. As he watched her eyes, hooded with desire, he began moving slowly.

She was having none of that. "Fuck me harder. I

need hard," she pleaded again. She grabbed his ass with her hands, pulling him forward as she moved her hips up.

Answering her need as their bodies slammed together, he leaned down to capture her lips again as his tongue began to emulate the movement of his dick. He had been with women in the past years but never had he felt this connection since the last time they had been with each other. Over and over, he plunged into her warmth.

The friction was building and she forced her hips up in the mating dance that she knew would bring relief. Sweet relief. More endowed than her few past lovers, he reached places deep inside that were longing to be stroked. With her hands moving back and forth from his ass to his back, she reveled in the feel of his muscular body connected with hers.

He knew he was about to come, but wanted her satisfaction first. He ground his pelvis against her clit, eliciting more delicious moans from the beautiful woman writhing beneath him. Leaning on one arm he slid his other hand down her body, over her breast and stomach until reaching that swollen bud. Moving his fingers around the wetness where their bodies were connected, he gave her clit a little pinch and that was all it took.

Her slick inner walls began to tighten around his cock and she threw her head back onto the mattress as her orgasm roared through her.

With a few more thrusts, he felt his balls tighten and as the muscles in his neck corded and the veins threatened to burst, he powered through his release as he pumped through his orgasm.

Panting and bodies slick with sweat, he fell on top of her before he could remember that he would crush her. Forcing himself to roll to the side, he pulled her along with him so that she was sprawled partially on top of him. They lay for a long time, neither saying anything as coherent thought was impossible.

As the air around them began to cool their bodies, he reached over to grab a light blanket and pull it up over them, making sure it was tucked around her.

As reality slowly returned, she lifted her head to peer down into his face. Wondering what she would see, she was surprised…his expression showed vulnerability. Sucking in her lips, she fought the desire to lean over and kiss him. *I just wanted a fuck, right? That's all. I don't need anything else from him. But…*she felt a tear slide down her cheek and she quickly lay her head back on his chest to keep him from seeing it.

Jobe knew she was trying to hide her emotions. *She thought she just wanted sex to forget what was going on. Yeah, right. That's not Mackenna.* He knew for himself that what they had just done was no casual fuck, regardless of what she tried to tell herself.

Before she could begin to make excuses, he gave her a little squeeze forcing her to look up at him once again. "Doll, hard and fast may have worked for right now, but you gotta know that's not how I wanted this to be."

She wanted to give a quick, flippant response. An "it was great, thanks for the sex" kind of answer. But he deserved more. And if she was honest with herself, so did she. So, she just nodded.

He sat up and tossed several pillows against the headboard before sliding up and resting against them. Before she could process what he was doing, he pulled her up, tucking her into his side, enveloping her in his embrace.

"You wanted to forget and I've been dying to be close to you again. I guess we both got what we needed at the moment."

He felt her nod against his chest and wondered what her thoughts were. *Was that really all she wanted?* He felt moisture on his skin and could not hold back the smile as tears slid from her eyes down onto his body.

"Doll, it's time. We gotta talk. You deserve to know everything. Then and only then can you decide what you want. What you need. What place I can have in your life."

She leaned up again, peering deeply into his eyes, finding uncertainty again. *I've held onto my hurt for so long. Can I possibly let it go and take a chance again?* Fear wrapped around her heart but, seeing his expression, she knew that his fears were just as real.

Nodding, she slid out of bed and grabbed his t-shirt

from the floor since hers was still by the front door. Sliding the soft material over her head it settled down her curves, hanging to her knees. She crawled back onto the bed and faced him. Armored, she sat quietly with her arms around her middle, waiting to see what was coming.

Jobe watched in fascination as she put on his t-shirt and climbed back into bed. His heart ached at seeing such a familiar sight. *Familiar...and different.* This woman was harder, more closed than the Mackenna of old. *She hides her vulnerability from me. From everyone. And I am the only one that can take that away.*

Suddenly unsure as to how to start, he realized that of the many times he had practiced this speech, now was different. Because she was staring straight into his eyes. And the words choked.

She saw the struggle in his face. That handsome face that haunted her dreams. No matter how much she cursed him over the years, she never forgot his face. Reaching out her hand, she palmed his jaw rubbing her thumb over the stubble. His eyes held hers as he leaned his face into her palm.

Now or never, he realized.

He looked at her and blurted, "This may take a while. I haven't spoken about all of this to anyone other than the Army psychologist or counselor." He watched her carefully for signs of discomfort.

She settled against some pillows on the bed, gazing up at him with trust in her eyes. "Okay," she said softly.

Sucking in a huge breath, he let it out slowly as his mind went back. To a different time and place.

"You know my family. We never had much money, but my parents gave me and my sisters nothing but love. I was the oldest, and a boy. It was my responsibility to help take care of the girls. I walked them to school. Settled their squabbles. Threatened their dates. I had a part-time job in high school to help pay the bills even though my parents wanted me to save for college. I just wasn't sure that college was what I wanted…not when the military called.

"See, when I was about eight years old, we went to a Fourth of July parade and I saw soldiers marching. I'd never seen anything so amazing. Perfect uniforms. Perfect unison." He gave a little smile as he looked back down at her, "That was it, doll. I knew at eight years old what I wanted to be. I began to study everything I could about the military and knew I wanted to be in the Special Forces. So I got my grades up in high school, went to a community college and then enlisted.

"The training for SF was the hardest thing I'd ever experienced but when it was over, I understood real responsibility. Real duty. The team and the mission were everything. That kind of discipline was perfect for me.

"The first tour was difficult, but I was in Tony's squad and those men were the best of the best. I wanted to always make sure I deserved to be there. Put them first. Put the mission first. We all clicked as a group and were successful."

He shifted in the bed to find a more comfortable position before continuing. "I met you and thought I had it all. Perfect career, perfect woman.

So far, his recitation had been impressive, but nothing that she did not already know. When they had first gotten together, she was around his family and knew how close they were...how his sisters leaned on him for strength and protection. They were so proud of his military career. His father would nearly burst with pride when talking about his son.

"It took years for me to realize that my life was about control. My control helped protect my sisters. Helped my family. Helped my squad. Absolute control. If I left nothing to chance, then nothing could go wrong. When I left to go into the military, I had my best friend look after my family. Took over my duties." He hung his head for a moment, the memories washing over him. Feeling a small hand on his arm, he looked up at Mackenna's concerned expression but could not find the words to reassure her.

Like ripping off a band-aid quickly, he blurted, "I got an email from my parents telling me that Hannah had been hurt. My goddamn best friend tried to rape her."

Mackenna's gasp slipped out as she saw Jobe's face contort in pain and anger. She watched as he slowed his breathing, regaining the control he so desired.

He swallowed several times before continuing, "She wasn't hurt badly, at least physically. He was supposed to be escorting her home from the library when he took advantage of her. When she rejected him, he drug her into an alley...someone heard her scream and called the police."

The silence in the room crept over them, each to their own thoughts. "What happened to him?" she asked softly, her fingers still stroking his arm.

"Asshole served some time. Got back out but isn't in the area anymore. I dealt with him when I got out of the Army."

She did not ask him how he dealt with it...she was too afraid of the answer.

"I was so angry. Stuck overseas. Couldn't help my parents. Couldn't help my sister. It was as though all of my control was slipping away."

"You never told me any of this. We were together at this time. I could have helped—"

"No," he barked. "Don't you see, it was my job. My responsibility. And part of that job was to keep you safe as well. How the hell was I going to dump on you if I couldn't be around to make it better?"

She wanted to retort, to fight back. She wanted to argue that if they had a genuine partnership, he would not have had to worry about control. But instead she just pursed her lips tightly, letting him finish.

"So I tightened up." He lifted his eyes to hers and saw the confusion on her face. "I started trying to control everything. I became immersed in our missions. I was known as having the most control of anyone on the squad. If they needed something or someone, they turned to me." He sighed, shaking his head slightly. "Then it all went to hell."

She watched as he rubbed his hand over his face as though to wipe memories away. This man who had always seemed so strong...*what happened?*

"We were out on a mission. We'd finally accomplished the rescue and were on our way out of the village. I was the last to leave, bringing up the rear. I was to make sure that no one was seeing us leave—that we slipped out as quietly as we slipped in. If anyone noticed, I would have taken care of it."

She continued to move her fingers along his arm, totally involved in the story knowing that something dreadful must be coming. Like watching a scary movie, knowing you should shut your eyes but kept them foolishly open anyway.

"I heard cries from the same hut as before, so I made my way to the window to peek in, to make sure there was no one who had seen us." He closed his eyes tightly to shut out the scene...but it came back anyway. It always did.

"A man was on top of a woman, her gown pushed up to her waist and he was...at first I thought they were just fucking but I could see her crying as she tried to push him away. Fighting him. I froze, Mackenna. I just fucking froze.

"My job was to get the fuck outta there without letting anyone see us, but that woman turned her face toward the window and I heard her gasp as she realized I was standing there."

He hesitated as he brought his gaze back to hers. "I realize that you can't possibly understand the code. The mission. But my job was to neutralize any threat. Any threat. And right then, I should have shot them both."

She held onto the gasp, knowing that the last thing he needed was censure from her. *It's not my place to know what their code was, knowing that he did what he was trained to do to keep the squad alive.*

Licking her lips, she just nodded, willing him to finish his tale.

"But all I could see was Hannah."

Her eyes widened at this revelation.

"It was as though I were looking at Hannah underneath that rutting bastard and I wanted to kill him." Rubbing his hand over his face again, he continued. "I hesitated. Special Forces never hesitate. We are so disciplined and trained that we never hesitate. Whatever the mission calls for that is what we do, or else my brothers could die. But I hesitated. I made it personal. Then I saw red and started to go to her. I looked at the woman's eyes and saw fear. Embarrassment. Pain.

"And then I totally fucked up. Instead of killing him and her too or at the least, leaving quickly...I actually moved toward the window thinking to help."

Jobe turned his anguished eyes toward Mackenna

and said, "All I saw was Hannah laying there. It was as though I was moving toward my sister. "Then swear to God, that woman moved quicker than anything as she rolled over, grabbed the man's gun and before I could get to her, she put the gun to her head and pulled the trigger."

Closing his eyes tightly, he could still see the blood and brains splatter the room. Opening his eyes, his vision cleared and he saw Mackenna looking at him, hanging on his every word. *I have to have her understand. I lost it then. I lost the me that she knew then.*

"My weapon had a silencer...hers did not. So as I stared at her broken body, still seeing my sister, I heard Tony on my radio to get the hell out. So do you see? I compromised the mission, my brothers, because I lost control. I allowed my emotions to rule and almost got everyone killed."

"You did what you needed to do, Jobe," she whispered, wanting to give him absolution. "What anyone should do. You tried to help."

He shook his head slowly, disagreeing. "To the average Joe, yeah sure. But to a soldier, I was wrong. Dead wrong."

"What happened then?"

"We got out of there, most of the team not realizing what occurred and we made it to the rendezvous point intact. Got back to the base and then I lost it. Went on a rampage. All my anger and rage came out. Rage over not being there to help my sister. For putting her in the hands of someone I trusted who turned out to be a rapist. Rage over almost killing my squad. Rage over anything that made me feel like I could not control."

He held her gaze, refusing to look away. "And that included you. I...I knew that I couldn't keep you safe or have thoughts of you invading my mind when I was on missions. Just having a relationship that I couldn't control and would possibly take away my concentration...I went berserk. I ransacked my bunk. Grabbed your letters and tore them into a million pieces."

Her gasp cut into him as he knew he was giving her more pain.

"The others had no idea what was happening except for Gabe, Vinny, and Tony. By the time they intervened, I had already sent you the Dear John email and destroyed most of my room."

He felt her fingers still on his arm and wondered if she would take away her touch now. Slowly, they began their movements again and he let out the breath he had not realized he was holding.

"Tony told me I had to get immediate counseling before he would let me go back on another mission and I readily agreed. Nothing was going to keep me from the squad. So I did exactly what he said. Three weeks of intensive counseling by the Army shrink." Giving a rueful snort, he said, "The guy was okay but honestly, his job was to get me back in the field. So while I did learn about control with him, I went right back into missions with the idea that ultimate, absolute control was everything."

He held her gaze, wondering what was going through her mind, but found the words to ask were stuck in his throat.

"And...I...did not fit into that picture any-more...did I?" she asked, pain lacing every word.

CHAPTER 12

JOBE STARED AT the woman that he had never stopped loving. Even when he tried to deny it. Even when he convinced himself that loving was the same as losing control. Even when he got out of the Army and knew that he had thrown away the best of him.

Swallowing hard, he said, "At that time…no, there was no room for the uncertainty of love." He saw his words slice into her and he cursed.

"But fuck, doll. I was wrong." Seeing the tears well in her eyes, he rushed on. "When we got out, I'd been decorated, praised for the dedication to the Forces, revered by my squad members as being the cool, level-headed one in all missions. But I was empty on the inside. Came home, spent time with my family.

"Hannah was married with a baby on the way. She had gotten into counseling and I envied her. She was stronger than I'd ever seen." The silence slid over them for a few minutes, each processing their memories. "She was the one that got me into counseling. I started going to a VA counselor who finally broke through my messed-up priorities."

He shifted again slightly, hoping her hand would stay on his arm. He was not disappointed. He was not even sure if she were aware of her touch on his skin. But he was. That little touch. That human contact. That tiny evidence that maybe, just maybe she would be able to learn to forgive him.

"What," she hesitated as she cleared her throat, "what did you learn?"

"I learned about Post Traumatic Stress Disorder and how it affects different people in different ways. I didn't have nightmares...well, sometimes I did. But not as much as many others. I didn't become disabled...instead, I went in the opposite direction. I became a workaholic. If I became the best goddamn SF, then I could make up for not being there for my sister. For not being there for my family. For almost fucking up the mission with my squad. I had substituted control for my own humanity."

Nodding slowly, Mackenna knew that what he said fit some of the patterns she had read about. Licking her dry lips, she asked the question that had been plaguing her for weeks since he had come back into her life.

"Why did you not try to find me? Reach out to me?"

"Would it have made a difference?"

Her gaze jerked up to his, a sharp retort on her tongue.

He quickly added, "Not that I blamed you. But I knew you hated me. Hated everything I had thrown away. Everything I had done." Her silence was his acknowledgment that what he said was true. "I thought about you all the time. I could have so easily found out where you had moved to once I was working with Tony and we had all the resources needed at my fingertips. Where you lived. Where you worked."

"But you didn't?" Her question was more of a statement of what she knew. He had not even tried to find her.

"I could not stand the thought of seeing you with someone else. A Facebook page showing you happy in another relationship. I know that was selfish because I did want you to be happy. I…I guess I was a coward. I just did not want the evidence of you without me. But I also didn't feel like I could try to get your forgiveness. It took me a helluva long time in counseling to see what had happened to myself. How could I even try to get you to understand?"

"I wish I'd known," she said, wistfulness filling her voice.

She stared down at where her hand rested on his arm, the feel of his warm skin underneath her fingertips.

"I just wanted sex earlier. No emotion, just sex," she said absentmindedly. He said nothing. "I just wanted to feel…something besides being sad." He still remained quiet. Her eyes looked back into his. "I guess I should have known I couldn't just have sex with you, no matter how much I told myself that it was just that."

Sighing deeply, she continued, "I did hate you for a while. When I got your email…that was the same week that dad was diagnosed with cancer. In fact, if you want to know about shit timing, I had sat down at my computer to send you a message telling you when I opened your email breaking up with me."

"Baby, I'm so—"

"No, Jobe. Let me get this out. Please."

He sighed, knowing he owed her much more than that. He found his hand had wandered to her blanket covered leg and he felt the warmth radiating from her body through the material.

"I finished college while dad underwent chemo. I spent every weekend with them, watching him get weaker and weaker." Her gaze met his but held no anger. Just resignation. "I tried to write you back, sure that you had just reacted out of a bad mood or some-thing. I couldn't believe that you could just set me aside so quickly. So callously. But the emails were not answered. The letters were unanswered.

"I couldn't let my dad see my pain, so I didn't tell my parents. Dad would talk about how he wanted to live long enough to walk me down the aisle and I let him keep dreaming. It broke my heart, but I let him plan while all along I knew you were gone."

Swallowing several times to keep the tears from coming, she continued, "He finally passed, slipping away peacefully in the night. Hospice had come in and his pain was controlled by morphine. Mom and I were there, each holding his hand." A lone tear escaped her tightly shut eyes.

"I let you go then, Jobe. I had no room in my heart for more grief. More pain. So all the hope I had clung to...just slipped away." Her pain-filled eyes searched his. "I allowed myself to become bitter. That's what kept me going."

Shaking her head slowly, she said, "And for about four years that worked. I got a job in social work, we sold the house that was way too big for us and moved into a smaller condo. Mom wanted me to have my own life, but I just couldn't leave her alone. Maybe the truth is that I didn't want to be alone either.

"I thought I had gotten over you, but sometimes, in the middle of the night, when all was quiet...the tears would come again."

The pain in his heart was so piercing, he moved his hand over his chest, rubbing absentmindedly as though to ease the ache.

"And just when I thought that life was getting back to some semblance of order, mom had her stroke. I was terrified, Jobe," her voice cracked. "I didn't know how I would survive another loss. First you and then dad. If I lost mom too, I knew I'd give up."

Wiping another stray tear, she plunged on, "So I got a job in Richland that actually dealt with women's issues, moved us here so that she had better rehab care and...well, that's where my story ends. I had finally worked to put you completely behind me when you popped back up."

Giving a little shrug, she said, "I guess that's all there is."

"Not all, baby," he said, reaching over to wipe a tear. Her eyes found his again. "We had a past. I fucked it up, but that's still in the past. What about now? What about the future? Is there any way you can forgive me? Give me another chance? Give us a chance?"

He left his hand on her face as he stroked her cheek with his thumb, wiping the tears that continued to slide down. He wanted nothing more than to pull her in. Kiss those tears away. Change it all. *Giving in to life is learning to hand over some control...*the words of his counselor came back to him. Staring into her light, brown eyes, he knew he was lost. Lost in her. And it was perfect. *Come on, doll. Please give me a chance.*

Mackenna's chest rose and fell with each breath as he held her gaze. Squeezing her eyes shut, she tried to dredge up the anger. The hate. The feeling of having lost everything. But it was not there. She could not find it. Her chin quivered as more tears streamed from her tightly closed eyes. All she wanted...all she needed...she opened her eyes...was right there in front of her.

"I..." her voice cracked. "I forgive you," she whispered so softly that he was not sure for a second what she had said.

She saw his expression of uncertainty and repeated, "I forgive you, Jobe. But I've got to tell you that I'm scared. I can't go through having my heart shredded again."

"I'm not the same man I was, Mackenna. I can't promise that I won't ever make you mad or do something stupid. But I swear on my life...I'll never walk away. I'll never hurt you like that again. If all you can do is start with forgiving me, then I'll take it from there. I'll work every day to make sure you know that you're the center of my world. Always."

Her chin continued to quiver as she stared at the man in front of her. The anger and hate had disappeared with her forgiveness. He was not the same man she fell in love with seven years ago and she knew for sure that he was not the same man who fractured her heart two years after that. As she peered into his eyes, searching for the truth...she found it. And it wrapped around her soul.

"I...I choose us, Jobe," she said, her voice choking with tears. "I choose us."

He gasped as he broke into a sob, finally pulling her in tightly where she belonged. His head rested on her chest, her heartbeat steady in his ear. Unashamedly, he cried. Tears for the time that had been lost. The innocence surrendered. Time wasted fighting a battle that never should have been fought.

Her arms cradled him close to her as she realized that this strong man needed her. Wanted her. Using the edge of the blanket, she wiped his tears as she rocked him back and forth, offering comfort as much as taking it.

After several long minutes, Jobe lifted his head and placed a kiss on her lips. A whisper of a kiss. Reverent. Quiet, while speaking volumes.

He moved back, settling her against him now, with their positions changed. This time her head was cradled on his massive chest, his strong heartbeat underneath her cheek.

A slow smile curved the corners of her lips as the feeling of peace descended over the room. She melted into his embrace, knowing that she had missed this closeness most of all.

Moving her head back, they stared at each other for a moment before he leaned down and captured her lips once again. This time, as rediscovered lovers. Her lips were soft and pliant under his, allowing him to control the intensity, the depth.

He slid his tongue back inside in a slow exploration, as though he had never known such ecstasy. Her taste was as familiar to him as always. As her tongue slid across his, he felt his erection growing. His hand moved from her cheek down to her neck where he could feel her pulse beat wildly. His lips followed the trail of his hand, moving to that spot in the hollow of her neck where he nipped and licked.

She shivered with the sensations, knowing this was different from earlier. Then, she had just wanted sex and, while she knew he would have never agreed to just that, she tried hard to keep her emotions at bay. But this? This was the dance of lovers.

He felt her shiver again as he slid her shirt off and his hand moved to her breast. Tweaking one nipple as his lips found the other, he alternated between the breasts, sucking, nipping, tugging, and licking until both nipples were elongated with need.

As his mouth continued its ministrations, he slid his hand lower until her soaking folds were discovered. Inserting one finger, and then two, he moved them slowly, exploring her sex once more, finding just the right spots that had her squirming and moaning. He moved his fingers in a circle, deep inside and then pulling them out to swirl them around her clit before plunging back inside. His lips made their way back to hers, as his tongue mimicked his fingers.

She felt strung as tight as a bow, the waiting excruciating. Her hips undulated next to his as her hand moved down toward his cock. Before she could have her next coherent thought, the waiting was over as her inner walls grabbed at his fingers deep inside.

He watched as she leaned her head back, her hands fisted at her sides as her body jerked its response when the orgasm ripped through her.

"Baby doll, let me see you," he whispered, eliciting her eyes to open. As she was coming down from her bliss, he moved on top of her, a question in his expression. Barely able to nod, she gave her silent permission as she clutched him closer to her.

With his dick at her entrance, he held her gaze as he pushed in slowly, inch by inch. Her eyes hooded with passion. Her lips plumped from their kissing. Her perfect teeth biting her bottom lip.

The urge to pound into her waiting channel once again was strong, but he maintained a steady pace. Wanting her to have pleasure again, he moved excruciatingly slowly out before plunging in quickly. Over and over he did this until she was mad with desire.

He lifted one of her legs over his shoulder to gain deeper access and looked down to where their bodies were joined. Moving his cock in and out of her slick cavity, he watched with fascination at their coupling, then lifted his eyes, seeing her watch as well. *Oh, hell, that's hot.* Her gaze moved up and captured his, a smile curving her beautiful mouth.

She tantalizingly slid her hands up to cup her breasts, pushing them together and then pinching the nipples, making them stand out further than he could have imagined. His breathing increased as he felt his balls tighten.

"Babydoll, I'm gonna come," he rasped. "Touch yourself."

She kept one hand on her breast and the other moved to her clit, where she tweaked the swollen bud. Just as her orgasm flooded over her, tears escaped, and she cried, "I need you. I've always needed you."

Need isn't the same as love, but it's a start, he

thought. Hearing the words he had longed to hear for four years tore into him just as his own release had him emptying himself deep into her warmth. "I need you too, Mackenna," he whispered against her hair, as his body fell just to the side of hers, pulling her over with him.

Arms wrapped around each other, they held on tightly as though afraid the moment would be broken, and the magic would disappear.

Her heart pounded as her sweat slicked body lay across his. Her limbs were weightless as fatigue overtook her. Closing her eyes for just a moment she allowed the exhaustion of the day to ease her into slumber.

Not able to believe the turn of events, Jobe lay with her in his arms, her declaration of need still ringing in his ears. The evenness of her breaths told him she had fallen asleep, exhausted by physical exertion, mental strain, and emotional turmoil. *Oh, Jesus, let me be worthy of her forgiveness...and love.*

"I love you," he whispered, closing his eyes.

Not quite asleep, she heard his words.

CHAPTER 13

I T WAS LATE AFTERNOON by the time Mackenna awoke, sated from sex and sleep. Jobe allowed her the privacy of a shower, knowing that if he saw her naked again they would move straight to shower sex.

Running his hand through his hair, he could feel the pounding fear of the loss of control. *That's what love is—giving control to someone else knowing that with love comes a helpless feeling.* A few deep breaths later, he looked up as she emerged from the bedroom, wet hair hanging down her back, fresh face and all smiles.

He stood, nervously waiting to see what she would do. He did not have to wait long. As soon as her gaze hit his, she strolled right over...straight into his arms. Wrapping her once again in his embrace, he kissed the top of her head.

"Baby doll?" She gazed expectantly, as he continued, "I thought you'd like to go over to my parents and you can see your mom."

If he thought the smile she graced him with earlier was incredible, it was nothing compared to the blinding smile that she now bestowed on him.

"Thank you," she effused, jumping up to kiss his

cheek.

He turned his head and captured her lips with his in a deft maneuver. When the kiss reluctantly ended, she saw his smirk.

"You're good at that," she accused. "And you'd better not say that practice made perfect."

"Only with you, doll. Only with you," he assured.

An hour later, they arrived at his parents' house. She glanced nervously over at him. "Do you think they'll know?"

He lifted his eyebrow waiting for her to explain.

"You know," she said in exasperation. "That we were...um...just had sex." This last statement came out in a whisper.

"Babe, they don't have a listening device in my truck so I don't think you need to whisper."

"You know what I mean," she said, giving him a playful slap on the arm.

He saw her nervousness, and his heart melted again. "Mackenna," he said, gaining her attention. "We can tell them as much or as little as you're comfortable with."

Smiling her appreciation, she nodded. "I think I'd like to talk to my mom first before we make a big deal about anything."

He sobered, realizing that her mom must surely harbor resentment towards him, although she did not show it the other day. *But she'd have to. I mean, I broke her daughter's heart just when her husband was dying of cancer and then wasn't around when she had her stroke. If she doesn't hate me, she must be a saint!*

Now nervous himself, he alighted from the truck and walked around to assist Mackenna out. Letting his hand span around her waist, he leaned down to give her a quick kiss.

A scream erupted from the front porch as Rachel turned and called for Penny. "Hurry, they're here. And praise God, they're kissing. Our prayers have been answered Joseph—our Jobe has returned to us with Mackenna. Penny, Penny come on," she continued to scream as she ran down the front steps toward the couple.

"Uh…so much for being able to talk to mom first," Mackenna said, her eyes worried.

"Oh baby, I'm really sorry," he blurted, wanting to strangle his mother at that moment. "Ma, shush," he admonished as she reached them, seeing his father and Penny standing on the front steps now.

"We weren't ready to let—"

"Nonsense," Rachel announced, grabbing her son in a heartfelt hug before letting him go so that she could turn and clutch Mackenna in an equally huge hug. "Too much time has been wasted for two people who need each other."

She tucked Jobe's arm under one of hers and took Mackenna's arm under the other, propelling them toward the house.

"Joseph, Penny! Look who's here," she yelled.

"Woman, the whole neighborhood can tell who's here," he admonished, looking at his son carefully to see how he was taking the attention. Seeing the corners of Jobe's mouth curve up, he let out a sigh of relief. Clasping Jobe firmly by the hand, he shook it as though he had not seen him in a long time. "Glad to see you again, son. Good to have *you* home."

Moving over to Mackenna, whose face was bright red, he bent to kiss her cheek. "My darling girl, I've not seen that smile in a long time. It does an old man good to see you like this."

She felt tears spring to her eyes as she realized how much Mr. Delaro knew about his son's life. "Thank you," she whispered. Turning, she saw her mom standing with Rachel holding on to her tightly. Whether to support Penny or herself she was not sure.

"Hey, mom," she said as she moved to hug her.

Penny patted her back and asked, "Ya a-right?"

She nodded against her mom's shoulder. "Yeah, I'm great."

Standing back she allowed Penny to move toward Jobe. He reached out to steady her, enabling her to stare deeply into his gaze. A lopsided smile beamed across her face and he let out the breath he had been holding. Pulling her in, he gave her a hug, whispering in her ear, "Mrs. Dunn, I'm so sorry for all the hurt I've caused."

She patted his back with her right hand and said, "Ya a goo man, Jobe. Ya a betta man than ya were."

Smiling again, she added, "Age brins wisdom."

"Yes, ma'am," he agreed, kissing her cheek. "I promise you, no more pain, Mrs. Dunn. I'll guard her heart with my life."

Seeing the tears in everyone's eyes, including her own, spurred Rachel into action. "Dinner! We need to eat. Joseph get your son a beer and the women can head into the kitchen with me. Rebecca, call Hannah and tell her to get her brood over here. We're celebrating. Miriam, get in the kitchen. We've got a meal to fix."

The dinner turned out to be a crowded affair with nine adults and two children. Mackenna kept an eye on her mom knowing this was much more than she had been used to, but Penny seemed to enjoy the gathering. The Delaro family was loud and boisterous, but the love among the members was palpable.

Jobe managed to get his mother alone for a moment to tell her to not make a big deal about him and Mackenna.

She patted his cheek as she smiled, "I know, baby boy. I was just so happy to see that you two had talked."

He grinned back, saying, "It's a start."

"Ah thin it is mor than a star," Penny said, walking up behind him smiling.

Jobe turned and allowed Penny to hug him as well. Nodding to his mom, he walked with Penny out to the back deck for a rare moment of privacy.

"Mrs. Dunn, I assume that you have some fears about this. I hurt your daughter once and I know I lost your trust with that. I don't blame you at all. In fact, if I'm lucky enough to ever have a daughter and someone hurts her as badly as I messed up? I'd pound the shit outta 'em."

Penny nodded, her genuine smile still in place. "Ah know. But ah prayed ya coul both fin hap-e-ness agan."

"I won't go into all of the details, ma'am, and Mackenna can tell you those as you want them, but suffice it to say that when I broke things off, I truly wasn't in my right mind. The choice seemed right at the time, but it took a while...and honestly, some counseling, to help me see that I was just reacting to a fu—um, messed up situation."

"Sometime, love ha to fin its own way," Penny acknowledged.

Just then Mackenna walked out onto the porch, seeing her mother and Jobe deep in conversation. "Hey, you two. Is everything all right?"

Penny stepped over to her daughter, hugging her close and said, "It is now." Winking at Jobe, she moved inside.

Mackenna walked to the edge of the porch and leaned her hip against the railing as she turned to watch the man in front of her. He did not move. He just stood. Staring.

"You're beautiful, you know?" he said, softly.

Ducking her head, she smiled as she heard him step

closer. And closer. Until his boots were directly in front of her shoes. Lifting her head, her eyes were in line with his massive chest before moving up to his square jaw and beautiful eyes. His muscular arms came to the railing on either side of her, pinning her in.

"Are you okay? With us, I mean?" he asked, concern etched on his face.

She realized that he was suddenly insecure. A smile curved the corners of her mouth as she nodded. "Yeah. I am."

"Baby doll, everything happened kind of fast and—"

She put her fingers to his lips, shushing him. "Jobe, I didn't have sex with you just to forget about work." She glanced to the side for a few seconds before looking up, blushing. "Well, okay, I kind of did. At first," she quickly added. "But it's really been building since you came barreling back into my life."

"So initially, I was just a body?" he said, rubbing his nose along hers temptingly close to her lips.

"Yeah, soldier boy. You got a problem with that?" she purred, jutting out slightly to allow her breasts to just barely rub against his chest.

"No," he growled. "As long as I'm the only one you come to when you need someone to fuck the stress away." He captured her giggle in his mouth as he devoured hers, stepping forward until their entire fronts were pressed together, knees to chest.

She soon felt the evidence of his approval and started to move her hand between them to palm his crotch.

With a swift motion, he grasped her hand, stilling it. "Oh no, baby doll. You do this and I'll be sporting the biggest hard-on you've ever seen as we walk back into my mom's kitchen." He stepped back, to give his body a chance to cool, as he continued to hold her hand.

Looking back up, she said, "Jobe, just so you know—all kidding aside, I did need you to take away the stress of work, but it was you I needed. Not just anyone, but you. I...I think it's always been you."

"Ya'll coming back in for dessert or just having it out there?" Joseph called out, startling them.

"We're coming, pop," Jobe said, throwing his arm around her. Looking down at her sparkling eyes, he said, "Come on, doll. Let's get mom's dessert before we go home and have some of our own."

A FEW DAYS later, Jobe took Mackenna to the Alvarez picnic—an event that occurred whenever the group felt the need to let off steam and have fun. As they pulled up to the riverside park, she tucked her long hair behind her ear in a nervous gesture. Reaching over, he took her hand in his, giving it a gentle squeeze.

"You okay, doll? You know all of these people already."

"I know, but...well, it's kind of different now," she

replied as she turned to face him. "Have you told them? About us, I mean?"

"I haven't said anything officially."

Her expression was one of confusion as she cocked her head to the side and repeated, "Officially?"

Ducking his head, he explained, "Well, let's just say that for the past couple of days, I've been grinning a lot more than usual."

"Hmm," she replied with a smile. Sucking in a huge breath, she said, "We'd better go. Several of them are looking over at us."

Laughing, he got out of the truck and with a wave to his friends, he rounded to her side and opened her door, plucking her out. His eyes scanned the sky-blue t-shirt she wore down to the jeans that fit just right. Her long, thick hair was secured in a low ponytail with the breeze lifting the loose tendrils about her face. Setting her down on the ground, he leaned over to kiss her forehead. "Remember, you're with friends here."

She gifted him with her brilliant smile as she linked her fingers with his. He stared down at the public announcement she was making and smiled back as they made their way over to the picnic tables. Both noticed the huge grins on the women's faces and the nods of approval from the men. He felt her fingers tighten on his and he gave a reassuring squeeze.

They quickly joined the others, where she was engulfed in hugs from Jennifer, Sherrie, and Lily, before being introduced to the rest of the women. BJ's wife,

Suzanne, was there with their toddler twins, as well as Annie, a local veterinarian who was married to Shane. Both Annie and Lily were feeding their babies. Last, a beautiful woman approached offering her a hug as well. Vinny's fiancé, Annalissa, was a shy musician and McKenna instantly felt a rapport with each of the women.

The men manned the grills while the women set the rest of the food out. Jennifer had already filled in the others about Mackenna's work with the women from gangs, and the questions flowed. Mackenna had no problem talking about her job and found the others to be comfortable to talk to. Several questioned her badass attempt to handle the threats with a baseball bat.

Mackenna blushed. "Yeah, not my finest moment," she admitted.

"Well, I think you're incredibly brave," Annalissa said softly, with a smile.

Jobe overheard and shouted, "Don't encourage her!" as the other men nodded, no smiles on their faces.

"You just keep grilling over there and stop eaves-dropping," Sherrie yelled back. The women laughed and continued their conversations.

Annie said, "If you ever have someone interested in working part time at my vet clinic, let me know. Since Suzanne here," she shoulder-bumped her friend, "had twins, she's cut her hours way back and I can always use some help."

Mackenna's eyes grew round at the generous offer.

"That'd be amazing. Thank you!" Just then, a bee buzzed around her head and she shrieked, throwing her arms into the air, waving them about her head as she ran in a circle, screaming, "Beeeeeeee!"

One of the women quickly swatted it away, leaving Mackenna nervously looking around, feeling ridiculous.

"So much for the badass," Jennifer laughed. Much to Mackenna's embarrassment, the others could not contain their mirth either.

Jobe had started to run toward her when he heard her scream, but stopped in place as he realized what had happened. His heart pounded as he shook his head incredulously at the women all bent over in laughter. The other men, equally startled, had to chuckle at Jobe.

Vinny patted him on the back. "Your girl charges after gang members with a baseball bat and yet is afraid of a bee?"

Jobe, hand over his pounding heart, smirked. "Now, I just need to get her as afraid of the gangs as she is a fuckin' insect!"

The conversations began again, all talk of gangs put aside. The group sat at two picnic tables pushed together as they ate while keeping an eye on the children.

Jobe, looking over at Mackenna, felt at ease. For the first time in a long time...serenity. This beautiful woman was giving him a chance. At forgiveness. At love. At a future. Reaching over, he wrapped his arm around her shoulders, taking her weight as she leaned into him.

She smiled up at him, her hand going over her mouth as she tried to swallow her bite of hamburger. He kissed her forehead as he whispered, "Love you, baby doll."

Swallowing hard, her eyes sparkled as she realized what a gift she had received. Giving forgiveness to this man had taken nothing away from her. Instead, it allowed her to move forward. With him. With them. Face planting into his chest, she felt his steady heartbeat against her cheek.

His eyes wandered over the group, noticing that they had become the center of attention and was glad that her eyes were on him and not the others, to save her from embarrassment. But for him, it was everything. Smiling, he gave a slight nod in acceptance of their silent approval and continued to hold her as the conversations flowed once again.

THAT NIGHT JOBE showed Mackenna the indoor pool in his apartment building. Dipping into the warm water, she watched him as he swam a lap from the deep end to where she was standing. Long, sure strokes of his arms brought him closer and closer until he broke the surface right in front of her. Rising from the depths, like Neptune, he shook his head sending water droplets from his hair flying in all directions as others slid down his torso.

She watched the trail of water as it made it way over his pecs and abs, licking her lips as she thought of running her tongue along the same path.

"Baby?" he said with a growl, moving closer, eyeing her bikini clad body. The scraps of material barely covered her tits as the hankie-sized bottoms covered the treasure he intended to explore later.

Her eyes jumped to his, a guilty blush moving from her chest up her face.

"You keep looking at me like that, and I'll be obliged to jump you right here in the water."

Her mouth formed an "O", but no words came out. He chuckled as her light blush darkened to a deeper red.

"I don't think the management would like that very much," she finally said with a grin.

"Vinny taught Annalissa how to swim in this pool. Somehow I can't see him not giving her some business right here."

Mackenna gave him a push, just enough to off-balance him, saying, "But I can swim and you'd have to catch me first." Then she quickly dove under the water and kicked off, swimming with all of her strength.

Laughing, he gave her a short head-start, then dove under after her. Just when she thought she had made it to the other end, a firm hand grasped her ankle and pulled her under against a strong, hard body. Twisting, she was lifted under her arms as her head broke the surface and pushed against the side of the pool. As he moved closer, with each arm on either side of her, she was trapped. And loving the feel of him pressed against her once more.

He looked down, seeing her eyes staring back at his, her chest heaving with the combination of exertion and lust. He took her mouth, hard and fast. His tongue immediately delving into her warmth as her tongue vied for equal access. Claiming her with his kiss, he devoured her as he explored every crevice, swallowing her moans as his hands moved to the ties on her bikini top. With a quick pull, the material fell away, freeing the rosy-tipped mounds he had been eyeing. Palming one with his hand, he then shifted her higher and kissed a trail from her lips to her nipples, sucking one in deeply.

She lifted her legs around his waist, allowing his hard cock to nestle into her core, aching with need. Leaning back as he ravished her breasts, she luxuriated in the feelings of weightlessness and excitement. She could not help but glance around, having never had public sex. The realization that her breasts were bared for anyone to see had her moving her hand up to cover the one he was not latched onto.

He noticed the motion and stilled, lifting his head. "Doll, if I'm giving you a chance to be concerned about where we are, then I'm not doing enough to take your mind off everything except me and you."

Giggling, she replied, "I can't help it. What if

someone comes in?"

"They won't," he promised, moving back to feast on her breast.

"B...but..." she started, before becoming lost in the feelings as his hand untied the scrap of bikini at her hips and tossed it up on the side of the pool. She heard the slap of wet cloth hit the concrete but could not seem to care.

"It's after hours, doll. I locked the door from the inside. No one's around." He slid his fingers into her waiting body, eliciting more moans. "Just you. Me. And this," he said, guiding her hand down to his engorged cock.

With one more effortless heft, he lifted her out of the water and onto the side, moving quickly between her legs. With one hand on her stomach to hold her, he dove in tongue first. Licking her folds before nipping on her clit, he felt her writhe under his ministration. Chuckling, he moved in again, this time with his tongue buried inside.

She felt his pleasure as the waves deep inside had her throwing her head back in ecstasy. With this man pleasuring her between her legs, she opened her eyes and glanced around. She had never had daring sex with any partner, but she quickly loved the feeling of danger and excitement. Knowing he had locked the door did not dampen the thrill. Just then, a finger was reinserted deep into her core as he latched onto her clit with his lips and that was the last coherent thought she had.

As her orgasm rushed over her, she felt her inner walls pulsate against his fingers. With her legs over his shoulders as he floated in front of her, she watched him as he watched her. Screaming his name, she tried to grind her hips closer to his mouth as the ripples moved from her core outwards.

Before she could come back to earth, she was lifted once more and pulled back into the water. Directly on his straining cock. How he managed to get his swim trunks off without her noticing was a tribute to her level of distraction.

Jobe guided her body to his, holding her gaze and gaining her approval before he moved up inside of her. She grabbed his shoulders as he pumped in and out, her channel still grabbing at his cock. He watched her tits bounce in the water as he kept one hand behind her back to keep it from getting scraped on the side of the pool. He found his rhythm and as she became more accustomed to the movement, she joined him by pushing up against his shoulder to increase the friction. *God, this woman is beautiful.* Knowing that she was giving herself to him after all that he had put her through was humbling. And vowing to take care of her in all ways, he watched as her pleasure once again filled her expression.

With her body balanced against his protective hand, he slid the other hand down to her clit knowing he was close. With her tits right at his face, he latched onto one extended nipple and sucked it deeply. At the same time as giving her clit at a pinch, he felt her inner walls grabbing his cock. His balls tightening, he felt the rush as he poured himself deep into her, thrusting until the last drop was emptied.

She dropped her head onto his shoulders, keeping her legs around his waist, as her sated body crashed in post-orgasmic bliss. He wrapped one arm around her as he propelled them through the water toward the shallow end. As soon as his feet touched the bottom of the pool, he enveloped her in his arms, pressing her naked form against his. *Perfect fit. She's a perfect fit. But then, she always was.*

Climbing up the steps, with her body still latched onto his, he now felt her slight weight as they rose from the water. He bent, with her still in his arms, and grabbed their towels. Not wanting to let her go, he also did not want her to cool. He slowly let her slide down his front, holding her until her shaky legs were steady underneath her. He wrapped a large towel around her body, tucking it tightly at her breasts.

Peering down at her, he saw the light in her eyes staring back. Tender. *Full of...* He so wanted it to be love but knew that still had to come. "Let's get you upstairs and into a warm shower, doll," he said, kissing the end of her nose.

Grinning mischievously, she nodded toward the locker rooms. "They've got showers in there," she said seductively.

Turning her toward the deep end where their bathing suits still lay on the side of the pool, he gave her ass a swat. "Not this time, baby. I've got things I want to do to you tonight, and squeezing both of us in a tight, metal shower stall when I've got a huge, multi-head shower with a seat upstairs, where I've got room to do all the things I want to do...no contest."

At those words, she glanced over her shoulder up at him as he propelled them to pick up their suits. "Ummm," she purred. "And I won't even make you chase me," she promised.

Tucking her into his side as they entered the back elevator, he said, "I'm not ever letting you go again, Mackenna." With that promise, they headed into the shower in his apartment. And he proceeded to show her just how creative he could be with a large, multi-head shower with a seat. And she loved it.

CHAPTER 14

JAZZIE WATCHED THE night watchman enter the center, noting the huge size of the man known as Little John. His eyes moved to the cameras installed over the front door and the new bars on the first-floor windows. Knowing the back alleyway was just as covered, he sat for a minute pondering his choices. *Gotta get the bitches out of the center at a time when they aren't expecting anything.* Determined to think on that, he drove back to their meeting house.

Walking through the front room, he saw a naked girl, bent over the couch with one of the brothers pounding into her. As she turned, he saw her bruised face and knew she had already had her beat-in by the girls around. The next man in line, his cock already out and being palmed, nodded to Jazzie indicating that he knew he was to give up his place to the man with the higher rank.

Jazzie looked at the girl whose face was turned toward his. A flash of steel moved through her eyes, quickly replaced by subservience. So, fast that he could not swear he saw it. He palmed his cock for a few seconds but decided her tiny tits just were not going to do it for him, so he gave a quick shake and continued into the room where Tito sat.

Tito glanced up as the signals were exchanged. "You're late," he clipped, irritation in his voice.

"Sorry. Got detained in traffic."

Tito just nodded, then turned back to the others. "Got a new shipment coming in tomorrow night. I want you and Waldo on it," he ordered to Jazzie. "Then got some guns coming in three days. That gives you the next two nights to get the stash in, get it cut up and out to the girls. I want it in the buyer's hands before you gotta deal with the guns."

Jazzie nodded, pleased to see Tito back into the business end of things.

"Now for other business," Tito announced. "I was willing to let things rest, but got some inside news. Some bitch at that center is ratting out the Kings. She wasn't a Sixer, but no one wants that to get out. And I sure as fuck don't want Gabby to get any ideas."

"Gabby didn't know our shit, did she?" Jazzie asked, concern in his expression. Tito did not answer and that gave Jazzie a bad feeling...and solidified his desire to take care of the problem.

"We been courting the Kings," Tito continued. "Gonna sell some guns to them at the end of this week. Like to hand them something else on a platter if we can."

That peaked Waldo's interest, as he leaned forward eagerly. "What's on the table?"

"Kings got another girl there. Thought we give her back to them. In a way that sends a message."

Waldo grinned. He liked the sound of that. Jazzie's interest was sharp as well.

Pushing a scrap of paper at them with a computer image and a name on it, Tito simply said, "Get her. Take Poco and one other you choose and get her. Then make her pay. All the way. Then deliver her to the Kings with a note that they can thank us for the gift."

The men laughed, anxious to do Tito's bidding. Jazzie watched him carefully. Getting this King's girl out would give him a good chance to see how best to get to Gabby.

The next morning, Jazzie could not believe how easy it was. The young woman left the center, walking to the bus stop to go downtown. He watched her in her clean, job-hunting clothes, knowing she was trying to shake the image of the River's off her. Glancing to the side, he saw Waldo's eyes glued to the girl's ass.

"That all you think about? Fucking?"

Waldo grunted as his eyes never left the girl. "Hell, yeah. Nothin' like sinkin' my dick in some sweet pussy."

"Who cares if it's sweet as long as it's pussy?" Poco called out from the back seat.

A bus pulled up, taking the others in line while the girl looked down at her watch. She was now the only one waiting for the downtown bus. As she stood, her hands nervously smoothing down her new skirt, she never heard the sound of soft footsteps behind her. Until it was too late.

"SO WHERE DID SHE go?" Mackenna asked Carla.

"I don't know. Teresa was dressed and out of here in time to make it to the bus stop for her interview. But they called and said that she did not show up."

Rubbing her temples, Mackenna shook her head. She had just gotten into her office when Carla gave her the news. "I've spent two weeks lining up that job interview for her." Looking up at Rose, who had joined them, Mackenna said, "I'm going to have to let Teresa go if she doesn't have a good reason for missing that interview. I've got two more girls who want into New Beginnings and I already have room for two of them since Selena left."

"Well, I've got more news," Rose said sitting down. "A couple of the other girls are nervous hearing that Teresa missed her interview this morning. They swear she was excited about it and they think something happened to her. I think Selena's situation has them afraid of gang retaliation."

Mackenna sighed heavily. "A week ago, I'd have told them that that was ridiculous. Now I don't know what to think."

The three ladies were quiet a moment before Mackenna looked up, shaking her head. "All right, enough about this. Let's get to work. I'm calling the social worker and telling her to let the two new girls know that they can come on over."

TWO DAYS LATER, Mackenna was sitting in her DSS cubicle in the downtown office, having just finished a staff meeting. Calling her mom to check on her, she was glad to hear the happiness in her mother's voice.

"Mom, I was thinking that we need to get back to our house," she said tentatively. "I talked to the detectives this morning and they said that the house is no longer being processed as a crime scene, so I am heading over there now to check it out. I think we'll just need to patch the holes and do a little touch-up painting. I made a call to our landlord so that he could make sure a window company came to measure the windows for replacement."

She noticed the quietness of her mom. Biting her lip, she said, "Are you still there?"

"I heah. I know we nee ta ge back."

Mackenna could hear the hesitation in her mom's voice and knew that she was enjoying her time with the Delaros. "Well, we can't move back until the windows are replaced and I'm sure it's all secure. So if you're happy, then there's no reason to not stay with Joseph and Rachel for a little bit longer."

"Oh, tha wou be lov-ly," Penny said, the excitement in her voice evident.

After a few more minutes, they hung up and Mackenna sighed, knowing she needed to head to the house. She did not tell her mother that when she talked to the landlord, he was not happy that her job had ended up having the ramifications of a drive-by. In fact, he had indicated that he would prefer them not to move back in. *Now I may have to find another place to live that can accommodate mom.*

Several hours later, waving to Jennifer, who was still in her cubicle talking to some friends, she walked to the elevators when her cell phone rang. Seeing Jobe's name, she smiled as she answered.

"Hey, sweetie."

"Where are you, doll?" came the clipped response.

"Well, hello to you too," she joked.

"Sorry, but I need to come pick you up and need to know where you are," he explained.

"What's wrong? Is it mom?" she asked worriedly.

"No babe, but I need to get you now."

Realizing that he would tell her when the time was right, she said, "I'm just heading out of the DSS building."

"Stay there and I'll pick you up out front in about ten minutes."

"Okay," she agreed, the uncertainty evident in her voice, as he hung up.

Hurrying to the elevators, she took one down and then waited until she saw the Alvarez black SUV pulling up. Without giving him a chance to double park and open the door for her, she rushed over and hopped into the front seat.

Jobe pulled into traffic, glancing at her, silent but knowing she had a million questions. "I appreciate you cooperating. This needed to be done in person and not over the phone."

Licking her lips nervously, she twisted her body so that she was facing him. Silently waiting, but not patiently.

"Got a call from Shane. A girl's been found and they think it may be one of yours. You missing someone and didn't tell me?"

She blinked slowly, digesting what he was saying. *Picked up? Picked up for what? Is he talking about Teresa?*

"Babe?"

Her eyes jerked back to his.

"Did you forget to tell me something? About one of your girls going missing?"

"Forget? I…I do have one of the girls who left, but sometimes they do that, Jobe. They don't all stay, although most of them do and finish the program. But a few get some skills, some new clothes and walk out the door. I…and what do you mean forget?" she said, angrily. "I don't report to you!"

His lips tightened into a thin line as he maneuvered them through the end-of-day traffic. "I'm trying to protect you, Mackenna. You have someone go rogue, I need to know that."

"Why? That doesn't involve you. Or Tony. Or the police. It just happens sometimes," she retorted, pushing her hair back in frustration.

"When you've got yourself and your center in the sights of some gangs, then yes—it does involve us."

She sat for a moment sulking, then realized how childish that was. Sighing heavily, she said, "Three days ago, I had set up an interview for Teresa Yanez. She had been with us for about two months. Fast learner, smart. She left us with a full breakfast in her, new business clothes on her, and she did not get to the interview."

"Did you call the police?"

"No, because they won't do anything," she said in a huff. Seeing him cut his eyes over to her, she continued, "I tried that before, Jobe. These girls are over eighteen years old. They do not have to stay at the center or in the program. Most that do stay in are successful when they get out. Others leave and go back to the life."

They sat in silence for a few more minutes when she looked around at the buildings. "Where are we going?"

He pulled to the back of a brick building and she saw the words over the doors. **City Morgue**. Her gaze snapped back to his as she silently begged for his denial.

Sucking in a huge breath as he parked, he turned to

face her. "Doll, I'm sorry. You're the only one who can make a positive identification right now."

"Dead? She's dead?"

Shane walked out of the building and seeing them both in the vehicle, he started for the passenger door. Jobe hopped out and rounded the SUV, assisting her out.

"I...I don't know if I can do this," she whispered.

He pulled her close, tucking her into his side as he shook Shane's hand and gave a head nod to Matt.

"Baby, I'll be with you every moment. I swear if there were another way, I'd do it."

Thirty minutes later, they retraced their steps back to the SUV, this time his arms held her trembling body. He assisted her into the vehicle, buckled her in and rounded the front.

As they drove in silence, her numbness wearing off, she said, "Can you take me to Jennifer's?"

He glanced to the side, willing to do anything and pulled out his phone, dialing Gabe. As soon as it was answered, he said, "Jennifer home? Can we come by?"

"Yeah, Mackenna needs to talk to her. We've been at the morgue. One of her girls ended up here." After a quick goodbye, he changed directions heading out to Gabe and Jennifer's subdivision.

Pulling up to a neat, two-story house with a fenced in yard they turned into the driveway. Jennifer's brother, Ross, was outside tossing a ball with Gabe.

"Jennifer's inside, Mackenna," he called out.

Jobe nodded and walked her up to the front door. Kissing the top of her head, he said, "I'll be right out here, doll."

Before she could nod, the door flung open and she was embraced in Jennifer's hug.

"Mac! Oh honey, come on in." Jennifer gave a small smile to Jobe and then shut the door after ushering Mackenna into the kitchen, seating her at the breakfast bar.

"Okay, Mac. I've got beer or wine. Or if you prefer, I can make a mean cocktail."

Mackenna had to smile at her friend's penchant for trying to fix everything. "I think this calls for wine. We'll save the cocktails for a celebration."

"Right," Jennifer said, pulling out the bottles and glasses.

Lifting an eyebrow, Mackenna asked, "How much wine are you planning on us drinking?"

"Honey, that all depends on how much talking we've got to do. So start spilling!"

Moving to the living room, settling into the comfortable sofa, Mackenna began doing just that. She told her about the problems with the New Beginnings Center and ended with the trip to the morgue.

Jennifer listened carefully and by the time Mackenna got to the end, she was shaking her head in sympathy. "Oh, Mac. How horrible for you to have to do that."

Lifting her gaze to her friend, Mackenna said, "You know, the morgue wasn't even like in the movies. They had me sign in, fill out forms on how I knew Teresa and then they showed me a picture of her face. I was able to identify her from that and told them so."

"Oh, thank God you didn't have to actually see the body," Jennifer said, leaning forward to grasp Mackenna's hand.

Squeezing Jennifer's fingers in response, she said, "Jennifer, is it all worth it? I thought so. I went into social work to make a difference. To help others. I was so interested in women's studies and empowering women. The more I learned about how to assist women in moving from poverty to productive lives and then learned about breaking the cycle of gang women, that's all I wanted to do."

"You are doing that, Mac. You have to know you're making a difference."

"I've got one girl who was taken away because she was witness to a horrible gang crime and who knows what the safehouse will allow her to do to keep her studies up. I've got a girl who has now confessed to being pregnant by a gang leader, who may be the one behind the drive-by shooting of my house. I now have another one that was kidnaped on the way to a job interview and was killed, before being dumped literally at the door of a gang. And to top it off, I have two others that are now thinking of leaving because they are scared of retribution. And that was before what happened to Teresa!"

Tossing back the rest of the wine in her glass, Mackenna leaned forward and poured another drink. She looked over at Jennifer and shook her head. "Pretty pathetic, isn't it?"

"Nope. Not at all," Jennifer stated. "I see in front of me a tireless, active, fellow social worker who is burning out due to being in a high-stress environment."

"Good God, you sound like one of our professors!"

"I know, but I now know that they knew what they were talking about. Almost fifty percent of social workers suffer from job-related stress and burnout. Look, Mac. You're making a difference, but right now all you can see is the negative. Tell me, how many girls have you had go through the center and actually graduate to jobs outside the gang system?"

"We've been open about eight months and have had seventeen girls finish the program and move out after their three months are up. And we currently have six more."

"How many failures have you had? And that does not include the girl who had to leave for crime witness protection."

"Just two who decided after a week that they wanted to go back to the life."

"Mac, you're running a program that is so far at

about a ninety percent success rate. That is amazing. Think of those seventeen girls who are out of a gang and living productive lives."

"I know, but…"

"But what?"

"Will you think less of me if I confess that I'm kind of scared? Now that I understand more of what I was up against when I went running out onto the stoop with a baseball bat, I'm terrified."

Finishing her glass, Jennifer poured another one for herself also. "You should be scared. Hell, Mac, I'm just working with a darling group of senior citizens. I would be petrified to go up against gangs."

"Yeah, well, that wasn't my intent. When I started the center, I stupidly thought that as long as the girls left the gang and came to us, then their old lives would be left behind. And for the first months, that's what happened. But now, it seems like we are definitely on the gang's radar. And that makes me wonder about the future success of what I'm doing."

The two women sat in companionable silence for a few minutes, letting the wine relax them a little. Mackenna finally said, "I just keep seeing that picture in my mind. When Teresa left for the interview, Carla said she looked great. New haircut, the professional clothes. Even one of the other girls did a little makeup for her." She gazed at Jennifer over her glass and said, "She was on her way to start a new life. And didn't deserve to end up as a photo that someone should have to look at to identify."

"No, she didn't," Jennifer agreed. "But, that's not your fault, Mac. That's the responsibility of the people who actually did that. And why your work is so important. For every horrible case like Teresa, there will be so many more that you can save, train, and they are successful."

The two finished their second glasses of wine and walked to the kitchen to place them in the sink. Mackenna gazed out the window as the evening sky was darkening. "I've kept the men out too long."

"Oh, posh, Gabe and Ross could stay out there all night. I'm just glad that you wanted to come here and Jobe brought you."

The two embraced in the kitchen before Jennifer pulled back and looked at her friend. "Mac, here's what this social worker thinks. You need a break. You need to take care of you or you'll suffer burnout. And I would hate to see the profession lose a talented counselor."

They walked out on the front porch, looking at their men. Mackenna admired Jobe's physique as he tossed and ran with the ball. The old, familiar feeling swept over her and she was transported back about seven years ago when she watched him play ball on the beach with some of their friends. Knowing then that he was the man she wanted to spend the rest of her life with. *And now? Can I possibly feel that again with all the craziness swirling around?* She gave herself a mental shake as the men made their way to the porch.

Jennifer kissed Ross' head as she told him to head inside to take a shower. Then she turned to Gabe, who wrapped his large frame around his tiny wife. His eyes found Mackenna's and he sent her a questioning gaze.

Mackenna smiled and nodded, gaining a head jerk back from him. Jobe noticed, glad that she had Jennifer to talk to, as he kissed her forehead before pulling her in for a hug as well.

"Jobe?" Jennifer called. As he turned toward her, she said, "Professionally and personally speaking, Mac is facing some burnout. It'd be good if you two could get away for the weekend."

Jobe smiled at his friend's wife, loving that she cared about Mackenna as well. "Sounds like a plan," he responded.

The four friends said their goodbyes as Jobe loaded Mackenna back into the truck. Driving home, he said, "What do you think about Jennifer's getaway idea?"

"You know, I believe I'd really like it. You mom told me that she wants Penny to stay as long as she can. Your mom likes the company and I think she also likes that Miriam comes by every day. I talked to my mom and she's happy for now with your parents. I was going to go to my house to sort things out today when all the craziness happened. Maybe a couple of days away would be good."

"You got anywhere special you want to go?"

Smiling at him, she shook her head. "Nope. Surprise me."

Returning her grin, he said, "That I can do, doll. That I can do."

CHAPTER 15

THE FOUR MEN sat down at a scarred table in the back room of a dingy bar, eyes darting around, carefully noting everyone's positions. Four other men stood behind the ones seated, their eyes just as alert. Two men stood on their side of the door, feet apart and arms crossed.

Tito waited. He did not call the meeting but expected it just the same. The leader of the River Street Kings, Goldie Washington, sat across from him, his gaze penetrating. Suddenly Goldie smiled and Tito knew where the nickname came from. The man had had every one of his teeth fully capped in gold. The brilliant yellow glistened against his dark skin, creating an otherworldly appearance and Tito was glad he had been warned. Otherwise it would have unsettled him—exactly what Goldie wanted the effect to be.

"You left us a present," Goldie stated, referring to Teresa's body.

"Thought you'd appreciate it."

"Dicks got her when we threw out the trash."

Tito's eyes grew dark at this admission. He had planned on the Kings disposing of the girl's body somewhere where she would not be found by the police. "That was careless," he growled.

His gaze caught the miniscule movement of the King's men in the room immediately followed by the same from his men. He did not take his eyes off Goldie, but with a slight jerk of his head he communicated to Jazzie to stand down. The last thing he needed was for the Kings to go on the offensive.

He softened his voice slightly as he amended his last statement, "But then a gift is for you to do whatever the fuck you want to with it."

Goldie eyed him a moment and then broke into laughter. The other men in the room, still wary, seemed to relax.

"You looking to do business or just givin' a gift for the fuck of it?" Goldie inquired as his mirth died down.

Tito then smiled, knowing the preliminaries were successfully out of the way. Jazzie sat next to him, comfortable that Tank and Waldo standing behind them would see to their safety.

"Moving into guns. Looking to see what you need. Thought you'd be interested in a business arrangement."

"I got guns," Goldie replied defensively.

"You got what you take. You got guns you use. But unless I've been told wrong, you ain't got new shit to sell."

At this, Goldie's gaze penetrated Tito's carefully, looking for a sign of disrespect. Tito held firm. The air in the room became charged again, each man assessing the climate.

Tito opened his hands on the table in a gesture of conciliation. "No dis, King-man, but the Sixers are moving into other areas besides the C-game and pussy," indicating wanting more income than just cocaine and prostitution.

Goldie sat for a moment, his mind racing with the possibilities. The Kings were growing, but he knew that a collaboration with another successful organization could open doors for them. But he was suspicious. "Why the Kings?"

"Easy," Tito answered. "You own the riverfront. That's prime. We'd like to use it for transport when needed. You give us access...you get what you need. Win-win."

Goldie sat silent for a moment, slowly nodding his head. "More. You got more than that."

Tito smiled knowing the King-man was not stupid. "Fuckin' pigs are closin' in. Stepped up in my area." Seeing Goldie's eyebrow lift, he continued, "Nothin' we can't deal but with the new business, we need a new place to get shipments. You give us access, we give you guns." Holding his gaze steady again, he repeated, "Win-win."

The brilliant gold smile split the King's leader's face as he nodded. "Like it. Gotta talk to my boys, but you'll hear."

Tito smiled in return, still cautious knowing his

rival could not be trusted entirely. "Don't got forever. Got a package waiting to come in."

"Our seconds can deal," Goldie announced.

Tito's head jerked toward Jazzie, then he nodded in agreement. Goldie did the same to his second.

Goldie hesitated for a moment, then asked, "Where'd you find our present?"

"Cunt was hiding out. A place on 91ˢᵗ street. Some bitch's got a place for our bitches to hide if they want."

Goldie heard more than the words Tito had spoken. Cocking his head to the side, he asked, "You got any bitches there? You need the marker?"

Tito shook his head. "We got it. We're taking care of the whole fuckin' place."

The men stood, clasped hands in a semblance of a shake and left the room, leaving the two seconds and two lieutenants behind.

DAYS LATER ANOTHER GROUP of men gathered around a table, the atmosphere completely different. Jobe, Tony, Gabe, Vinny, BJ, and Lily sat with Shane and Matt as they discussed the recent events.

Shane looked up, saying, "Chief needs Alvarez Security again."

Tony gave a slight nod, knowing that the detectives already knew that whatever was needed would be given.

"We're hitting the gangs hard right now. Finding

where they meet and shutting them down. If we can find them with guns, stolen goods, or drugs, we're charging them with that."

"It's causing some unrest on the streets, but most of the citizens are applauding the police crackdown," Matt added.

"But?" Jobe prodded, unable to keep quiet knowing Mackenna was in the thick of things.

"We're stressed staff-wise, doing all we can. We'd like to run some of the data through BJ and Lily's databases and see if we can narrow our focuses down a little. The main players are not leaving, just moving deeper underground. Hideouts we don't have a finger on yet. And the word out is that the Sixers have moved into guns."

"How do the Kings figure into it all?" Tony asked.

"Never been good blood between those two but seems like they may be moving toward a detente. At least for now. Protection for both and widens their areas. But, gotta tell you, I'd be surprised if either trusts the other much."

"Besides BJ and Lily, anything else you need?"

Matt and Shane's gazes cut over to Jobe and he stiffened.

"Know you've got eyes on Mackenna's center. After looking at the kidnapping and murder of Teresa, knowing that Tito's pregnant ex-girlfriend is there, and Mac's on their radar..."

"Got her and them covered," Jobe declared.

Nodding, Shane said, "Knew you did. But the chief wants to make sure you're in the loop."

Jobe felt his heart pound uncharacteristically and the familiar feeling of losing control of a mission swept through him. Pulling in a deep breath, he let it out slowly utilizing one of the methods taught by the counselor in dealing with stress. He could feel the eyes of his comrades on him and it pissed him off. "I've got this," he growled.

"What's going on?" Tony asked, turning the attention back to the detectives.

Shane hesitated. "The dead girl had words carved into her stomach. *The bitch is next.*"

At that, the air in the room changed. The temperature dropped. Ice. Cold.

"At first, it was assumed by the homicide detectives that it was just a random threat, but they had nothing to tie it to."

"And now?" Jobe asked, his voice barely recognizable to himself as he sat up straighter, hands clenched into fists.

"Got intel that says it's about some woman who's running a center. Something to do with the Sixer's leader's girlfriend."

"Fuck!" Jobe growled as he stood quickly, his chair falling backward in his haste. He started around the table to head toward the door when his way was suddenly blocked by the massive twins.

Looking at his two best friends, he said menacingly,

"You do not want to be in my way, bros."

Tony stood quietly and turned toward the men squaring off next to him. "Stand down, all of you."

The stance of the three barely relaxed, but the military training was too hard to ignore. Jobe's body was locked, his mind centered on one thing and that was taking Tito Montalvo down.

"Jobe, I gotta have your head in the mission."

Jobe's gaze cut over to his former Captain's, seeing understanding, not censure. But also a determined stare that brooked no question.

"We got Terrance, Doug, and two others in the surveillance room twenty-four seven watching the center, along with our other video feed contracts. You know Mackenna agreed to talk to the residents and those that have business outside the center are getting escorts. We've grown and got the manpower to take care of it."

"She and the center are on the radar of the police as well," Matt assured. "Hourly passes with marked patrol cars."

The room was deadly silent for a moment, all eyes on Jobe. Using all the training he could muster, he controlled his breathing, his mind beginning to clear of the consuming rage he felt. Then, uncharacteristically, he confessed, "Fucked up years ago. Been breathing but not living for a long time. I just got her back and I'll be goddamned if I lose her to some shithead punk."

Tony walked the three steps that it took to get to

Jobe, standing right in his space. The two were almost the same height, so eye contact was easy to obtain...easy to hold. "We all fucked up years ago, one way or the other. Mine was knowing you needed help to stay in the field but not pushing you harder to take care of home. That's on me. That's on all of us that were there."

Jobe jerked back at Tony's words, shaking his head. "No, sir. That was squarely one me. My decision. My fuck up."

"Not in my book. Brothers don't let brothers fall without taking care of everything—and that included the girl back home. If you'd broken up with her for the right reasons, we would have been good in standing down. But we all knew it wasn't right and not one of us took it upon ourselves to help that situation. We just took care of you in the field. And that, Jobe...is on us."

Jobe was silent as his gaze moved from Tony's to Gabe's to Vinny's, seeing the same guilt in each one. No words came past the lump in his throat...so he stood tall giving them a head nod in acknowledgment.

Tony continued, "We didn't take care of Mackenna then, but we sure as hell will now. I promise you— promise—we will see her safe. But we plan, we work together, and we keep our heads in the mission."

Blinking hard, Jobe nodded. This time was different. This time, he was not afraid of losing control. This time, he agreed that his brothers had control as well. This time Mackenna would be protected...her heart as well as everything else.

Sitting back down to the table, the group began to plan.

ANOTHER GATHERING SAT at a table, finding little comfort with the news being shared, but comfort in each other. Mackenna, at the New Beginning's dining table, was surrounded by Rose, Carla, Jenita, Gabby, Little John, and the other women staying at the center. She had just told them about Teresa and sat as they processed the information. After the tears, now came the fears.

Gabby sat stoically for a moment before asking, "Do we know who did this?"

Mackenna felt all the eyes looking at her as she sucked her lips in, trying to think of what to say. Slowly letting out the breath she was holding, she said honestly, "I was told by the police that they suspect her former gang, the River Street Kings to be involved. But…" she said, turning to Gabby, "they also suspect the Sixers."

Gabby sucked in a quick breath. "They're sending a message to me, aren't they? He is, I'm sure of it."

"We don't know what they're doing or what the message is."

One of the newer girls, face pale, said, "I don't want to go back, but…"

Mackenna pierced her with a hard stare. "Tina, don't think about going back. Don't you see, if you go back now, you could easily have it worse for having left."

"Oh, great. So I'm dead if I stay and dead if I go back," the girl retorted angrily.

"No, that's not what I mean. You don't have to stay here, but you don't want to go back to that life."

"What other options are there?" Jenita asked gently.

"I talked to my supervisor after this happened. If I can work up a new grant proposal and get help with fundraising, we are thinking of moving the center."

"Moving?" Rose asked.

"Look, we got this building because the city was taking it over and it needed little work to make it fit our needs. Plus, we thought that being close into the downtown area would be good. But maybe not. If we were out somewhere…we would be away from the local gangs."

The group was quiet for a moment, so Mackenna plowed ahead. "We've got police protection and the security in place from Alvarez Security. Now, we're safe here, so for those of you still in our educational program, you're good. We just need to change the rules a bit for when you go out. For those of you who are already working and looking to graduate from this program within the next couple of weeks, I've been told that Alvarez security will get you to and from your jobs."

"Do you think it'll be enough?" one of the women asked.

Mackenna thought back to the conversation she and Jobe had the previous night where he pledged his protection...of her heart as well as the center. Looking at the women sitting at the table, she replied honestly, "Yeah, I think it will."

"Then that's good enough for me," Carla said, gaining nods from the other women.

"Okay then," Mackenna said with the first smile on her face in days. "Rose, you're back in the classroom. Carla, those of you learning culinary skills, I've got someone to take you to the restaurant together at ten, so be ready. The rest of you should be with Rose." Turning to Gabby, she said, "I know you've got an appointment at the health department and I've got a nice man from Alvarez named Doug that will be taking you so be ready by nine-thirty." Looking around as she stood, she said, "By the way, this afternoon I'm picking up a new girl. I got a call from a school counselor and she has a girl that needs out badly. She survived her beat in but wants out. Seems like she may need some extra help and so I'm picking her up. Then I'll start finding us a new home."

Several hours later, Mackenna returned with Paulina, a small woman whose face was still yellow with bruises. The girls circled around welcoming her and worked to get her settled in. Paulina's eyes darted around nervously as Mackenna went over the rules of

New Beginnings with her.

"Do you think that you'll have a problem with any of these?" Mackenna asked.

"No, ma'am," Paulina replied softly.

Leaning forward, she patted Paulina's leg and said, "I know you've been through a lot. I'll be working with you as far as counseling goes and you can tell me whatever you want to. Miss Rose will get you in the computer room tomorrow to start your classes. And the other girls will be here to help you settle in."

The young woman nodded as she looked at Mackenna with a small smile. "I can do this," Paulina promised.

Mackenna hesitated for a moment before continuing, "Paulina, most of the women here have been through what you've been through. We don't talk about what gangs they're from usually because the whole idea is to put that life behind them. But you should know that the police are watching us carefully. I know you are from a gang that has made threats against us."

Paulina's eyes grew wide. "They can't get to us?" she asked, fear in her voice.

"No, no. Don't worry. We have security cameras around, bars on the windows, and an excellent night watchman who's a former soldier. The police drive by several times a day and we're escorted. In fact, I'm going this afternoon to look for a new place for us to move to so that we can be even farther away."

Paulina let out a sigh of relief. "I...I can't go back to what I left," she said. "I can't do...that again."

Smiling her assurances, Mackenna stood. "And you don't have to go back to that. I'll make sure of it." With that, she headed out to scout for a new location.

CHAPTER 16

JOBE WALKED INTO the apartment, the smell of dinner cooking immediately hitting him. It dawned on him what he had been missing where he lived. *Home.* It had been a place to crash. A place to eat. A place to sleep. But now with the woman he loved here with him…it was home.

An idea had been forming in his head, but he was uncertain how Mackenna would take it. *Is it too soon? Is it something that she wants?* He had mentioned it to Penny when he dropped by his parent's house.

Rounding the breakfast bar, he stopped as he saw Mackenna in the kitchen with her mother as they both worked around each other seamlessly preparing dinner. Mackenna's reddish-gold mane was pulled on top of her head with some curls escaping and falling down her shoulders. Her gorgeous ass was shimmying in yoga pants as the music from her phone played. Penny was laughing at something her daughter had said as they worked side by side. Smiling, he felt the uncertainty of the day slide away, leaving a warm place deep inside. One he wanted to keep alive. And safe.

"Sweetie!" Mackenna called as she turned and saw

him standing there. He was leaning against the bar, one tree-trunk leg crossed in front of the other. His thick arms mirrored his legs, as they were casually crossed over his chest, pulling his black polo tightly across his body. His dark hair, just long enough for her to run her fingers through when they were—*whoa, time to shut down those thoughts.*

She peered up at his smiling face, seeing his twinkling eyes. *Damn, he knows exactly what I was thinking.*

And he did, having to adjust himself when Penny turned back to the stove. Narrowing his gaze at Mackenna, his expression promised retribution for giving him a hard-on in front of her mother.

Giggling, she pranced over to him, rising on her toes to press a kiss on his lips. "Hey, sweetie," she repeated.

Wrapping his arms around her, he pulled her tightly against his chest in welcome. "Hey yourself, doll."

"We thought we'd eat early and then take you up on your offer to let mom try out your pool if that's okay," she said.

"Absolutely," he enthused. "I think that'll do you a lot of good, Mrs. Dunn," he said, winking at her over the top of Mackenna's head. He knew Penny was perfectly happy with his parents, but he wondered if she was amenable to the idea that he had mentioned.

Mackenna noticed that he was introspective during dinner but was afraid to ask him why. She so wanted to stay with him but did not know how to bring it up.

Her mom had to take priority and they could not continue to rely on the Delaro's kind offer, nor could she possibly ask Jobe if he wanted them to stay.

The meal finished, the three of them headed to the pool where Jobe assisted Penny into the water and worked with her in using her weaker limbs. Mackenna swam laps for a few minutes and then moved over to where they were. She watched the expression on her mother's face as Penny floated with weightless ease in the water. It was so nice seeing her mom enjoying herself again.

The trio made their way back upstairs where they quickly changed into dry clothes. Walking out into the living room, Jobe said, with what he hoped was enough casualness to not be obvious, "You know, Mrs. Dunn, if you lived in this building, you could have the pool, hot tub, and sauna whenever you wanted."

Mackenna shot him a strange look, wondering where that comment had come from. *Does he want mom here? Does that mean he wants me here too? I don't want mom to think I don't wish to live with her.*

"They have the elevators so there are no stairs to deal with. And on the second floor they have smaller, one bedroom condos that are affordable."

"Jobe," Mackenna admonished. "Mom needs to live with me. I admit that our landlord is afraid for us to come back, but I was going to start looking for a new place."

Penny chuckled as the two walked over to her.

Reaching up with her good hand to cup her daughter's cheek, she said, "I can see tha wheels tu-ning in ya mind. It okay if you wan ta be with Jobe."

"Mom, I never minded sharing a house with you," Mackenna proclaimed.

"I know. Bu thi way, I can be close bu have ma own place too."

"You're considering living here?" Mackenna asked with a smile.

"Maybe. I don wan to be in ya way," she said with a wink.

Jobe rushed to say, "Mrs. Dunn, like Mackenna, I don't want you living somewhere else. I'd like you to live here. If you wanted to stay with me that'd be fine."

Penny saw the uncertainty written on both of their faces and shook her head. She took Mackenna's hand in hers and walked her over to Jobe. She struggled to take his hand in her left one, but he made it easier by placing his hand on hers. Smiling, she brought their hands together. Looking at them both, she said, "Tha time is o-va for not say-in wha is on ya mind. Ya par-ens are pick-in me up, so I nee to get downstairs." With that, she kissed them goodbye and left the apartment.

Mackenna glanced down at her hand, still holding his, and said, "I think we've been dismissed."

Jobe chuckled and pulled her along before tugging her into his lap as he sat on the sofa.

"Penny's right. The time is over for us to keep things inside, even if we're afraid," he said, holding her gaze. "Mackenna, I know everything has happened fast…or so it seems. But the honest to God truth is that I never stopped loving you for the past five years. And I have loved having you in my house."

He watched her carefully, but so far nothing that he had said seemed to have her running for the hills. *So far, so good.*

"I ran by to talk to Penny, the day after she went to stay with my parents, to let her know that we had a great place in this building that was affordable. We got to talking and she admitted that she loved being with you, but wished that she had her own place too."

Mackenna nodded, knowing it was the right thing to do for her mom. She reached up and cupped his jaw in her hand, feeling the stubble underneath her fingertips. "You're so amazing, Jobe. You saw something that I hadn't even seen…her need to feel more independent."

"Oh doll, you don't need to thank me. If I hadn't been in such a fucked-up state of mind, I'd have been here all along when you needed me."

She sighed, thinking of the past.

"Babe, if that sigh is any indication, I'm still fucking things up."

She lifted her eyebrow, confusion written on her face. "I…I'm not sure I understand."

Jobe pulled her over so that she was straddling his lap, one hand on her waist and the other cupping her cheek. "Mackenna, for the past week, we've lived in my apartment as a couple. But I knew that it wasn't home to you. Hell, it wasn't much of a home for me. Just a place to hang. But I want you to move in with me. Bring your stuff so that we can put it all together. Make it our home."

His words slid through her, moving into barren places, long empty and cold. A slow smile curved the corners of her mouth, as the full meaning of what he was saying penetrated her mind.

"You want to be here with me?" she said, almost afraid that he would immediately retract his sentiments.

Chuckling, he leaned forward and placed a kiss on her lips. Chaste. Soft. "Yeah, Baby doll. I'm back in your life and I'm not about to give that up. You and me, with your mom close by…that's home."

"So instead of a weekend getaway, how about we get your friends to help us move? That would be the perfect thing to take my mind off of work—making a home here."

He smiled as he pulled her back in for a kiss. This one deeper. Wetter. Hotter. And then he showed her just how much having a home together meant. All night long.

THE WEEKEND FOUND the Alvarez crew loading furniture and moving while the women all pitched in to help unpack. Most of Mackenna and Penny's furniture was moved to Penny's new second-floor condo. She had signed the paperwork with the condo management and since the apartment was empty, she was granted an immediate move in.

Her furniture fit perfectly and Penny's pleasure showed on her face. Knowing her mom was just two floors down gave Mackenna peace of mind, while knowing that her mom had gained a little of her independence back was priceless.

BJ's wife, Suzanne, along with Lily worked in Penny's new place, unpacking the kitchen items and getting them into the drawers and cabinets as directed. Jennifer, Annalissa, and Sherrie took care of clothes and linens. Mackenna ran between the two apartments, making sure that things were going well for her mom and chatting with her friends, before seeing that the items the men brought over for her new home were going to fit.

Jobe could tell she was fretting and finally stopped her in mid-run, with his hands on her shoulders. "Babe, slow down. This weekend was supposed to be non-stressful for you and you're about to run yourself ragged."

"It's all good, Jobe, I promise. This is good stress and I just want to make sure mom's taken care of."

Jobe held her stare for a moment. "Seriously? She's got four other women down there helping. My mom, Miriam, and Rebecca are bringing dinner for the entire gang. I think your mom is fine."

She puffed some of her reddish-gold curls out of her face and said, "Well, what about here? I don't want them dumping all my things in here and making you crazy. I mean it may not mesh with your stuff."

Standing up straight, he lifted an eyebrow. "Mesh with my stuff? Look around, babe. Does it look like I have a style to you? Hell, bring whatever and we'll make it work. If we don't like something, we can dump it and buy new shit."

By the end of the afternoon, Penny's new apartment was completely set up with her furniture, cable, and the internet. Her books were in shelves, her kitchen was in order, and her clothes were in the closets. Mackenna gazed at her mom's beaming face with its lopsided grin and her heart melted. Walking over, she hugged her tightly saying, "Mom, I want you to be happy."

"Oh, bab gir. I am so hap-py," she said, obviously proud of her improving speech.

Jobe walked over to envelop both women, kissing Penny's cheek before kissing the top of Mackenna's head. "Mrs. Dunn, I think you're going to enjoy living here. And remember, we're just two floors up."

His phone vibrated and after glancing at the text, he announced to the large group, "My mom's here with the food so let's get up to our place."

The friends moved out of Penny's condo to go upstairs, quickly settling into his apartment. Mackenna looked up into his eyes and smiled.

"What's that smile for?"

"You called this *our* place, not just your place."

"Well, hell yeah, doll. It is our place," he said with a twinkle in his eyes. Looking around, his mom was running the show from the kitchen, bustling around and giving orders. And smiling so wide, Jobe thought his mother's face would break.

The group pitched in and the food was laid out on the table so that everyone could grab a paper plate and get what they wanted before settling down anywhere they could. Conversation flowed as old friends and new friends mingled.

Mackenna studied the gathering as she sat on the floor with her plate on the coffee table. She had not been with this many friends since her father became ill. As her eyes moved around the room, they landed on Jobe sitting a few feet away, his gaze on hers. Smiling, she realized that she was home.

That evening, she knelt over a box of clothes that she was placing in drawers as Jobe lounged on the bed. He loved seeing her things in his drawers and closet. As she reached in, her fingers touched the packet of letters that she had thrown in the bottom of the box when packing up her old house. Looking down, she saw the familiar bundle, tied with a ribbon. Letters from the past. Letters that had represented what she had...and what she lost. Now as she wrapped her fingers around them, they no longer gripped her in misery.

He noticed that she had stilled, wondering what she

was pondering. Her gaze lifted slowly to his as her hand raised out of the box. She was holding the packet of letters that he had discovered weeks ago. His breath caught in his throat, fearful of what those memories might do to the relationship they were forging now. The cold dread wrapped around his heart as surely as her fingers around the evidence of their past love that he had thrown away.

"It's okay," she whispered, seeing the fear and anguish written on his face. "I'm not afraid of these anymore."

He rose from the bed, walked to the closet and knelt at his locker in the corner. She watched him with curiosity, then her heart pounded as she saw him moving back toward her with his own small packet of letters in his hand. He saw the confusion on her face, knowing that he had confessed to shredding all of her letters.

Kneeling down before her, he said, "These I kept. After...I foolishly destroyed the others. These were the ones you sent me afterward."

She honestly could not think of a response as her eyes gazed at the worn envelopes, wrapped in a rubber band. Licking her lips, she lifted her gaze to his. "What should we do with these? Mine represent who we were, but we're no longer are those two people. And yours," she said, once more staring at the envelopes in hand, "represent the bitter end of what we were."

He shook his head slowly, "I don't know, doll. You

tell me what you want to do with them? I kept these because they were my constant reminder of what a desperate dumb-ass I'd been to throw away the most important person in my life out of fear. I honestly don't need them anymore, now that I have you again."

Sucking her lips in as she moved her gaze down to the ribbon bound, tear-stained letters in her hand. "I think I'd like to keep them, just because they are a part of our journey." She quickly amended, "But if they bother you then we can get rid of them."

He took her hands in his as he stood, helping her up from the floor. Placing the small sheaf of letters in his hand onto the stack that were in hers, he wrapped both of their hands around the entire packet. Holding her gaze, he said, "These represent who we were. We can keep them to remember another time and as a reminder of what we never want to be again…and that is apart from each other."

Offering him a small smile through teary eyes, she nodded. "I think that's a good idea. We can get rid of them sometime in the future." She allowed him to gently take the stack from her fingers and watched as he placed them in the footlocker in the back of the closet.

He walked back, stopping long enough to wrap his arms around her, pulling her in for a sweet kiss. One of promises of the future. Then he settled back on the bed as she grinned and moved on to the next box, continuing to hang her clothes next to his.

MILES AWAY NEAR the river, the Sixers brought in their first load of guns, delivered from Miami. The gun runners slipped in unnoticed and docked at the back of an old, unused pier. Jazzie, Waldo, Tank, and a few others were there, along with some of the River Street Kings. Tension ran as high as the distrust among the two gangs.

The ones delivering the firearms stepped off of the boat looking for the one in charge. "Jazzie?" one of them called out.

Jazzie swaggered forward, making a sign. He nodded toward the men behind him and they moved to begin unloading the boat. The wooden crates were opened as Jazzie was allowed to inspect. Smiling, he jerked his head to the Kings standing back and they hustled over to take possession of one of the crates. The others were for the Sixers and with another jerk of Jazzie's head, his men moved to quickly load those into the vans parked nearby.

The payoff made, the Sixers jumped into the two vans and drove away. As they headed back to the rendezvous point, Waldo looked over at Jazzie.

"What the fuck you staring at?" Jazzie barked.

"You think that girl's got Tito's head?"

Jazzie warred between being pissed at a fellow officer questioning the leader and knowing that he felt the same. After a few tense, quiet moments, he asked,

"What's got you thinking?"

"Tonight. Tito seemed…I don't know. Distracted. When I was about to ask if it was about the delivery tonight, he said something really random and it shocked the shit outta me."

Jazzie spared him a glance, not saying anything.

Waldo shook his head. "Probably nothing. But he suddenly said that he wondered how far along that Gabby bitch was and when he'd know if it was a boy or not."

"Goddamnit!" Jazzie cursed, his hand slapping the steering wheel. Trying to negotiate a deal with an international organization at the same time as having to work with the Kings and moving into a new venture was not the time for their leader to be distracted with some pregnant pussy.

They continued driving for a few more minutes in silence. Finally, Jazzie said, "Keep your goddamn eyes open and your mouth shut. Don't say nothin' to nobody." He glanced over, seeing Waldo nod. "Good. I'm workin' on how to get rid of that skank so that we get our leader back to thinking with the head on his shoulders and not on the end of his dick."

As they pulled into the secure rendezvous location, Jazzie knew that it was time to take on Gabby…and that white bitch as well. But only when the opportunity came along. He had to play this smart.

CHAPTER 17

FOR THE NEXT several weeks, Mackenna and Jobe settled into a routine. She still divided her time between New Beginnings and her DSS office, but spent more and more time trying to find extended funding. Even with the new security at the shelter, she felt as though they would all be safer if they were away from the area that gangs were near. Of course the more she learned about gangs, the more she realized that they were everywhere—even in suburbia.

Penny was getting out more, utilizing the pool for exercise and visiting with the Delaros and other friends. She only had the home nurse come once a week for about an hour and her speech therapy sessions were only twice a week. She now traveled by taxi to the physical therapist and loved her new independence.

Matt and Shane had kept Tony's group in the loop about what was going on in the city. The police were keeping up their vigilance and on the surface, things had cooled down. But they also knew it was only a front.

Meeting one morning, they all gathered around to find out what intelligence Lily and BJ had been able to ferret out.

Lily smiled as she reported, "It didn't take much. These guys aren't very sophisticated when it comes to their money. Tito Montalvo himself has a rather meager bank account. But he does move money through it to his uncle's grocery store business. Then there are withdrawals from that account into various others, including Waldron Perkins and Thomas Jazine."

"Waldo and Jazzie," Shane said. At Lily's lifted eyebrow, he added, "That's the street names of the Sixer's officers under Tito."

"But knowing who did the drive-by shooting at Mackenna's place should make a difference, doesn't it?" Jobe asked in frustration.

"We got Poco in jail. Of course, he admits to everything but won't roll on anyone else."

"He admitted?" Vinny asked. "He didn't try to punk out?"

Matt shook his head. "Nah, man. It's their creed. They can't deny the gang."

Tony's men stared at the two detectives in disbelief. "So, if they're doing gang work and get caught, they admit to it and go down. No pleas, no bargaining."

"If you're in a gang and took their oath—it's thicker than anything. You get caught, you openly admit you're in the gang. To deny the gang is to disrespect it."

"So you got this Poco kid and nothin' else on

Mackenna's drive-by?" Jobe asked.

Shane nodded, "Sorry, man. He confessed to the spray painting, the driving, the shooting…says it was all him."

"That's bullshit," Jobe muttered, running his hands through his hair.

"Agreed," Matt said. "It's only one more off the street, but at least it's one."

"Well, I don't have to worry about her and her mom not being safe in their beds now since they're in my building, but, it's just the rest of the time."

Turning back to BJ and Lily, they continued to discuss their findings.

"ATF and FBI are working on the case as well since the transportation of guns has both of them nervous."

BJ said, "Well, while Lily was following the money, it looks like the cameras have given us a bit more of a clue as to where they hide out. For the Sixers, Tito's uncle's grocery holds some kind of importance. Our cameras pick up guys going into the building across the street in groups of two or three. That building is an old apartment complex, but a quick look inside shows that they are heading to the basement."

"Underground tunnel over to the grocery basement," Matt surmised.

"We saw that with another case," Tony added. "Seems like old-town Richland is full of steam tunnels between various buildings."

"The chief will be glad to get that intel," Shane

said. He and Matt stood to leave as the meeting came to a conclusion. As they were walking out of the door, Shane turned his attention back to Jobe. "Hate like hell to remind you, but we're still considering Mackenna to be at risk. Take care, man."

Jobe's jaw ticked with anger as he nodded toward the detectives. The others were silent for a moment, knowing that nothing they said would have any effect on Jobe's mood. Or loss of control.

MACKENNA MADE HER WAY into New Beginnings after waving goodbye to Terrance, who had dropped her off. Planning on working with the women today, she told him that she would text him when she was ready to leave.

Rose came by her small office an hour later to find Mackenna slumped back in her chair. "Are you all right?"

"I'm exhausted. I feel tired, sleepy, kind of nauseous…just generally yucky. And I don't have time to get sick!" she complained. "For the past three weeks I have worked on the new grant proposals and I may have stumbled onto a real deal."

"Girl, you're working too hard," Rose admonished.

"Yeah, well, there's so much to do."

"If you get sick, then none of this will matter."

Just then Carla stuck her head in and said, "Hey,

Ms. Dunn. I'm packed."

Inwardly wincing, Mackenna had forgotten that Carla was graduating from the program today and was moving out. Standing, she embraced the girl tightly. Pulling away, she felt the sting of tears in her eyes, always loving it when the girls left while acknowledging that a part of her went with them as they moved out into their new circumstances.

The three walked into the kitchen, where the other women had made lunch. Gabby had been in the kitchen, whipping up her specialties and as Mackenna approached the table, her stomach lurched. She broke out into a sweat and tried to discreetly wipe her brow. Pretending that her phone was vibrating, she left the room and headed to the bathroom.

A bit later she returned, having dry heaved for several minutes. Begging off of the meal, she sat with the others as they laughed and talked about what life would be like for Carla and for Jenita, who would be leaving the next week. Finally, it was time to say goodbye. Mackenna had arranged for one of Tony's men to escort Carla to her new apartment across town. She stood on the stoop waving as the official SUV left the road.

Rose walked up behind her and said, "You do good work here, you know?" Mackenna just nodded, unable to speak over the lump in her throat. "You fight an enemy that hides and attempts to overtake everything, but you never give up. And girl, one by one those women who leave here to a better life, do so because of you."

Taking a shaky breath, Mackenna returned the hug and said, "Carla makes nineteen and then when Jenita leaves next week, that'll be twenty who've made it through."

"We should celebrate," Rose enthused. "But first," she stopped as she looked at Mackenna's pale face, "you need to take care of yourself."

"I think I'll call Terrence to pick me up and head home. I just feel so drained," Mackenna admitted.

Her mother came by Mackenna and Jobe's apartment an hour later, just as Jobe was getting off of the elevator. "Ah came ta check on her. She did na come to see me," Penny explained as Jobe let her into the apartment.

They found Mackenna asleep on the couch. Touching her daughter's forehead out of motherly habit, she was pleased to see that there was no fever.

Mackenna stirred, opening her eyes slowly. "Oh mom, I'm sorry. I meant to come straight to your place. Not come up here and fall asleep."

"You shou see a doc-ta," Penny said.

Jobe moved to sit next to Mackenna on the sofa, pulling her into his arms. "Absolutely," he agreed, concern showing on his face.

Mackenna snuggled up close to him, pushing her long, thick hair out of her face. "She'll probably tell me it's stress or not enough sleep." She looked into her mother's worried face and realized that as much as she hated the idea of anything happening to her mom, Penny felt the same way about her. "I'll go. I promise. I'll go tomorrow."

Placated, Penny kissed her daughter and patted Jobe's shoulder as she walked out.

Yeah, it's probably just stress, Mackenna thought. *What else could it be?*

DOUG HAD DRIVEN HER to the doctor's office since Jobe was out on an installation job and eyed her carefully when she came out. She appeared pale and distracted when she left the building. Seeing her almost knocked over by others on the sidewalk, he jumped out of the SUV and moved to her side. She looked up at him, a slightly confused expression on her face.

"Mackenna?"

"Oh, yes, Doug. I'm sorry, I was…um…not think-ing."

He assisted her into the vehicle and turned to ask, "Where to?"

Mackenna's thoughts were in a whirl, thinking of all she had to do. *I've got a gang after me, trying to find a new home for the center, still helping mom, and a new relationship to work on. And now this?*

"Home, if you don't mind. I'd like to go home now."

JOBE WAS INSIDE ONE of the larger estates in a new subdivision in Richland. The owners had hired Alvarez Security and he was working with Gabe and BJ to get the system correct. The installation was taking forever because the owner's bored wife had been salivating over the three gorgeous men inside of her house all day.

Finally finished, they packed up and left to head back to the office. "Jesus, I feel like I've got to take a shower," Gabe complained while the others laughed.

After a few minutes of companionable silence, Gabe said, "You know, before Jennifer came into my life, I would've thought of tapping that. Wouldn't have done it because she's a client, but I would've been thinking about it."

BJ laughed, "Yeah, I hear you. And now?"

"Oh, hell no," Gabe growled. "I see that and all I can think of is how glad I am that that part of my life is over." He glanced at Jobe driving and said, "And now that shit's over for all of us."

Jobe grinned, admitting, "Thank God! I was running out of places to hide from that cougar. Now I get to go home to my own tiger."

The men laughed as a call came in. Gabe answered it, saying, "Yeah, he's right here. Okay, got it. I'll tell him."

Jobe looked over at Gabe, his eyebrow lifted in silent question.

"Doug just got back from taking Mackenna home. Said he escorted her to the doctor's today and then she wanted to go home."

Jobe glanced sharply at his friends, worry immediately creasing his brow. "Fuck, I knew she was going to the doctor's today but I forgot to check on her afterward. Goddamnit!"

"What's going on?" BJ asked from the back seat.

"She's been tired, no energy. Kind of pale." Jobe gripped the steering wheel tighter. "I know it's fucked, but with her father having died from cancer and her mom having had a stroke, I can't help but worry. It's kind of like her family is a walking medical risk."

"Head to your place. We'll take the company van back and one of us will drop your truck off," Gabe ordered.

"Thanks, man," Jobe nodded.

In a few minutes, they pulled up to the front of his building. Hopping out, he glanced back at his two friends. Silent communication all that was needed. With a head jerk to both of them, he dashed through the doors.

Once inside of their apartment, he found Mackenna standing in front of the bank of windows in the living room. A solitary figure, she stood quietly looking out at the park near the apartment building. His fears of earlier began to build. *Whatever this is, we can do this* he silently vowed.

Crossing over, he startled her when he approached.

Jumping, she placed her hand over her pounding heart. "Oh, honey. I didn't hear you come in," she said, with a smile.

He watched her carefully, studying her face for signs of concern. "I'm sorry, doll." He placed his hands on her shoulders and continued to peer deeply, looking for whatever had been on her mind. "Um, are you okay?" he asked. "You seemed really lost in thought."

"Yeah," she said, leaning into his embrace. She felt his arms wrap around her tightly, enveloping her completely. *Safe. Here, I'm safe.*

She leaned back and held his gaze, a nervous look now filling her face. "Jobe? We need to talk."

His heart began to pound as his control shook, making it hard to steady his breathing. "Sure," he managed to choke out, inwardly cursing that his voice was betraying his fear. "Whatever it is, we can deal," he promised.

Keeping his arm around her shoulders, he turned them and walked to the sofa. Sitting down, he carefully pulled her in close to his body.

"You know I went to the doctor today and—"

Before she could continue, he blurted, "Baby, whatever it is, I'll be here. Whatever is going on, we can face this together."

Her eyes widened in surprise at his outburst and then slowly understanding filled her expression. "Oh no, honey. I'm not sick."

His eyes closed in relief as he pulled her in closer,

pressing her face into his chest. *Thank God!*

"Mmm pena," she said, her face still held firmly planted against his chest.

He felt her hands move from around his neck to his shoulders where she pushed away. She was smiling as he said, "What did you say? I couldn't understand you."

She licked her lips nervously, forcing herself to hold his gaze. "I said that I'm pregnant."

THE LIGHT FROM the full moon beamed down on the bed, illuminating Mackenna's sleeping form. She was curled on her side with one hand tucked under her cheek and her long's mane streaming behind her across the pillow. Jobe had rolled to his side facing her, but sleep did not come. The events of the evening filled his thoughts.

He had sat dumbly as the words that had left her mouth slowly managed to penetrate his foggy mind. *Pregnant?* He stupidly said the first thing that came into his head. "How?" he blundered.

"Um, the usual way, I'm sure. You know...sperm, egg, all that stuff we learned a long time ago?"

Then he managed to blurt out, "Are you sure?"

The smile on her face began to drop as she answered, "Yes. The doctor is sure."

He saw the doubt move over her face, and cursed in

regret that he had put that fear in her. "Shit, doll. This is amazing. I know it's unexpected, but baby...this is everything." Suddenly realizing that she might not be well, he jumped in, "Are you okay? Is the baby okay?"

She giggled as she moved her hands up to cup his face as well. Leaning in she kissed his lips gently. "Yeah, I'm all right. It's too early to know about the baby, but," she said with a little shrug, "I'm good."

After the words she had gifted him with finally sunk in, he pulled her closely once again, holding her right against his chest. Thoughts swirled through his head. *Gotta tell our parents. Gotta turn the spare bedroom into a nursery. We need to go ahead and get married. And her job—Jesus Christ, I need to get her out of—*

His anticipations were interrupted by her cupping his face once again.

"Jobe, I can practically hear those thoughts as they fly through your mind. And I know because they've been flying through my mind also. But honey, we can deal with them one at a time."

With that, he pulled her in for a kiss once again. One that he hoped poured all of his love into her, desperately wanting her to know what she and this child meant to him. *Healing. Hope. New life. Forever.*

Now he lay, quietly watching her as she slept. And he vowed once more to keep her safe always.

CHAPTER 18

TITO, JAZZIE, AND WALDO sat around the unfamiliar table in the dimly lit room, trying not to show their excitement...or their nerves. With the police dogging their moves, the meeting had been relocated from the basement of Tito's uncle's store to the basement of one of their brother's houses. Across from them sat the envoy from Florence 10, one of the larger gangs in South Los Angeles that had been making inroads in Virginia. This was what Tito had been leading the Sixers toward—a chance to be recognized by an organization as big as the F10s. This could mean an opportunity to move in the circles that could make some serious money.

Jazzie watched carefully, noting the F10's seconds that were running the show. Three of them had arrived to negotiate, with five more of them as backup. One, street named Oz, was introduced as the man in charge. Oscar Portillo—a reputation as a slick killer as a teen, now given the command of the envoy. Jazzie licked his lips in anticipation, eager for the negotiations to begin. They waited, respect being given to the larger gang. Finally after several minutes of silence, making the

Sixers more nervous, the talking began.

"Not happy having to relocate," the man sitting next to Oz said.

"Havin' some trouble with the crabs," Tito replied, referring to the police.

"You don't got trouble. You give it."

Not wanting to appear weak, Tito smoothly said, "Wanna give you the best."

The silence extended for another minute, the Sixers sweating out the time.

"Done," Oz announced, and Jazzie found himself releasing the breath he had been holding.

For a while, the session began with an immediate discussion of the drug trade that the Sixers were bringing in. Tito had played it smart—he had his figures written down and spreadsheets of who they traded with, how many runners he had, and their costs vs. profit. Jazzie's admiration for his leader rose again as he realized that Tito had done his homework.

The F10s were impressed with the management of large shipments of stolen guns, noting that smaller gangs usually just dealt with what they had stolen off of the streets.

As Tito handed over the information, the expressions of the F10 seconds relaxed slightly, seemingly to be satisfied that their time was not being wasted. The meeting continued for another hour, going over the details of a merger negotiation. The Sixers would remain autonomous, but have the F10 as a distributor and supply line for both the drugs and weapons.

Tito had hoped to impress them more with his dealing in bringing the Kings on board, but was unable to hide his surprise that the F10s already knew that.

"We don't waste our time, so we know all your shit," Oz said. He stared at Tito for a moment, once again letting the silence of the room unnerve the Sixers.

"Heard you gave them a present?"

Tito smiled as he nodded. "Some bitch needed to return home," he said with a chuckle.

"From what I hear you got several bitches that need to get home."

The smile left Tito's face as a question formed on his lips. Jazzie stepped in, "We're dealing."

The F10's gazes all moved from Tito to Jazzie, holding his stare.

"You can't take care of your own house, how you gonna take care of our business."

At the risk of showing disrespect, Jazzie reiterated, "We're takin' care of our business."

Oz shifted his gaze between Tito and Jazzie, silence filling the darkness. Slowly nodding, he said, "We can bring you on board. Drugs, guns...we can deal. But you take care of your house first."

The F10s stood from their seats, the metal chairs scraping noisily on the concrete floor. One of them bumped the lightbulb hanging from the ceiling, causing it to move back and forth shooting shadows across the men. Tito, Jazzie, and Waldo stood as the others left, giving shakes and signals.

The other gang members moved out into the night leaving the three Sixers facing each other, not knowing whether to celebrate or curse.

NOW THAT CARLA had graduated from New Beginnings and Jenita was almost ready to move out, Mackenna thought that she needed to step up her efforts to find a new place. *One with more rooms so that we could expand.* Sitting in the small office in the center, she continued her online searches for appropriate housing that the city would continue to fund. Several seemed promising and she took note of those.

Rose wandered in having finished her class. Leaning against the door frame, she watched Mackenna concentrate on the computer screen.

Glancing up, Mackenna smiled, saying, "Hey, what's up?"

"I've had three daughters you know."

Mackenna's brow creased in confusion. "Yeah, um, I know."

"Two of them have given me grandbabies."

Mackenna cocked her head to the side, still waiting for Rose to continue.

"Something you want to tell me?" Rose asked, her lips curving into a smile.

Eyes widening, she whispered, "How can you tell?"

Throwing her head back in laughter, "Oh honey, it's just a mom thing." Settling her gaze once again on Mackenna, she said gently, "And it looks like you're going to be finding out all about mom things."

Mackenna rose from her seat and the two women embraced. Tears filled Mackenna's eyes as she pulled back away from the older woman. "Oh, my goodness. It seems like I keep tearing up."

"That's normal," Rose said, patting her hand. "How's Jobe?"

Shaking her head, she gushed "I swear, he's over the moon with excitement. We've only known a week and haven't told our parents yet. I wanted to wait for a bit to make sure that things were going well." Sitting back down in the chair as Rose settled in the other one, she continued, "In fact, you're the only one who knows!"

"Then you'd better stay away from your moms because they'll ferret it out of you as soon as I did. Have you thought about down the road? With this place, I mean?"

"Not really. My first concern right now besides finding a new location is keeping these girls safe."

The two women looked at the computer screen for a moment together as Mackenna scrolled through the options she found. "There's actually a house that is currently being used as a battered woman's shelter and they're moving. So...I think that it might be perfect. There are five large bedrooms, and with bunks in there, we could house ten women at a time."

She glanced up at Rose's smiling face and asked, "Would you come with us?"

"Oh honey, you couldn't keep me away."

"I would like to give up the running of the shelter, though," Mackenna confessed, then seeing the distress on Rose's face she quickly added, "But I'd like to just focus on the counseling."

Rose's face immediately melted into a smile again, as she leaned over and patted Mackenna's leg. "That'd be perfect for you," she agreed.

"By the way, don't tell anyone else, please. At least not now," she begged.

Standing, Rose moved toward the door looking back over her shoulder and said, "I promise."

"THAT CENTER BITCH is knocked up," Jazzie said as he came into the room, out of breath.

Tito looked up sharply, his mind immediately working through the information Jazzie had blurted out. "How'd you find out?"

"I got my ways," Jazzie said. "And it's by one of those security guys that was hanging around."

A slow smile crept across Tito's face. Jazzie noticed and began grinning as well. "Prez, you thinkin' what I am?"

Tito nodded, "Fuck yeah. We got us a chance for some payback."

Jobe, Vinny, Gabe, and Terrence were out once again securing cameras in some of the areas noted by the Richland Police as heavy with active gangs. Wearing utility uniforms, they worked on installing cameras near traffic lights and, slipping inside several older buildings, they managed to locate some of them on rooftops. Working seamlessly, they made quick work of the task and were heading back to headquarters by the end of the day.

Tony had called a staff meeting as soon as they returned, so Jobe phoned Mackenna on his cell as Gabe drove. "Hey doll, are you home yet?" Receiving an affirmative, he told her that he would be a little late.

Gabe asked, "How's she feeling?"

Jobe, unlike Mackenna, told everyone that she was pregnant immediately. Rounds of congratulations, back-slapping, and "join the club of little sleep" rang out at Alvarez Security. Smiling, he looked over at his friend and said, "She's great. So far no morning sickness, just a little nausea at night."

Jobe's good feelings continued until they reached their destination. Striding into the conference room, the group saw that Tony was standing with Matt, Shane, and…much to his surprise, Jack Bryant. Jack, a former member of their Special Forces squad had retired and started his own protection and investigative services and had recently assisted them when Vinny and

Annalissa needed help.

None of the men had happy expressions on their faces. Everyone quickly settled around the table, all eyes on Tony.

"Matt called me today to tell me that they had more news and about the same time, called to let me know that he had gotten a request from the Governor. Jack gave me enough info that I surmised that both he and Matt had some of the same concerns. So I brought us all here together to find out what's going on and what we can do to assist." With a nod toward Shane, he turned it over to them.

"The Sixers are different from some of the local punk-ass gangs. A bunch of the others are just teenagers breaking into houses, selling pot, or petty crimes likes smashing car windows, vagrancy, etc. But Tito Montalvo's got a real eye for making a name for himself. He's smart and has figured out a way to move into the big time.

"We knew he ran drugs and puss—um," Shane glanced apologetically at Lily, "girls. But as we've been tracking them, we now know that they've moved into guns. And not just stealing guns from houses, but running stolen military guns."

Matt continued, "We've got inside information that they made a deal with the River Street Kings to use some of their river front property to bring the guns in by the water and they give the Kings a cut of the profits. The Kings are more punk-ass, but control a decent spread right on the river, so this is a win for them. They align with the Sixers, they get some guns and money, and the Sixers get a place to run."

Alvarez's men listened intently, eyes occasionally moving to the screen on the wall where Lily projected some aerial views of the river's old wharf area.

Shane added, "All this adds up to the Sixers becoming the most powerful and dangerous gang in Richland. The mayor is concerned; an election year is coming up and there are rumblings in the Richland Times about gangs in the area and how politicians have turned a blind eye to the problem for years. To combat that, he's having the Richland Times do a huge article on Mackenna's New Beginnings program."

All eyes moved to Jobe, as he nodded slowly. "Yeah, she said she was interviewed yesterday for the newspaper and it'll run tomorrow. She was excited because she's wanting to move the location to a safer place and said the publicity will be great for donations."

Shane added, "Yeah, but it puts her right on the front page with a powerful gang's pregnant girlfriend hiding there."

The sick feeling that started in Jobe's gut when a mission was not going as planned began to creep over him and while no one else would notice, his brothers knew immediately what he was experiencing.

"Before you ask, no, we can't get the article pulled," Matt said. "The mayor's too involved now. 'Course he said that the police'll make sure the center is safe."

Looking sharply at Jobe, he added quickly, "and, we will, but you gotta know there's no way it'll get twenty-four hour police protection."

The group was quiet a moment while BJ took over the technology side and projected pictures of Tito Montalvo on the screen.

At this point, Tony looked over at Jack and gave him a nod as well. Jack opened up a file that was in front of him and after glancing around the table, focused on Jobe and began.

"The governor's now gotten involved. He had a state drug task force, which one of my men served on. The guy's got a background in undercover work with gangs. It seems the state has a bigger problem. One of the larger LA based gangs that have national ties is the Florence 10. They're about as badass as the Crips, Bloods, or MS-13. They go by F10, an old throwback to the Air Force fighter jets known by that name."

The feeling that had been growing in Jobe became sharper, more pronounced. His mind flashed back to the multitude of times that he had sat around a conference table being briefed before a mission. In the Army, with his squad, and here at Alvarez Security. *This feels different. This is personal.* Giving himself a mental shake, he knew he needed to focus. Mackenna's safety depended on him knowing all of the intel he could gather.

Jack's gaze landed on Jobe as he continued, "They're on the FBI's top-ten list of most dangerous gangs. And now the F10s have been making inroads into Virginia. They checked out DC but have settled on Richland being their new place of business. The river, the I95 corridor of drug traffic between Florida to DC to New York is too lucrative for them to pass up." He paused for just a moment before dropping the news that he knew would most upset the group.

"And now they've made contact with the Sixers here in Richland."

The rumbling and cursing around the table grew louder, both with indignation that their city was being overrun and infiltrated but also for the knowledge that by her vocation, Mackenna could find herself in the crosshairs.

Shane shook his head, saying, "Fuck, as though we didn't have enough to deal with. If the Sixers have gained national attention to get someone as big as the F10s to be interested in dealing, that's going to spread our police force even thinner."

Jack nodded and added, "That's why the governor has contacted me. He's got a job for us." He said no more, but the group expected that. Jack's business took on the hard assignments...the ones that no one else would take. And he flew under the radar, not following anyone's orders or protocol other than his own. And from what they knew, his employees operated the same.

"What does this mean for us?" Tony inquired.

"The Richland police are stepping up their surveillance, presence in the gang infested communities, even some that are undercover, trying to get information. Tito's smart but not infallible. He'll make a mistake and we want to be there when he does. We're hoping to put more pressure on the Kings as well, to maybe discourage them from doing as much business with the Sixers," Matt said.

"But that money is a big pull," Shane admitted. He looked around the table at Tony's group, his gaze landing on Jobe. "Gotta tell you, the center that Mackenna runs is a concern. And she's not the only one. There are at least four other centers in the city that need someone to keep an extra eye on because they offer gang alternative places to be."

"We just got the last of the security cameras up on those locations that you gave us," Gabe announced. "That's what we did today."

Matt nodded, "Appreciate it, man."

Jobe's jaw ached with the pressure of clenching his teeth and with each comment he could feel his anger ratcheting up. Finally he said, "You gotta know this shit's killing me."

Vinny, sitting next to him, clapped him on the shoulder, promising, "Nothing's gonna happen to her. We got this. We got her."

Jobe turned on his friend and growled, "No disrespect, bro, what about Annalissa? We thought we had her too and your fiancé almost died before you could get to her." His eyes moved to the others, including Lily. "I could keep going, but you know what I'm saying." Immediately, understanding passed over every one of their faces. Most all of them had been in the same situation—trying to protect the woman they loved...and almost failing.

"Any chance she'll stop working?" Shane asked.

Hanging his head, Jobe asked back, "For how long?" There was no response. "I mean, drugs and gun running and gangs have been around for a long time. You think this mess with Tito is going to just go away because we're all watching them? I don't see that happening. This scares the shit outta me, but my girl's got a career where she's trying to help. Trying to fight for other women who don't feel like they've got anyone in their corner. You think she's gonna just walk away from that?" He hung his head, emotions flying through him as his hands balled into fists on the table.

Sucking in a deep breath before letting it out slowly, he lifted his gaze to his friends and said in a calmer voice, "I want to march home right now and order her to quit. The idea of losing her or the baby is unthinkable to me." Swallowing loudly, he continued, "But I gotta work with this. Through this. I...I...just don't have a clue how."

Tony, taking charge as always, said, "Not this time, bro. We got this." Looking at Shane and Matt, he said, "You know we'll help the chief as much as we can, but we've got the surveillance cameras in place on some of the gang hangouts for the police to monitor, and," he looked over at Jack, "you've got the task from the

Governor to try to take them on. But for us," he returned his gaze back to Jobe, "our primary job is to ensure the safety of New Beginnings and Mackenna." Then looking around the table at the rest of his crew, he reiterated, "That is the mission of Alvarez Security in this matter."

Jobe felt the sting of tears hit the back of his eyes, and he swallowed several times to bring himself under control. *Under control. Fuck, that was the whole reason I broke up with her in the first place...feeling out of control.* Taking a shaky breath, he knew the friends around the table knew what this meant to him, and he nodded to each of them as the meeting dispersed.

Driving home, anxious to pull her in close, the words of Tony rang over and over in his ears. "We got this." *Yeah* he thought, *I got this.*

CHAPTER 19

WALKING INTO THEIR APARTMENT, Jobe once again saw Mackenna in the kitchen pulling out plates. She smiled at him as he tossed his keys and some bags onto the breakfast bar and made his way around toward her. Her long hair fell softly down her back and he wanted to run his fingers through it. His gaze did a body scan, from her old, faded, tight t-shirt to her form-fitting yoga pants, down to her pink painted toenails. As his eyes made their way back up, they rested on her flat stomach.

"How ya doing, doll?" he asked gently as he closed the distance between them, taking her in his arms.

"I'm great," she replied, her smile touching his heart as he tucked her head against his chest. She leaned way back to stare at him, her eyes twinkling as she said, "I'm glad you called to say you were bringing Chinese. I'm starved and hated the idea of cooking tonight."

He leaned down to kiss her nose, saying, "Anytime either of us doesn't want to cook, we order out. Simple as that."

"I did put plates out so that it'll seem more like dinner."

He chuckled as he let her go so that he could grab the takeout food and they sat at the table to eat. He wondered how to bring up his concerns, afraid that she would feel as though he were trying to run her life. *But dammit, we've got a baby to consider.*

As she grabbed their plates to take to the sink, she stared at him. "Are you going to tell me what's on your mind or are you just going to scowl all night?"

Caught off guard, he looked up in surprise, a guilty expression on his face. Laughing as he stood, he grabbed her hand and gently tugged her into the living room. Sitting down on the sofa, he settled her on his lap, her back against the arm and her legs draped along the pillows.

"I was just wondering about…you know…plans. Your plans. Well, I mean our plans."

"Plans? Honey, what kind of plans?"

Looking around evasively, he said, "Well, like this place? Do you want to stay here or find a house? Do you still want to tell our parents together this weekend? I want us to get married as soon as we can, so have you thought about that anymore? Have you thought about a replacement for when you're on maternity leave? In fact, have you thought about quitting once you have the baby? Or maybe before?"

The smile that had been growing as she listened to his questions slowly fell from her face. "Jobe, I'm not quitting my job! What on earth made you think of that?"

"Because you're in danger. The whole fucking place is in danger and I'm not going to go through what all my friends did."

She pushed against his chest in an effort to move back, but his arms held firm. Huffing, she glared as he continued.

"I wasn't willing to take a chance with just you and I'm sure as hell not going to now that you're carrying my baby."

"Well, my quitting isn't going to happen, so you can get that idea out of your head."

"Mackenna, you're being unreasonable," he growled.

"Me? Me? I'm being unreasonable? Jobe, you're asking me to quit my job. This isn't how a relationship works. You can't just pull the macho, 'I'm the man so we'll do it my way' act."

Sucking in a deep breath, his jaw tight with frustration, he said, "I'm not trying to argue or take over. I had a bunch of concerns and you jumped on this one."

"Okay, fine. Let's talk about the others. No, I don't think we need to move right now. A baby can have everything they require right here and doesn't need a house yet. My mom's downstairs and we can turn the study into a nursery for now. Down the road, we can move." She glared then said, "There. Does that make you happier?"

Hell, I went about this all wrong. How the hell do I make this right? he wondered. The silence poured over them, each stewing in their own frustration.

She watched him struggle with his emotions and then finally lay his head back on the sofa to stare at the ceiling. Looking away, she allowed her eyes to move about the room. The table still loaded with the boxes of Chinese food that he so thoughtfully brought home. The shelf over the flat screen TV that now held silver picture frames of them—some recent and a few from their lives years before. She glanced at the coat rack that stood by the front door holding his leather jacket snuggled next to her woolen coat. This place represented both of them. What they have as a couple. Who they are together. *I don't want him changing me, but I can't ask him to be less than who he is,* she realized.

Turning her head back to his, she leaned forward and kissed his stubble covered neck. He lowered his head, his eyes on hers in question.

"I'm sorry, Jobe," she said softly. "I don't want to argue."

"I don't want to either," he replied, capturing her lips in a gentle kiss.

"I really do want to stay here for now and have us buy a house later when the baby is bigger or we have another one."

That thought brought a smile to his lips as the future lay before him. "I'd like that. Both. Have lots of children and wait to buy a house."

"And as far as our parents go," she continued, "let's get them all together this weekend and tell them then.

Do you think you can get your parents to have everyone over without them getting suspicious?"

Chuckling, he replied, "Babe? My mom need an excuse to get the whole family together? Not a problem."

She felt his chest rumble against her side as he laughed. Loving the feel as much as the sound, she relaxed in his arms as they tightened around her.

He kissed her once more, this time with more of a promise of things to come. "What about getting married? I want to as quickly as possible but know that these things take time."

Mackenna sat quietly in thought and he began to worry about what was on her mind. She finally lifted her gaze to him, licking her lips nervously.

"Um, I was thinking a lot about this and I really need you to hear me out, okay Jobe?"

His heart pounded as he grew fearful of what she was going to say. "Okay. I'm listening."

"Well, here's the thing. I…I don't need a big wedding. I know that years ago we were planning a huge wedding with all the trimmings. You know, princess dress and veil, big church, everyone we knew, big reception." Her voice choked, "Dad walking me down the aisle. All that."

A tear escaped, and his heart broke knowing that his stupidity had kept her from that dream. Wiping the tear with his rough thumb, he said, "Baby, I'm so sorry—"

She quickly interrupted, "Oh no, I'm not looking for an apology. Please let me finish."

He nodded, so she continued. "Five years ago that was important to me. The wedding that, when you're a little girl, you dream about. But now life is so different. Those things just aren't important to me anymore."

Wanting to take away his confusion, she plunged ahead. "Jobe, I just want to be married to you. That's it. Period. That's all I want. No big wedding. No big, expensive reception. Just you, me, our families and a few friends. We can even go to the Justice of the Peace if you want." Grabbing his face in her hands, she said, "Are you getting this, honey. I just want you. Just married. That's all. And if you want to do it this weekend when we tell our parents then that's fine too."

Before he could respond, she pulled him in all the way, her lips melding with his. She moved her mouth over his, knowing the taste, the feel, the sensations that always engulfed her when they kissed. He allowed her to take charge for a moment, her words resounding in his head. *"I just want you. Just married. That's all."*

As the realization washed over him that she was his—truly, passionately, wholly his—he pulled her tighter and took over the kiss. Angling her head for maximum contact, he thrust his tongue into her mouth, tasting every inch.

His hand moved from cupping her face to slowly sliding down her arm to the bottom of her shirt. Grasping the material he peeled it off of her gently, dropping it to the floor. The creamy skin of her breasts spilled out of the top of her lacy bra and he trailed his lips from hers as he kissed his way tortuously down her neck into her cleavage.

Mackenna's head fell back as her skin came alive from his lips. He reached behind and with a flip of his fingers her bra was unsnapped and she shifted her body so that the scrap of material could slide down her arms and join her shirt on the floor.

Standing with her in his arms, Jobe strode toward the bedroom, his lips fused once more to hers. Reaching the bed, she was lowered to the mattress when he finally halted the kiss. Standing over her, he tugged her pants down past her hips, snagging her panties as he went. With her body now naked for his perusal, he leaned over, resting his weight on one hand as he admired her perfection.

Her rosy tipped nipples beckoned and he obliged. Sucking one deeply into his mouth, he halted when she jumped. "Was I too hard, doll?" he murmured.

"Ummm," she replied. "No, they're just sensitive. More so than usual."

Realizing that her pregnant body was already responding differently, he moved back to her breasts, this time licking her nipples before sucking gently on them. She writhed underneath his ministration, feeling each pull on her breasts send a jolt to her womb.

She smiled in delight as he stood up before grabbing her ankles to pull her to the side of the bed. She raised her head to watch as he laid a trail of open-mouth, wet kisses from her breasts down her stomach, ending between her legs. Her legs spread wide, he feasted on her wet folds, sliding his tongue deep inside. *She tastes sweeter than anything I could have imagined.*

Her head fell back on the bed as the sensations swept over her, threatening to drown her in their intensity. Her sex throbbed as his tongue continued its thrusts. She began to rock her hips up seeking more contact, more pressure, more...anything.

He chuckled, placing his large hand on her hips to keep her still. He continued to lick her folds, pressing his tongue inside her sex, then moved up slightly to pull her clit into his mouth. His hand slipped up towards her breasts, lightly pinching a nipple at the same time.

She cried out as her world exploded in a shower of sensations, sparks flying out from her core in all directions. He lapped up her juices as the orgasm created the flow he had been waiting for. She lay boneless, not sure she could move until he stood and leaned over her, dragging her body up higher on the bed. Lifting herself up, she admired the physique towering over her. She would never get tired of seeing him naked, his muscular body proudly on display. Over six feet of sinew honed from years in the military. His six-pack abs led downward to his massive legs, with his cock standing out ready to meld his body with hers.

He crawled up her body. With the scent of her sex

filling the air, he nipped at her still flat stomach and suckled her breasts gently. Lowering his hips between her legs, his dick strained to enter her as though it had a mind of its own. Jobe gazed down at the face of the woman he loved, marveling that such a perfect creature wanted him. Her eyes were closed allowing her thick lashes to touch her cheeks. Her pale complexion was reflected in the moonlight shining through the windows. Her shiny mass of thick hair laying on the pillow.

"Eyes, babe," he softly ordered. She smiled as her eyes opened and her gaze met his.

"Love you, Mackenna. You've got my heart," he whispered.

"You have all of me, soldier-boy. Always."

With that, he plunged his straining cock deep inside her, fully seating himself in one thrust. Her hips moved upwards to meet his as his thrusts became more forceful. With wild abandon, he pumped furiously inside as though reaching a secret place inside of her that he wanted to touch. With that intensity, it did not take long until she was screaming his name as her climax roared through her.

He pumped until her walls had stopped milking him, then he quickly pulled out much to her dismay. Before she could question him, he flipped her over onto her stomach and grasped her hips to pull them up and back.

"On your knees, babe," he ordered, voice raspy

with need, as he placed a pillow under her hips.

She quickly obeyed, desperate for his cock again. He held a handful of her hair in one hand, pulling gently as he slid his fingers back through her drenched folds, giving her clit a light pinch. Immediately, she felt her core clench and moisture pooled again. She moaned involuntarily, and he leaned over her back.

"Is that okay, babe?" he asked, wanting to make sure she was comfortable.

Moaning in pleasure was the only answer she was able to give, and he just chuckled again as he thrust his engorged dick into her waiting core.

This angle brought new sensations and she felt as though her world was tipping on its axis. His fingers gripped her hips, digging in to hold her as he pounded in fiercely.

She rocked back and forth as his body dove into hers, over and over. She loved the friction inside but wanted to feel the sensations on her clit. Slowly moving her hand down between her legs, she fingered herself.

"Oh, babe. Seeing you touch yourself is gonna make me harder," he panted, between thrusts.

Sliding her fingers back to her clit, she rubbed and pulled on the swollen nub, feeling herself race to the end, desperate for the finish line.

Wanting her to come again before he did, he reached around tugging gently on her sensitive nipple, sending her moaning.

"Are you close, babe?" he asked roughly.

"Yes," she panted. "Yes, yes." The gripping sensations from her sex was sending sparks outward as the pressure began to build. Like a volcano that needed to erupt, she was so close, straining to find her release. Her hands went back to the bed as his hard thrusts pushed her forward.

Her walls convulsed around his cock, and with a few more thrusts he felt himself give over to his own release. Head thrown back, thick neck muscles straining, he pulsated into her waiting body, experiencing a release unlike one he had ever felt in his life.

They both fell forward onto the bed, his large body completely covering hers. Sweating and breathing heavily, Jobe had never felt so sated in his life. Awareness slowly came back, and he realized that Mackenna was crushed under him.

Rolling to the side, he pulled her gently to him. "Babe, sorry. Didn't mean to crush you. You okay?" He brushed her hair away from her beautiful face, peering deeply into her eyes. What he saw stunned him.

Tears, shining in her eyes, glimmered back at him. Her face was lit with a smile that dazzled. Reaching up her small hand to cup his strong jaw, she gently rubbed the stubble.

"I'm all right, honey. That was so amazing. As though we were truly one person. One body. One soul." Looking deeply into his gorgeous eyes, she leaned in to place a chaste kiss on his lips. "I love you, always and forever."

He closed his eyes momentarily, realizing once again how lucky he was. "Love you back, doll."

The darkness of the night had blanketed the city, casting shadows over the couple lying tangled in the sheets. Her body half draped over his, he pushed her hair back from her face. With her head on his shoulder, he smoothed his hand over her body, ending at her flat stomach. His long fingers splayed out over the area that nestled their baby.

She looked up into his face, seeing the love mixed with awe at the thought of the new life they created. Sighing, she said, "Honey?" She watched as his eyes moved back up to hers. "I don't want to argue about my job. I know it shouldn't be dangerous, but I also know that things are happening that have gotten out of control. I want to do whatever I need to do to stay safe."

He released a breath slowly, feeling a sense of relief sweep over him. "I never want to take anything away from you. I just know I'd die if I ever lost you again."

Her hand moved up from his arm to his face, cradling his strong jaw. "I've been talking to my supervisor about how to stay involved without actually running the center."

"What did he say?" Jobe asked, hope building.

"I really like working with the women, Jobe. I like counseling them much more than trying to be the center's administrator. I've talked to Rose and she's agreed to continue to be the teacher when we make a move to a new location. If I can just be the social worker who counsels and maybe goes into the schools to see about counseling some of the girls there, then I'd be happier. And safer," she added quickly.

His arms tightened around her body, pulling her in as closely as he could, not willing to have any space between their heartbeats. "Baby doll, I think that would be amazing."

"I have found a place and I'm going to go see it tomorrow. It's more on the edge of town, in a house that's already zoned for this type of facility. It's about the same size, although the bedrooms are bigger so we might be able to accommodate more women at a time."

"This is just exactly what I needed to hear, Mackenna. I found out from a meeting at work that things are getting worse with the Sixers. More danger-ous." Leaning back, he said, "But you gotta know. Alvarez Security and I are on it. You're not only the most important person in my life, but Alvarez's priority mission right now."

She felt guilty that she had put up such a fuss earli-er, knowing that this was not about control but about keeping her safe. She recognized how hard this was for Jobe. "Oh honey, I'm so sorry that I've put you through this," she cried. At his look of confusion, she added, "I know this is hard for you. Hard for you to not feel control."

Giving a rueful snort, he said, "I'm honestly doing a lot better with that. I think it's your love that has made that better...not worse."

"Really?" she asked with a small smile.

"Yeah. When I was overseas, the idea of being in love and not being able to control anything, made me crazy. But now? I'm good. I'm dealing. I'm learning that I don't have to control everything. And most of all, as long as you're in my life...we got this, babe. We got this."

He leaned down and pulled the covers up, nestling their bodies tightly together. The stars twinkled over the city skyline, the moon now high in the sky casting a glow about the room. As they slid into peaceful dreams, they both had the same thought on their minds.

As long as you're in my life...we got this.

CHAPTER 20

THE NEXT EVENING found Mackenna and Jobe pulling up to his parents' house with Penny in the back seat.

Looking over her shoulder, Mackenna said, "Mom, the Delaro's are going to be so surprised at how much you've progressed since using the gym and pool at the new place."

"Ah know," Penny said, her lopsided smile exuding her pride. "An ah can speak so much bet-ta now."

As usual, Rachel ran out on the porch and was down the steps before Joseph ambled out of the front door. She grabbed Penny in a hug before turning to throw her arms around Mackenna in an equally exuberant greeting. Finally turning to her son, she beamed up at his face as she wrapped her arms around him. "Oh, baby boy, to see you smile does this old heart so much good."

"Let the man go, Rachel," Joseph admonished, offering his son a shrug. Shaking his head as he shook Jobe's hand, he whispered loudly, "You'd think your mom's never seen you before, the way she carries on."

A playful slap on his shoulder had Joseph turning

around, pretending to be surprised that Rachel heard him. Jobe laughed as he threw his arm around Mackenna, ushering her into the welcoming home. They moved into the large kitchen, where Miriam, Rebecca, Hannah, her husband and their children were all gathered. Cooking for a lot of people was no challenge for Rachel and within a few minutes they had all heaped food on their plates and settled around the dining room table that had been extended by a cloth covered card table at the end.

Good food and good conversation flowed as the family enjoyed each other's company. Miriam was pleased with Penny's progress while Rebecca enchanted them with stories of her fourth-grade students. Hannah's children ate quickly and then ran to the living room to play, leaving the adults to finish their meal.

Jobe and Mackenna continued to glance at each other, trying to decide on the right moment to tell their parents, but just when the time seemed right someone else would begin talking and the opportunity passed.

Joseph had been staring at his only son throughout the meal, knowing that Jobe was anxious. Not in the way he had been when he came home from the Army, but he noticed the way Jobe constantly sought out Mackenna's hand underneath the table. And the way her eyes cut over to Jobe's.

Mackenna finally rose from the table and grabbed her purse, still lying on the counter. Pulling out two small bags, she walked back over as Jobe stood as well.

The others watched them carefully, uncertain what was happening. Looking up at Jobe, Mackenna gave a nervous smile and he answered her silent question with a nod.

"Mom, Rachel," Mackenna began. "We wanted to give you two a little something, for…um…well, for just being great moms. We'd like you to open them together if you would."

Jobe took the two gift bags from Mackenna's hands and leaned over the table, offering one to Penny before giving one to his mom. "Mom," he said softly, capturing Rachel's gaze, "open it slowly, along with Penny."

Rachel nodded, understanding that Penny needed a little bit more time to get the gift opened. She kept her eyes on Penny as she reached her hand into the bag at the same time. Both women felt a piece of cloth in the bottom of their bags and pulled them out together. Their eyes landed on baby bibs with the words, "World's Greatest Grandma" printed on the front.

A quiet second of shock followed by shrieks of joy filled the room. Mackenna rushed to her mother as Rachel bounded out of her chair to throw her arms around Jobe. Joseph leaned back in his chair, fighting unshed tears as he held the gaze of his son over Rachel's head. Jobe smiled at his father, accepting his nod of approval, as his mother continued to squeal.

Penny held her daughter tightly as tears ran unchecked down her cheeks. His sisters all moved to hug Mackenna as well, filled with questions of due dates and if they knew the sex yet.

Suddenly Rachel reared back looking up at her son. "You're not married! You've gotta get married. No grandchild of mine is going to be born—"

"Rachel!" Joseph spoke sternly, never having raised his voice to his wife, instantly gaining her attention. "Our son's come back to us, now. Lost him for a long time, but he's back. And with this beautiful woman who brought him back into her heart has now brought him back to us. So whatever they decide to do is good by me."

Duly chastised, Rachel nodded her agreement. "Oh Joseph, you're so right," she agreed, but then turned to Jobe and said, "But you want to get married, right?"

Throwing his head back in laughter, he hugged his mother again before moving to Mackenna and wrapping his arms around her, pulling her back into his front. "Yes, we do want to get married. But we talked about it and we've agreed on doing things Mackenna's way."

The family all looked to her and she was glad that Jobe's arms were tightly embracing her. Licking her lips, she said, "I just want to be married to Jobe. As soon as possible. No big wedding...just a simple ceremony with family and friends. That's all. No dress, no cake, no big party. Just the people we love sharing the love we have for each other."

She braced herself for the moms' wails or the onslaught of protestations. She felt Jobe's arms tighten as well, knowing his thoughts were the same. But all that met them were smiles.

"I think thas love-ly," Penny said, standing to hug both Jobe and Mackenna.

"I do too," Rachel agreed, smiling. "I think you two deserve to have all the happiness in the world."

Letting out the breath she had been holding, she smiled back. "Thank you all. We were thinking about this weekend."

Jobe looked at his dad and asked, "Pop, would it be okay if we had it in your back yard? We can get our friends here and have a justice of the peace."

"Our minister will be glad to come, if you want him," Rachel added, hope filling every word.

Mackenna smiled and, gaining Jobe's approval, she said, "That'd be lovely."

"I can bake a cake," Penny said.

The women quickly pulled Mackenna out of Jobe's arms and hustled the men into the living room so that they could begin planning. Within a half an hour, the simple foods and decorations had been decided on.

"Mom," Mackenna said, gaining her mother's attention away from Jobe's sisters who were busy with food ideas themselves. "I'd like it if you'd walk me down the aisle."

Smiling, Penny said, "Oh, bab-y girl, I would love that. You dad would be so proud."

In the other room, the men listened as the women plotted and planned. Joseph went to his cabinet and poured a glass of dark red wine for Jobe, Daniel, and himself. He then turned to his son-in-law and said, "Daniel, you're a good man. You've loved my Hannah and brought her healing. You've given us two beautiful grandchildren and I can only hope that Miriam and Rebecca find men as good as you."

Jobe nodded to his brother-in-law as they took a sip. Then he turned to his dad as Joseph began speaking again, this time to him.

"Son, no man was prouder than me when you joined the Army and then when you graduated from Special Forces training. A family is always afraid, though, wondering if their child will return safely from a war. You did, but you weren't the same. I worried, but just prayed that God would bring you back." Lifting his glass again, he continued, "You were man enough to know what you had lost and willing to get it back. And that woman in there has brought you back to us. So my prayers have been answered."

The men lifted their glasses once more, this time the lump in Jobe's throat keeping him from tasting the wine.

"Pop? We're not having any attendants, but Mackenna is going to ask Penny to walk with her and I'd be honored if you'd stand up with me."

This time it was the lump in Joseph's throat that

kept him from answering. Instead he pulled his son into his arms, offering a hug as a response to Jobe's question.

TRUE TO THEIR WISHES, the next weekend found all of their friends gathered in the Delaro's backyard. The spring flowers in the flowerbeds provided the perfect backdrop. Miriam had hung Christmas lights in the trees over where the vows would be said. Borrowed card tables with white tablecloths and folding chairs were scattered around the yard. A long table held food that the women had prepared. Once the plans were out, Sherrie, Suzanne, Annie, Jennifer, and Annalissa all pitched in to provide dishes. Penny's cake sat in the middle of the food-laden table, making the perfect centerpiece.

Annalissa brought her harp and at the designated time began to play Pachelbel's Cannon in D, as the gathering turned to see Mackenna walking arm in arm with her mother down the makeshift aisle. Joseph reached out to place a steadying hand on his son, noticing that Jobe's knees almost buckled at the sight of her walking toward him.

She was radiant in a long, cream colored dress, the sweetheart neckline showing off the pearl necklace that her mother had given her. Her reddish-blonde hair hung in waves down her back, with only the front pulled away from her face. Her eyes sparkled as she never took her gaze off of the man waiting the end for her at the end of the aisle.

Handsome in his tailored suit, hair swept back, his face smiling at hers. For just a moment, her mind flashed back to seven years ago when she first saw him on the dance-floor. A younger version of the man in front of her. She quickly put that memory to rest, knowing that as much as she loved the man in the past, she loved the man that he had become even more.

Reaching his side, she smiled as she placed her hand in his. Within a few minutes, they had recited their vows of love, pledges of faith, and promises of forever. Jobe leaned down, placing a sweet kiss on her lips as they were declared husband and wife.

Then with a whoop, he scooped her up in his arms and swung her around while kissing her the way he had wanted to ever since he had seen her. "I love you, Mackenna Delaro," he said, still pressing his lips against hers. The kiss lasted until the shouts from their guests pulled them apart and, smiling, they walked back down the aisle to the good wishes of their friends.

That night, back at their apartment having chosen to wait until the New Beginnings Center had moved before taking a stress-free honeymoon, he pushed her hair to the side as he slowly unzipped the dress. As it pooled around her feet, he held her hand as she stepped out, wearing a strapless cream bra and matching satin panties.

"One of us seems entirely overdressed," she said, running her finger down his white shirt. He had ditched his jacket and tie at the reception, but she impatiently began unbuttoning his shirt while swatting his hands out of the way. Pulling it down over his shoulders, it landed on the floor, next to her dress. Running her hands down his naked chest, she felt each muscle underneath her fingertips as they trailed their way down to his trousers.

"Stand still, soldier-boy," she ordered, as her hands fumbled with his belt.

He lifted his eyebrow at her, smiling at her command. *I can play this game...at least for a few minutes.* She maneuvered his zipper down over his engorged cock then leaned forward to slide the pants down his legs.

Unhooking her bra from the back, she let it land on the growing pile of clothes on the floor.

Palming his dick, the silky thickness filled her hand as she wrapped her fingers around and began sliding her hand up and down his shaft.

He groaned, throwing his head back, the roaring in his ears drowning out the sound of her kneeling in front of him. Startled when her mouth replaced her hand, his head jerked back down to see her on her knees at his feet. Watching her slide his cock into her warmth, her hands on his hips, he fought to hold still and not fuck her mouth. His fingers splayed out on her head, the silken threads of her long mane sliding through his fingers.

She worked his cock, swirling her tongue around the head before sliding his length back down as far as she could go. She felt his hands move from her hair and down to grasp her shoulders, gently pulling his dick out of her mouth before lifting her to her feet.

"You done being in control?" he asked, a grin on his handsome face.

She sneaked a peek up, seeing his amused expression. "Yeah," she whispered.

"Good, 'cause tonight's about me making love to my wife, and doll, it's gonna be all about you," he promised.

He lifted her in his arms, carrying her to the bed and laying her down after tossing the comforter back. Lying beside her, he caressed her body from her neck down to her full breasts. Slowly. Tortuously. His mouth trailing behind his hand, he moved his lips from the sensitive skin where her heartbeat pulsed at her throat to her rosy-tipped nipples.

As he sucked one in deeply, she gasped as the electric sensations vibrated throughout her core. Clinging to his back, she stroked the corded muscles that rippled underneath her fingertips. She felt his hand continue its downward path as she opened her legs for easier access.

Sliding his fingers through her moistness, he inserted a finger into her sex then soon joined it with another finger, beginning a scissoring motion. Eliciting moans from her lips, he smiled as his teeth nipped her breasts.

Her hips rose off of the bed searching for friction and he chuckled as she pleaded, "Now. Please, I need you now."

Rolling his body over on top of hers, his cock stood at attention at her entrance. Resting his weight on his arms, he looked down into her perfect face. He waited until her eyes met his, a smile curving the corners of her mouth.

"We gave our vows today in front of everyone," he said, "but this right here is my promise to you. My heart is yours, Mackenna. All my love for all my life."

With that, he slowly pressed his cock into her slick channel an inch at a time until he was fully seated, holding her gaze the entire time. Watching as the gradual curve of her lips formed a smile, taking his breath away.

"You have all of me, soldier-boy. Always and forever," she whispered into the night.

With that, he pulled back out and immediately plunged in again, this time harder and faster. He felt her inner walls drag him back in every time he moved out, as though her body needed the contact. Her breasts bounced with each thrust and he leaned down to suck a nipple into his mouth, tugging slightly.

Her eyes closed as her head pressed back into the

pillow, the sensations taking her closer and closer to the edge. Her lashes lay on her blushing cheeks, her lips were making a silent "O" as she was surrounded by his body. She lifted her knees, opening herself up more to him, allowing him to plunge deeper and deeper.

He felt his balls tighten and knew he was close. She recognized it also, feeling his cock grow even thicker than imaginable. Reaching down to her clit, he tweaked the swollen bud bringing the desired result. Her core grabbed his shaft, squeezing it in a rhythm as she cried out his name. With a few more thrusts he emptied himself into her, his muscles corded in strain as he felt the orgasm down to his toes.

His arms shook with the intensity of his release and just as they gave out, he summoned enough presence of mind to roll to the side so as not to crush her. He immediately pulled her body into his, not willing for an inch of space to separate their heartbeats.

For several minutes they lay, legs tangled in the sheets and each other, the coolness of the night slowly penetrating their warm bodies.

Wife. She's truly, irrevocably mine. Mine to love. Mine to protect. His hand moved slowly down her body, resting on her stomach, fingers splaying out. *And so are you, little one.*

Pulling the sheets over their bodies, he tucked her in tightly to his side. Kissing her lips once more, he whispered, "Sleep, doll. We've only just begun."

She did just that and fell asleep a few minutes later. And then later in the night, he woke her again…continuing to worship her body until the morning light peeked through the windows.

CHAPTER 21

TWO WEEKS LATER, Mackenna sat down with the women from the New Beginnings Center and informed them of their impending move. Her excitement was infectious and they all began talking at once.

Mackenna laughed and quieted them down as she explained the new facility and the moving process.

"It's a large house, with five big bedrooms. We'll still utilize the bunk beds though because we want to have at least ten women there at a time. The kitchen also has room for a large table so the dining room will become another classroom. We should be able to get another teacher in as well. I will do the counseling and we'll have another administrator that will take over the day to day plans."

"I'm definitely going with you all," Rose said, smiling at the women around the table.

"Is it far from here?" Paulina asked. "I'll need to be able to get to the library."

"There's public transportation right down the street and it'll be able to get you to your job, but you may have to cut back hours until you're closer to graduation and that won't be for another two months," Mackenna answered. She noticed Paulina's worried expression but leaned over to pat the girl's hand. "Don't worry, it'll be fine."

"What about the escorts?" another girl asked.

"Well, Alvarez Security will still oversee our security until we move, but it's my hope that in the new location we'll all be safe. It's on the outskirts of town and, while anything could happen, it should be out of sight and out of mind of any of your former gangs. But to be on the safe side, they will be taking the security cameras from here and putting them in the new facility."

Looking around, she said, "I checked on Carla and she's doing well in her new apartment and with her job in the restaurant. Jenita will be leaving us this week so she'll be the last to transition out from this location." She smiled at the young woman who was beaming at the others.

"Jerika, you have only about two more weeks to go, so you should be the first to graduate from our program in our new home. You'll be able to make the city bus route work for you as you get to your job. So that leaves Gabby, Tina, Yesenia, and Paulina for right now making the move. As soon as we're in, I'll have three more women brought into the program as well."

They discussed the actual move for a few more minutes before the meeting disbanded and Rose took her group to the computers. Paulina hung back, her eyes darting toward Mackenna.

"What's up?" Mackenna asked.

"I'm just wondering about whether or not to make the move with you," she said, her eyes now darting to the side, not making eye contact.

Mackenna watched the girl carefully, contemplating what was going through her mind. Paulina seemed scared, but Mackenna wanted to hear what the young woman had to say. "I'm listening," she said.

"You got no idea what it's like, Ms. Dunn."

Mackenna did not correct her on the name, knowing that the last thing the women needed was to be reminded of her wedded happiness. "You're right, I don't. But I do know that if you go back, your life expectancy will be much shorter than it would be if you stay out. Your chance of an unwanted pregnancy will also increase. The same with illness, injury, venereal disease, and ending up in jail."

Paulina sucked in a huge breath, then slowly let it out. "Yeah, I know," she said, defeat leaking into her words.

"I know it's hard now. You've only been with us a couple of weeks. But give it time. In another month, you'll be able to transition to a full-time job and then things will seem better."

Paulina nodded, but her expression gave away her doubts. Standing, she started to walk down the hall toward the classroom. Suddenly turning, she ran back, throwing herself in Mackenna's arms for a hug. "I'm sorry," Paulina said, her face buried in Mackenna's neck.

"Oh honey, you have nothing to be sorry for!" Mackenna assured her. "Once we get the move over with, you'll feel so much better."

A little later Mackenna finished up and decided to meet Jennifer for lunch. Walking toward the front, she heard Rose speaking to someone on the phone.

"It needs to be soon. We're moving next week. Yes, we'll be at a different location."

Mackenna's keys rattled in her hand as she turned the corner, and by the time she came into view, Rose was putting her cell phone back in her purse. Looking up, she asked, "Oh, are you leaving now?"

"I'm heading out to meet Jennifer." She hesitated, wondering if Rose would tell her who she had been calling. When Rose said nothing, Mackenna nodded awkwardly, then headed on out of the building, letting Doug drive her downtown.

THE RIVERFRONT WAS dark, the dim streetlights unable to penetrate the inky blackness of a cloudy night. They only gave partial illumination to the water that was swirling past the anchored boats. This time Tito came to the old warehouse to oversee the arrival of the shipment of new guns.

As Jazzie and Waldo moved toward the boats to assist with the unloading and inspection, Tito stayed back with Tank. Eying the large Hispanic, he said, "You never talk much. Like that about you. And you're loyal. Like that too."

Tank just nodded, his eyes sharp on the procedure in front of him.

"You got plans for moving up?" Tito asked.

Tank nodded again, "Yeah." His eyes never wavered from Jazzie and Waldo.

Tito followed his line of sight and turned back, asking, "You got a reason to be suspicious? Something I should know?"

Tank allowed his gaze to drop to Tito, answering, "No reason, no proof. Just figure anyone close to you bears watching."

Tito turned back, now wondering if there was not something that Jazzie or Waldo had been saying...or planning. The transaction in front of them was concluded, payment and arms transferred without any problems. The Kings had skulked away like river rats and the boat crew slid their crafts back into the river's current, moving out of sight in the inky waters. Jazzie and Waldo, laughing together as they pushed the cargo toward the vans, never noticed Tito's intense focus now on them. He had no reason to be suspicious of their loyalty...but maybe it was worth keeping an eye on them.

"Watch them," Tito said quietly. He did not have to look at the big man next to him to know that he had been heard, and that Tank had nodded as usual.

JOBE MET WITH TONY and the others as they discussed the New Beginnings transition. "We need to get the new building's security set up before they move in," he said.

Tony nodded and asked, "They move on…?"

"Thursday," he replied. "So we've got two days."

"No problem," Tony said. "Vinny, you've been out there. Do you have a list of what we'll need?"

Vinny turned to Lily, who flashed the equipment list up on the white screen on the wall. "Shouldn't be a problem. Most of it's the same as what we have in place now. We'll just duplicate it and then remove what's at the old building on Friday."

"Equipment issues?" Tony asked Gabe.

"Shouldn't be. We've got most of it in stock, except parts for a few of the cameras. That shipment is coming in tomorrow, so we're good to go."

"Any news from Matt or Shane?" Jobe asked.

"Latest I heard was that they know for sure that the Sixers are running guns as well as drugs. They even know where the Sixers are getting the shipments in— some warehouse on the King's riverfront."

"If they know where the fuckers are landing and buying this shit from, then why in the hell don't they shut it down?"

Tony shook his head. "I know. Let's face it, we'd go in the middle of the night and deal quickly and get this taken care of."

"If you tell me bureaucratic bullshit is the reason—
"

Tony threw up his hand, silencing the group. "Here's what I've been told. The guns they're buying? From the military. And not just stolen off of the bases, but actually someone in the military selling them to whoever will pay the highest."

For the men sitting at the table who had served in the military, they simultaneously reared back, appalled at what Tony had said.

While the others cursed, Jobe tried to choke back his rage. "That's why the FBI won't move against Montalvo. They want to figure out who's selling him military guns." The room was silent for just a second, before erupting into rounds of cursing once again.

Tony let the men get out their frustrations before adding, "Jack's on it." That brought silence, as they turned their attention back to him. "His group's been asked to infiltrate and find out who's selling the guns from the inside."

Gabe and Vinny nodded as Gabe said, "Well, if anyone can ferret out the asshole, Jack'll be able to."

Jobe pinned him with a stare. "Yeah, but in the meantime, Montalvo's still after my woman's place of business."

"He won't get her, man," they all vowed. "Not on our watch."

JAZZIE AND WALDO unpacked the crates inside the storage area that Tito had indicated. Underneath an unoccupied building near his uncle's grocery, it provided a safe location until the guns could be re-sold.

"You thought any more about doing something to that bitch?" Waldo asked.

"Which one?" Jazzie asked. "We got lots of bitches."

"Tito's distraction."

Jazzie was quiet for a few minutes as they continued to work. "Don't know. He's been focused since working on the deal with the F10s, but if they get picky about him not taking care of his business, then we may need to step in."

Waldo worked silently, willing to let Jazzie work the problem and take the lead.

"I got news. The bitches are moving day after tomorrow. Thought it'd be a good thing, getting Gabby out of Tito's reach. Now...if the F10s want a clean house then maybe we ought to give it to them," Jazzie said after a few minutes.

"Tito'll be pissed," Waldo warned.

As they finished the work, they covered the crates before moving toward the door, missing the person who had been listening on the other side. Tank, quietly observant as always, slithered out of sight.

"If we do it right, then maybe he won't have to be,"

Jazzie continued.

"Right?"

Jazzie stopped, turning toward Waldo. "Yeah, we kill that white bitch, then hey? Gabby gets in the way and gets it too, then that's on her."

Waldo smirked. "Like the way you think, Jaz-man."

The two walked out of the building and into the dark alley. Jazzie looked over his shoulder before turning back to his companion. "Just takin' care of business, man. That's all. Just takin' care of business."

LYING IN BED that night, Jobe held Mackenna as the bliss of their love-making lasted long after their bodies cooled.

"Always heard about pregnancy hormones making a woman horny," he joked, "but you're amazing."

Grinning, she pushed back her long hair, damp around her forehead, and asked, "Where'd you hear about pregnancy hormones?"

"Seriously? Between BJ, Matt, Shane, and Tony, I've heard plenty about the subject. I'm just waiting for Gabe and Vinny to start in with it."

She placed her hands on his pecs and gave a slight shove back. "Hmmph. You men sit around and talk about sex with your wives?"

Laughing, Jobe answered, "And what do you and your girlfriends talk about? Never talked about us men?"

"Oh…well, when you put it that way," she said, blushing. "We do talk, just a little."

"So if it makes you feel better, men don't go into details about their wives. But I admit that the words pregnancy hormones and sex have been heard around the office."

Mackenna just smiled, the relaxation almost sending her into sleep. She scooted back closer, allowing him to tuck her in tightly. She loved the feeling of falling asleep with his hand on her stomach.

"Baby?"

"Hmm?"

"The next couple of days are going to be busy. I want you to take it easy and let others do the hard work."

"Uhh-hmm," she replied, sleep pulling her in.

He gave her a little squeeze, saying, "I want to hear you agree, doll."

"Mmmkay. I'll take it easy," she promised, just before her breathing slowed and slumber finally won out.

Jobe lay there a few more minutes, his mind going over the tasks of the security for the transfer. *Should be smooth. We've got this.*

CHAPTER 22

MACKENNA SAT IN her office at DSS, a tension headache causing her to rub the back of her neck as she dialed Jobe.

"Hey, babe," he answered jovially.

"Honey, we've got problems."

His voice immediately became serious. "What kind of problems? Hang on, I've got the group here so I'm putting you on speaker."

"My supervisor said that everything is scheduled properly for the move tomorrow, but that the security system has to be in place first. That caveat was added to the grant due to the problems we've had with gang threats. I know you all were starting tomorrow but weren't going to finish until the next day when you could get some of the cameras from the old place."

Jobe heard the worry in her voice and immediately reassured her that they'd be ready. "Let us work the problem here for a bit, and I'll call you back. Meanwhile, take care of yourself. Go home if you have to."

Jobe hung up, looking at the Alvarez group for answers and support. "What do ya'll think?"

Tony turned to Vinny. "Can we get new cameras in

over at the new location and then just recycle the ones we take down tomorrow at the old place?"

Vinny nodded, "Yeah, the new ones should be coming in today."

"Guys, I hate to be the downer, but we've got more problems," Lily said, hanging up her phone. "BJ can't come in today. One of the twins has the croup and they are taking him to the hospital now. It's not serious, but they want him checked out. We can't use him today to check the new feeds."

Tony took out his cell and immediately sent a text to BJ. "I'm telling him to let us know the minute he hears anything and to not worry about us." The others around the table nodded, understanding the parental fears of a sick child. Looking over to Lily, he asked, "Can you do it?"

Lily bit her lip nervously, answering, "Truthfully? Yeah, I'm sure I can figure out what he does, but never having done that type of programing or checking before, I'll want BJ to re-check it as soon as he can."

Tony nodded, irritation evident on his face.

"I'm sorry, Tony," Lily added.

His gaze jerked to hers, noting her concern. "Lily, I'm not upset with you at all. I'm upset with myself."

Seeing the confusion on the faces of those around the table, he replied, "In SF, we had a medic but we also had a backup medic. We had someone trained in communications, but a backup. Same with sharp-shooter."

The others nodded in understanding, but Tony continued, "Most of you are trained in multiple areas so that we can pick up the slack in any situation, but I've only used BJ to go out into the field and that was poor management on my part."

Everyone clamored to contradict Tony's assessment, but he raised his hand. "No, this is on me. But Lily," he said, turning to her, "we'll definitely use you today and I'm having the office manager start looking for another programmer we can hire."

"You know," Gabe added, "Just installing the cameras outside of the new place will be a deterrent until we can have BJ test them out."

"Good point," Tony conceded.

"Oh, no."

All eyes at the table turned toward Lily, seeing her dismay.

"The shipment of new equipment that was coming today won't be coming in after all. The shipping company is on strike so the dealer is now sending them through the Post Office, but they won't get here for three more days."

"Goddamnit," Jobe shouted, his jaw tight with frustration.

"Okay folks, work the mission," Tony ordered.

After another hour, the group had their assignments. Deciding that they did not want to delay the move, Jobe, Vinny, and Gabe would start removing the cameras from the current New Beginnings location and install them today at the new home. Lily would go with them when the systems were in place to provide the video-feed check. The bars would remain on the bottom floor windows of the current location and they would have Terrance spend the night at the old location along with Little John, to provide more security.

"Jobe, you okay with this plan?" Tony asked when the details had been hashed out.

"Yes, sir. It looks like we've planned for all contingencies. This will get the new place wired so the city can move the women tomorrow, plus the old place will have extra manpower tonight for their last night in the old location."

We got this.

FUCK, WHAT ELSE can go wrong? Jobe thought angrily. Getting a late start due to the change in plans, he, Gabe, and Vinny had just removed the security cameras and driven to the new location when it began to rain. The men had worked in the soaking weather until the thunderstorm rolled in. Heavy rain, lightning, and strong winds kept them in the van for over two hours.

Jobe glanced at his watch as the storm finally began to pass on. "We've got just enough time before it gets dark to get these cameras up and then call Lily to come check them so they'll be ready. I'll have Tony send Doug over with another ladder and that'll make it go faster.

Getting off the phone with Tony, he reported, "Gettin' the ladder and Lily's coming on over. Terrance has headed to the old center to get some instructions from Mackenna before she heads home." *Okay, we've got this.*

MACKENNA HAD TOLD the women at the center that morning that they would be on a tight schedule for the next couple of days. "The cameras have been taken out and are being installed at the new home," she said, looking out of the windows at the impending storm. "Hopefully they can get them installed in spite of the rain and we'll be good to go for tomorrow."

Forcing her eyes back to the group, she told them to finish packing their belongings.

"How safe are we going to be tonight?" Paulina asked.

"Alvarez Security is sending another man to stay with Little John so you'll have plenty of protection tonight," Mackenna replied.

The group soon disbanded, Rose heading to the classroom by herself to unplug and label all of the equipment. The girls moved upstairs to pack their clothes and toiletries as well as the linens. Mackenna headed down the hall just as Rose was finished.

"I'm going to head out early," she said to Mackenna. "If you don't mind. I'd like to get ahead of the storm."

"That's fine. I'm staying to make sure Terrance is settled in and then I'll head home later. See you tomorrow—it'll be a busy day."

Something flashed through Rose's expression, but it was gone so quickly that Mackenna could not be sure that she had seen it. *I wonder if Rose is all right. I hope she isn't changing her mind about staying with New Beginnings.*

An hour later, Jobe called with an update on the progress. "Hey doll, just wanted to let you know that I'll be a little late tonight. The storm has passed and we're getting back on the ladders to finish the outside installations. Had a delay also when the city inspector did not show up for the inside camera approvals, but that's finally done. We want to get these cameras up and running for tomorrow, so I'll be in late."

"Oh, honey, I hate that you're working so long on this. Tony's going to hate me."

"No way. He's glad to do it. Are you heading home?"

"I see Terrance pulling up now. Little John should come soon and I'll stay until I'm sure they're settled. Tell Doug he can pick me up in about two hours."

"Will do. Love you, doll," he said, his voice always going lower when saying the endearment.

Smiling to herself, she acknowledged, "Love you too."

An hour later, Terrance and Little John were sitting in the kitchen talking to Mackenna when Paulina walked in. Greeting them shyly, she moved to the coffee maker. Fixing two cups, she smiled as she handed them to the two men. Looking over at Mackenna, she said, "I know you don't need the caffeine. Is there something I can get for you?"

"No thanks, Paulina. I'm going to leave in just a little bit anyway and since Jobe is going to be late, I'll fix something when I get home."

Nodding her head, Paulina walked over and awkwardly hugged Mackenna before leaving the room as the three others continued to talk for a while. Little John began yawning, giving his head a little shake.

"I don't know what's wrong. I never get sleepy this early," he said.

Terrance laughed but stifled a yawn himself. He rubbed his eyes, trying to hold them open. He looked up at Mackenna, but the fuzzy image of her would not come into focus.

Just then her phone rang again and she saw that it was Jobe. Before he could speak, she rushed, "Terrance is here and he's falling asleep. So is Little John. Something's not right."

"Put him on," Jobe ordered.

Terrance reached for the phone but could not hold it himself, so she held it up for him and put it on speaker phone.

"Jobe, sumsin wron. Drug coff," Terrance slurred

before his head hit the table.

Mackenna watched in horror as the two men went from yawning to slumping over on the table. She jumped up, closest to Little John, shaking him as she called his name. No response.

"Girls!" she shrieked. "Help me!"

"Jobe, they're unconscious! What do we do?" she screamed into the phone.

"Get outta the house," Jobe growled. "We're on it." She heard him shout to Gabe to call Tony and to Vinny to get hold of Matt and Shane.

"Where do we go?" she asked, her heart thumping as fear threatened to choke her.

"Get out through the back. If you can find a building to get into, then go. If not, head toward the park."

She immediately heard the pounding of feet as the women in the house ran down the stairs and into the kitchen. The others crowded in, desperate to help but not knowing what to do. Mackenna's eyes darted around, quickly taking a count. "Where's Paulina? She was just here making the coffee!"

"She's not upstairs," Jerika said. "She never came back up after being down here."

Fear warred with anger as Mackenna realized that Paulina must have put something in the coffee. "Fuck!" she cursed. "Jobe? There is only so fast we can go. I've got a pregnant girl. And I think we were ratted out by Paulina Orchuro."

"Got it, now go!" he ordered again.

Mackenna glanced around the room at the girls' terrified faces then back down to the drugged men whose head still lay on the table.

"Oh, Jesus," she cried. "Help me hide them and then we've got to get out of here!" The girls moved forward and within three minutes managed to drag the two unconscious men into her office. Then, stepping gently over the two men on the floor, she locked the door behind her.

Sprinting to the back door, she ordered, "Outside. We're leaving." The women ran out of the kitchen door and to the back gate. MacKenna quickly unlocked it and they dashed through. Once into the alley, the women all turned toward her.

"We're heading to the park." Just then the sounds of gunfire at the front of the center could be heard along with sirens that seemed too far away to assist the girls at the moment. Jerika and Yesenia grabbed each of Gabby's arms and assisted her as they jogged down the street. Tina reached the corner first and waited for the others.

Making a quick decision, Mackenna said, "We'll do better separated. Tina, run up to the street first because you're faster. If you can hail a cab or get on a late bus, then do so and have them take you to the police station. Don't worry about money. Tell them who you are and where you're from."

Tina nodded and with a flash of sympathy in her eyes, she took off to the right running as fast as she could. Makenna then turned to Gabby. "Honey, let's face it. They're after you and me." Turning to Jerika and Yesinia, she said "Follow Tina. Run as fast as you can. If you find a business or person who will take you in until you can call the police, then do so, but stay together. I think there's a bar about six blocks from here. If you run in screaming for the police, then no one'll mess with you!"

Once again, with sympathy on their faces, the two women began running down the street, as they held hands.

"It's you and me, girl," Mackenna said. "Let's go try to outsmart these fuckers." Gabby gave a nod and the two women hurried across the street. Making their way into the dark park, illuminated by only the path lights, Mackenna diverted Gabby off the path and into the shadows. "We've got to stay hidden as much as possible," she whispered.

After just a few minutes, Gabby stopped suddenly, bending over at the waist and moaning while clutching her stomach. With tear-filled eyes, she looked at Mackenna and gasped, "I can't go, I can't do it."

Mackenna wanted to rail at the girl to keep going, but one glimpse at her tortured face and she knew they needed an alternate plan. Just then a huge, dark figure loomed over them, the light behind his body casting his features into shadow.

Just as Mackenna opened her mouth to scream, he pointed a gun right at her. The scream died in her throat as she moved protectively in front of Gabby. The pregnant woman dropped to her knees, a slight moan escaping her lips.

"Don't, please don't kill us," Mackenna pleaded, knowing her words were falling on deaf ears.

The figure tucked the gun back into his pants and stepped quickly around her, kneeling over Gabby. "No intention of killing you," he said, as he placed his hands on her stomach. He looked up at Mackenna, his face no longer in shadow, and she saw the handsome face of a large, Hispanic man, kindness in his eyes.

"You're Alvarez's. Jobe's woman, right?"

She stood numbly at his words, staring down. Licking her lips, she said nothing.

"Name's Tank for now," he said. "I'm undercover. Worked with a couple of friends of yours. Shane and Matt."

"Oh, my God," she breathed as she dropped to the ground next to him as he checked out Gabby. "You...you're here to help?"

"Yes, the police know I'm here and that some of the Sixers were planning on hitting your facility tonight. I'm supposed to be out with them, but followed you here."

"Can you help her?"

"Yeah, I can stay with her and keep her safe. If I have to, I can even take her on my motorcycle that's parked over there," he said, nodding off to the left.

Mackenna thought for only a few seconds, before

saying, "Do it. Get her out of here. I'm sure whoever is after us, is after her and you've got to get her safe."

Tank looked down, his expression torn in indecision. "I can't leave you here," he growled.

"I'll be okay," she said, hoping it was true. "Get her to safety and I'm going to find a place to hide." She stood quickly and then touched his shoulder. "Thank you. As soon as you can, tell Matt and Shane that the other three women headed down 42nd Street to find anyone who can help."

"Will do," he said, standing with one arm around Gabby, assisting her as well.

Mackenna saw regret in his eyes. Placing her hand on his arm, she offered a small smile of gratitude. "Thank you. For...everything." With that, she turned and started to head toward a small grove of trees.

Tank called back softly. He left Gabby and hustled over to Mackenna, pulling out his weapon as he approached. Turning it backward, he handed it to her. "Can you use this?"

Nodding, she stepped forward, taking the gun out of his hands. "Yeah, I think so."

He gave her quick instructions and then smiled. "It's not a baseball bat, but it'll do." With that, he rushed back over to Gabby and picked her pregnant form up effortlessly in his arms and jogged off to where his motorcycle was parked.

Mackenna stood momentarily in the shadow of a large tree, the eerie stillness of the night punctuated only by the sounds of far-off sirens and voices that were not too far away. And the rumble of thunder. Her heart pounded, as she ran between the trees, hoping for a place to hide until Jobe could get to her.

Alone. Utterly alone. That thought was broken by her hand gently rubbing her still flat stomach. *No, not alone, little one.* Vowing to protect her baby, she ran into the copse.

CHAPTER 23

J OBE BOUNDED OUT of the van into the underground garage of Alvarez Security, closely followed
by Gabe and Vinny. Tony and Doug were waiting for
him as he ran over to suit up. The Kevlar vests were
quickly donned, their weapons were already secured in
the SUVs.

"Matt and Shane are on their way, that's why I had
you continue here to get your equipment."

Matt had called Tony as soon as the alert came to
them that the New Beginnings Center was being
invaded. Since Jobe, Gabe, and Vinny were almost
back from the new location's job, Tony informed them
and ordered them in.

"Gabe, ride with Doug. Check the center first. I
know EMTs were on their way, but I want Terrance
checked out by you. Vinny, you're our best marksman.
You go with Jobe and me heading to the back of the
center. Let's roll," Tony barked.

The men quickly headed out, Jobe's heart pounding with fear. Trapped in a nightmare ever since
Mackenna called him, he tried to focus on the mission
of getting her out safely, but could not gain control.

Attempting to steady his breathing, he fell short of that goal, feeling his vest choking him.

Leaning over, he placed his head in his hands, trying to force the discipline that years in the military honed. But his mind was filled with her. *Her eyes when she laughed. Or filled with tears. The silly noises she would make when telling a joke. Or the warmth when looking at her mom...or him.* Licking his lips, he allowed visions of her to consume him. *To hell with control. This was about his life. This was about her.*

They drove by the center, now filled with police, and saw Gabe and Doug entering the building that had been secured by the gang task force. Within a minute, Gabe came over the radio, informing them all that Terrance and Little John were alive.

Matt radioed that three of the girls had been rescued and he and Shane were near the park, in pursuit of suspects. Jerika, Tina, and Jenita had been found after running into an open bar yelling for the police. The patrons had immediately assisted them and they were now picked up by other detectives.

All of the news was positive, but Jobe felt none of it. So far nothing had come in about Mackenna. Tony jerked the SUV to a stop at one of the side streets bordering the city's one hundred acre park. Grabbing their weapons and night vision goggles, the men exited in haste, running toward Shane and Matt.

"What've you got?" Jobe barked.

"One of our undercover detectives, who'd infiltrated the Sixers, found Mackenna and Gabby. Gabby may have gone into labor, so he took her and made it to the hospital."

"So, he just left Mackenna on her own out here?"

Shane nodded and said, "He had to make a call, man. Chances are the Sixers are after Gabby and he could only take one on his bike. He called it in, said Mackenna ran off towards the woods. He gave her his gun, though."

"Oh, Jesus, you've got to be fuckin' kidding me! She's got no goddamn idea how to fire a gun. Jesus, she'd be safer with a bat!"

Vinny stepped up, putting his hand on Jobe's shoulder, passing his strength to his friend. Shane nodded toward their night vision goggles and said, "With those, you're going to be a step ahead of us."

Tony reached into his bag and pulled out two more, tossing them to the two detectives. They had just started across the path when Jobe's cell phone indicated a text. **Tnis crts**

"Are there tennis courts near here?" he asked, showing the others his phone.

"About two hundred yards straight through the middle. But how do you know that's her? It could be someone who has her phone."

Fuck, he thought. Then his phone vibrated again. **Soldr boy**

A wave of relief almost dropped him to his knees as he saw her comment. "It's her. Only she calls me this."

Nodding, the men ran silently through the woods toward the tennis courts. Jobe noted the terrain was a million times easier than the rough treks through Afghanistan and, yet, he would trade anything to be on a mission that did not involve Mackenna. *Stay safe baby. Stay alive.*

THE BLACK, STARLESS NIGHT made running arduous for Mackenna. The rain had begun again, quickly soaking her, and she pushed her long hair away from her face as she moved out of the grove of trees and found herself near the tennis courts. She pulled out her phone, sending a quick text to Jobe, knowing he'd be looking for her. After texting with wet, cold fingers that she was at the tennis courts, she sent a secret message so that he would know it was her.

Looking beyond the courts, she could make out a walkway bridge nearby, so she headed toward it looking for a dry place to rest. Her foot caught on a limb in the path and she tripped falling flat on the ground. Looking down, she could see a tennis racket at her feet, long discarded with its strings broken.

With the rain slowing down, she struggled to her feet in the slippery mud, holding onto the racket to give her leverage to rise.

"Well, look what we've found. We may have lost Tito's woman, but we finally got the main bitch."

Mackenna startled, her feet slipping again in the mud causing her to land on her ass. Twisting around to see who was speaking, she could barely make out a man, dressed in black, stepping slightly from the shadows coming from the faint light pole near the courts. *How did he find me?*

As though he could read her thoughts, he held up a small electronic box in his hand. "You think that badass boyfriend of yours is the only one with shit? You've got a tracer on your shirt."

The cold was penetrating as she continued to shiver, desperately trying to make sense of his words. *Tracer?*

"Come on out, girl," he ordered.

Mackenna's brow crinkled in confusion and then in shock as a young woman stepped into the faint light. She gasped, both in surprise and hurt. "Paulina. What have you done?"

"I had no choice, please believe me. You can't know what it's like. What they do to you. But once you're in, you gotta stay."

Chest heaving, Mackenna stared the young woman in the eyes. "We all have a choice, Paulina. We all can choose."

The young girl's face fell as tears joined the raindrops on her cheeks. Looking back at the man still standing nearby, Mackenna licked her lips wondering where Jobe was.

His hand lifted, a gun pointing right at Mackenna

as he said, "Yeah, bitch. And Paulina here made her choice. She stuck a tracer on the back of your collar and made sure your goons were out."

The memory of Paulina hugging her earlier, bolted back into Mackenna's mind. Her gaze stayed on the gun as her body shook with a combination of fear and cold.

Tank's gun! It must have dropped when I fell. Hoping it was too dark for him to see what she was doing clearly, she tried to drop her gaze to the ground but was unable to see anything. Her fingers still clasped the racket. She was afraid to drop it for fear he would shoot at any movement.

Suddenly the pounding of feet could be heard and for an instance Mackenna imagined Jobe rushing to the scene to save her. Instead, another man, all dressed in dark clothing, came into view.

"Jazzie, Jazzie! Where the fuck are you?"

Jazzie turned, his face angry at the intrusion from Waldo. "What're you doin' here? You're supposed to be after Tito's bitch."

"She's gone. I saw Tank drive off with her on his bike."

"Tank?"

Mackenna could not see the man called Jazzie's face, but realized that they had no idea that Tank was undercover. *Oh, Please God. Let him get her to safety.*

"You think he's taking her to Tito?"

"Don't know. When I came running here, there'd

been firing at the front of that bitch's place. Cops may have gotten him."

"Motherfuckers! This is going to shit, man. Tank wasn't supposed to be in this. He takes that bitch back to Tito and we're no better off."

Jazzie turned his angry visage back to Mackenna, still on the ground.

JOBE AND HIS FRIENDS moved swiftly through the trees, the slippery ground and dim light not impeding them at all.

Hearing voices in the distance, they separated silently and began to circle the area. Vinny moved in front of Jobe, just long enough for him to make eye contact. Even through the goggles, Jobe knew what Vinny was looking for. *Needs to see I'm not losing my shit.* Understanding the action of squad members keeping a pulse on each other, he gave a curt nod. His heart pounded and he knew he was not in control. And for the first time in his life, he understood that that was okay. Another nod and Vinny shifted to his right.

Tony radioed, "Visual. Two females. Two males."

As they crept closer, they could hear the male voices raised in anger. Continuing to circle, they each signaled to the others when they were in place. Vinny, as the most accurate sharpshooter, moved to a position where he could take a shot when needed. As a civilian, he knew he had to wait, unable to just fire because the suspect was a killer asshole. He gritted his teeth, wanting to go ahead and take the shot he knew he had.

Jobe moved between two trees, still in the dark shadows, but able to see Mackenna on the ground with the other three standing nearby. The other female was looking down while the two males faced each other, one with a gun in his hand still pointed at Mackenna. Jobe nodded once toward Vinny, both understanding the silent code. Blinking his eyes once, he fixed his eyes on the target, slowing his breathing. *Come on fucker, make a move and you're mine.*

MACKENNA WATCHED AS JAZZIE turned back to her, and could see the desperation in his eyes even in the dim light. Adrenaline still pumping, she felt her muscles quivering, unable to stop the shaking.

A flash of movement to the side had her gaze jerking over in a panic, as Paulina dropped to the ground. Before she could understand what was happening, she saw the young woman kneeling with a gun in her hand. *Tanks' gun!* But Paulina was not pointing the weapon at her...she held it in front of her...pointed straight toward the man with the gun.

Jazzie's fury was evident as he growled, "You better use that bitch, 'cause you ain't worth my spit now."

With his focus on Paulina, Mackenna roared while

swinging the tennis racket toward his gun hand, which had lowered in his anger. The gun fired, sending a blast of light in the dark night, as Jazzie screamed in pain. Another shot rang out, he dropped to the ground and Mackenna tried to scramble away.

"Police!" Shane roared. "Drop your weapons," he ordered to Paulina. She shook in fear, but slowly knelt, placing the gun on the ground.

"Hands on your head," he ordered next as the others stepped into the dim light, showing themselves. Paulina immediately obeyed, as she stayed on her knees.

Waldo looked around as the detectives moved forward, then back to the area where Jazzie lay dead in the grass. He knew his life was worth nothing now. He had gone against the leader. He was dead if he went back...dead if he went to jail. Pulling his gun out of his pants, he aimed at the bitch still sitting on the ground. The last thing he heard on this earth was a shot being fired. Right before he dropped to the mud next to his brother.

Mackenna flung herself down as she instinctively covered her head. Vinny stepped from the trees, his weapon still in position as Shane pulled a handcuffed Paulina to her feet.

Jobe, throwing off his goggles, raced to Mackenna still huddled on the ground. Scooping her up in his arms, he pulled her into his embrace as he sat on the wet dirt. "Are you hurt?" he cried, trying to see if she were injured, but her wet, muddy clothes made that task impossible.

"No, no," she answered, her voice shaky as she twisted around to see his ravaged face. Lifting her hands, she cupped his jaw pulling him in close. "I'm fine. Honest, Jobe. I'm fine."

He lifted her up in his arms, but she insisted on standing. He placed her feet reluctantly on the slippery ground but held her tightly against his side. Her hand wrapped around his waist, thick with the Kevlar vest, glad for the protection but wishing she could feel him instead.

The area quickly filled with others as the police closed in, some with heavy lights to illuminate the crime scene. Jazzie and Waldo's bodies lay twisted on the ground as they had fallen and Matt ascertained that they were both dead.

Paulina stood, staring down at the two bodies, her hands behind her back in cuffs. Her shocked gaze lifted to Mackenna's, a tear sliding down her cheek. "I...I'm sorry," she whispered. Shaking her head slowly, she looked over at Shane standing next to her. "I'll tell you anything. Anything."

A policewoman stepped over and, taking Paulina by the arm, led her away. Mackenna watched her silently as the sight of Paulina disappeared into the night. Suddenly, her legs gave out as the adrenaline no longer pumped, leaving her weak.

Jobe's body took her weight as she slumped against

him before he scooped her up once more. Stalking over to the EMTs that had appeared on the scene, he gently laid her down on the stretcher.

"I'm all right, honey. Just tired," she said, her hands still holding tightly to his arms, unwilling or unable to let go.

He turned to the EMTs, barking, "She's pregnant."

They immediately began assessing, against her protestations. Jobe leaned down, his face directly in hers and said, "Not taking a chance, doll. Please," he begged, as his voice broke.

Nodding, she lay back still clasping his arm. Not letting go. *Never letting go.*

SWISH, SWISH, SWISH. The baby's heart monitor gave off the clear signals that it was alive and well, bringing both Mackenna and Jobe to tears as she continued to cling to him.

With her high blood pressure, the ER doctor admitted her for overnight observation. Once settled into the hospital room, she slept fitfully as Jobe kept watch, his hand still holding hers and his gaze moving between the monitor and her face.

A slight movement at the door had him swinging his head around, nerves instantly on alert. He relaxed as he saw Shane and another man enter. His eyes appraised the second man, his large frame filling the doorway as he hung back from the others. Dark hair, with an expression of hardness on his Hispanic features.

"Tank?" came Mackenna's soft voice.

Jobe's head jerked around, seeing her eyes open and a quizzical expression on her face.

"Yeah," the large man said, walking over to join the others. Looking down at Jobe, he extended his hand. Jobe glanced at it momentarily before taking it. "Real name is Cam," he said to Jobe, but his eyes shifted over to the woman in the bed. "Glad you're okay."

Jobe, wanting an explanation of who the man was, looked at Shane. "Undercover with the Sixers," came the short answer. "He got Gabby out of the park and gave his weapon to Mackenna."

Jobe stood, not used to looking up at anyone, but found himself directing his glare upwards several inches to Tank. "She didn't know how to use the gun."

Tank nodded but said, "She's smart. She'd done all right. And it was better than nothing." His gaze dropped back to Mackenna as he said, "But I hear that a tennis racket is almost as good as a baseball bat."

She blushed as the others tried to hide their smiles, while Jobe sat heavily in his chair again. "Fuck," he said, the fight leaving him as the thought of the danger she had faced sunk in once more.

After a moment, she stared past Jobe at the men in the room. Licking her lips, she asked, "How's Gabby?"

Receiving assurances of the young woman's health, she looked back up at the large man who had shifted to the other side of her bed. "What happens now? Now that your cover's gone?"

"I'll be okay. Got options. Anyway, just wanted to check on you." He gave a head jerk to Jobe and with a last smile down at Mackenna, turned to walk out of the room. Pausing next to Shane, he stopped. As the two men held each other's eyes, silent communication between them, he just nodded again before stepping into the corridor.

OUTSIDE OF THE HOSPITAL, Tank slid on his sunglasses just before climbing into the large, black SUV. The driver glanced at his passenger carefully before saying, "You ready, Cam?"

Tank nodded silently as the vehicle pulled into traffic. Several minutes passed before he spoke. "Yeah, time to make a change."

Jack Bryant just nodded.

SHANE STAYED IN the hospital for just a few more minutes, updating Mackenna and Jobe on the latest. With preliminary information from Tank and Paulina, Tito's gun running operation was going to be shut down. He had not been arrested yet, but indictments would be coming.

"From what Tank had seen, Gabby was Tito's

greatest downfall," Shane said, much to the surprise of Mackenna. "He hated that she left, but must've really had feelings for her—enough that the others were questioning some of his judgements. It's true that he wanted you out of the way, but he wanted Gabby back with him."

Shane left soon, letting Mackenna know that once she was out of the woods they would question her about the events of the previous night.

The sun was just rising as Penny, Rachel, and Joseph tiptoed quietly into the room. Jobe lifted his head from its position on her bed, giving a tired smile to their parents. Standing, he moved over to offer hugs to all of them, then took Penny by the arm leading her to her daughter's side.

Mackenna's eyes fluttered open and she smiled seeing her mother's face. "Mom, I'm fine," she assured as Penny leaned down to hold her.

After a few minutes, the parents left, with Rachel's vows of filling their refrigerator with food so that Mackenna would not have to cook.

Jobe watched Mackenna as his mother left, whispering, "You know what that means, doll? She'll bring enough to feed an army."

Giggling, Mackenna laughed. After a moment she sobered, looking at the monitors. "Everything still okay?"

"Yeah, babe. Your blood pressure's back down and listen," he said, encouragingly.

Swish, swish, swish.

Her expression gentled into a smile as she heard the baby's heartbeat. Settling back against the pillows, she asked, "When can I go home?"

"Soon, the last nurse who came in said." He brushed her hair back from her pale face, the dark shadows underneath her eyes stark in contrast. "Try to rest some more."

As soon as the words left his mouth, their room quickly filled with friends as Sherrie, Tony, Gabe, Jennifer, Vinny, and Annalissa came in. The women rushed to her bedside as the men moved over to Jobe.

"Good shot last night," Gabe said to Jobe, referring to his kill shot to Jazzie.

Jobe glanced over at Vinny, addressing him with a nod. "Thanks for letting me get that one. And for taking out that other asshole."

Turning to Tony, he asked, "Any problems?"

Shaking his head, he replied, "Nope. We had the police with us. Clear evidence. We're good."

The four brothers shared a look, no words needed.

CHAPTER 24
6 MONTHS LATER

"COME ON, DOLL. You're doing great," Jobe encouraged, trying to ignore Mackenna's glare. She panted through the contractions, anxiety mixed with hope spurring her on. Her thick mane of hair had been trimmed in layers around her shoulders and was currently pulled back with a headband, keeping the damp tresses from falling in her face. Jobe used a cool, moist washcloth to wipe her brow as her body relaxed. The epidural was easing her pain, but she was exhausted.

She looked into his face, as familiar as gazing into a mirror. His handsome features along with two days of stubble, piercing but tired eyes, had her smiling in spite of the exhaustion. Unlike Jennifer, who had only been in labor for about six hours before delivering a healthy boy, Mackenna was going on almost eighteen hours.

"I don't know how much longer I can keep this up," she confessed, tears in her eyes.

Before Jobe could call the doctor again, he appeared and checked her once more. The obstetrician's jovial manner had Mackenna wanting to punch him, but one hand gripped the bed sheet while the other clung to Jobe's instead.

"Looks like we're about ready to start pushing, little lady," he said with a smile, nodding to the nurse in the room who began moving equipment around.

Jobe saw Mackenna's glare turn murderous at the name *little lady*, and he could only smile, thinking that his tiger was about to show her fangs. Leaning down, he whispered, "Good thing you don't have any sport's equipment handy or I'd be afraid for the doctor's safety."

Her eyes jumped to his and she could not help but grin. For her birthday, he had given her a beautiful, silver charm bracelet with her first charm being of an envelope. Together, they had burned the old letters, choosing to not to be defined by their past, but by their future. The tiny, silver envelope charm was the perfect reminder of their earlier years. She had been even more surprised when Gabe and Jennifer gifted her with a silver charm in the shape of a baseball bat, followed by a tennis racket charm from Vinny and Annalissa.

After the events of that night, the New Beginnings Center moved to the new location and had not been bothered by gangs again. They had had eleven more women graduate from their program and were getting recognized at the local and state level as a premier facility for their purpose.

Gabby had given birth to a little girl, whom she was

raising on her own. Tito was in prison and Gabby was determined to raise her daughter in a way that would keep the allure of gang life from her. Even hearing that Tito truly had feelings for her, she had her own life…and the life of her baby…to focus on.

Rose had been in secret arrangements with a local church to take on the women in educational programs including child care. She had explained her phone calls to Mackenna after that night, saying that she had hoped to have a big surprise waiting for her when the new center opened. The extra help was welcome and new business partnerships had been created.

Mackenna, true to her vision, had resigned as the center's administrator and become the counselor only. She loved continuing her work and spent a lot of time in the local high schools reaching out to girls before they took the fateful step toward gangs.

Her mother had continued to thrive in her rehabilitation, her speech almost perfect and her left side much more functional. She, along with Rachel and Joseph, were outside in the family waiting room, eagerly awaiting her first grandchild.

And now, it was time to push. At this point, Mackenna's body took over and with Jobe by her side, they welcomed their baby girl into the world.

YEARS LATER

THE ALVAREZ PICNIC was in full swing, the area overrun with good friends. BJ's son had commandeered the playground's fort, along with Shane, Tony, and Gabe's sons. Matt's two girls played on the swings with Shane, BJ, and Vinny's daughters. Jobe's daughter was trying to attack the fort, much to the consternation of the boys.

When the boys tried to push her down, she roared a war cry, swinging a plastic baseball bat before the men could intervene. Tony and BJ continued to man the grills while the others refereed the children.

Mackenna rolled her eyes at her daughter's antics, saying, "I wish she would learn a little diplomacy instead of swinging a bat."

"She's just like her momma," Jennifer quipped, as Sherrie and Annalissa nodded.

The other women laughed as they continued to set out the food, waiting for the meat to finish grilling. As food was finally passed around, good friends joined in the conversation, comfortable in the intimacy of the group.

Each adult, in their turn, reflected on the years that had passed. Their career paths, old friends and new friends, and life as it evolved.

Makenna snuggled closer to Jobe on the picnic table bench, her small son in her lap as she watched her daughter play with the others. This was the dream she had had so many years ago—life with this man. She felt his warm breath on her neck, as he kissed her shoulder.

Jobe's arms wrapped around her as he settled her deeper into his embrace. Like the others there, he managed to keep up with the conversation and keep one eye on the children playing games in the grass. *Nothing like having children to make you feel like you've lost all control.*

Control—no longer a word that he had to live by...or live for. Life moved along at its own pace and as long as it was filled with friends and family, he was good with that.

Kissing the top of his wife's head again, he smiled down at her as she twisted around to gaze into his face. The beautiful face that he once tossed aside out of fear was now his to admire every morning. He had to agree with something that Penny had once told them. Sometimes, love has to find its own way.

THE END

If you enjoyed Jobe, please leave a review!

Keep up with the latest news and never miss another release by Maryann Jordan.
Sign up for her newsletter here!
goo.gl/forms/ydMTe0iz8L

Other books by Maryann Jordan

(all standalone books)

All of my books are stand-alone, each with their own HEA!! You can read them in any order!

Saints Protection & Investigation

(an elite group, assigned to the cases no one else wants…or can solve)

Serial Love

Healing Love

Revealing Love

Seeing Love

Alvarez Security Series

(a group of former Special Forces brothers-in-arms now working to provide security in the southern city of Richland)

Gabe

Tony

Vinny

Love's Series

(detectives solving crimes while protecting the women they love)

Love's Taming

Love's Tempting

Love's Trusting

The Fairfield Series

(small town detectives and the women they love)

Carol's Image

Laurie's Time

Emma's Home

Fireworks Over Fairfield

I love to hear from readers, so please email me!

Email

authormaryannjordan@gmail.com

Website

www.maryannjordanauthor.com

Facebook

facebook.com/authormaryannjordan

Twitter

@authorMAJordan

More About Maryann Jordan

As an Amazon Best Selling Author, I have always been an avid reader. I joke that I "cut my romance teeth" on the historical romance books from the 1970's. In 2013 I started a blog to showcase wonderful writers. In 2014, I finally gave in to the characters in my head pleading for their story to be told. Thus, Emma's Home was created.

My first novel, Emma's Home became an Amazon Best Seller in 3 categories within the first month of publishing. Its success was followed by the rest of the Fairfield Series and then led into the Love's Series. From there I have continued with the romantic suspense Alvarez Security Series and now the Saints Protection & Investigation Series, all bestsellers.

My books are filled with sweet romance and hot sex; mystery, suspense, real life characters and situations. My heroes are alphas, take charge men who love the strong, independent women they fall in love with.

I worked as a counselor in a high school and have been involved in education for the past 30 years. I recently retired and now can spend more time devoted to my writing.

I have been married to a wonderfully patient man for 34 years and have 2 adult very supportive daughters and 1 grandson.

When writing, my dog or one of my cats will usually be found in my lap!